THE
KILLER
STALKS . . .

He would need some time to find the right place and get himself used to the darkness. He had to be out of sight, in a place where he could be certain to get the drop on Wilson before the cop had the chance to draw his weapon. No gunshots—he couldn't risk that. It was going to be difficult . . . he'd have to get close enough to Wilson to overpower him with one blow, then disarm him and maybe tie him up before letting the cop's blood run.

He could feel the mist coming over his eyes as he planned the kill. Red and smokey, it squeezed hard at his temples, making his throat go dry and his heart beat very fast. He smiled. He had it under control now and relished the opportunity to wait a few more days. *Let it build*, he thought.

❏

In the tradition of Lawrence Sanders and Joseph Wambaugh, a crime thriller of gripping realism and unrelenting suspense . . .

RED MIST

RED MIST

A NOVEL BY MICHAEL O'TOOLE

POPULAR LIBRARY

An Imprint of Warner Books, Inc.

A Warner Communications Company

ACKNOWLEDGMENT

All too often in life, at seeing the end result of our endeavors we lose sight of the steps involved in getting there.

I would be remiss in not mentioning the magnificent support, caring and encouragement that brought *Red Mist* from conception to reality, and would particularly like to mention the contributions of a wonderful editor and friend, Rick Horgan; my agent, indefatigable in her belief in me, Sherry Robb; Sandy Miller (we miss you); and, not least, my supportive, compassionate "best friend" —my wife, Cindy.
Thank you all for sharing in this with me.

POPULAR LIBRARY EDITION

Popular Library® and the fanciful P design are registered trademarks of Warner Books, Inc.

Cover illustration by Ben Perini
Cover design by Jackie Merri Meyer

Popular Library books are published by
Warner Books, Inc.
666 Fifth Avenue
New York, N.Y. 10103

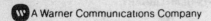 A Warner Communications Company

Printed in the United States of America

First Printing: April, 1989

10 9 8 7 6 5 4 3 2 1

The Raiders had lost again. *Damn*. It wasn't the losing that bothered him as much as the way they'd lost. They'd become pathetic.

Vic Perry had been a Raider fan ever since the glory days up in Oakland, when he'd commuted to each home game from Southern California. Jesus, once upon a time they'd made a person feel good; they took no prisoners and you could count on them to make the playoffs every year.

Now they were in L.A. And making the Rams—the Rams, of all teams—look good. It was a disgrace.

As he made his way to his car, Vic felt the hatred well up in him. They'd let him down again. What a world when you couldn't count on the Raiders. Shit, everything was going to hell in a handbasket. They'd become a bunch of pansy-assed wimps.

The parking had always been an annoyance, but today it was sending a red mist over his eyes. He could feel the ring of pain starting to squeeze at his temples, and the nerve ends in his entire body started to constrict. His heart was beating faster, and he remembered the last time it had happened.

The Raiders had actually won that day and the drive home hadn't seemed so daunting, until that selfish moron in the Cadillac had decided the traffic jam was for everyone except him. Vic had started to feel the same tightness around his temples and the frustration of sitting there in his turbo-powered Porsche, waiting, and seeing this stupid, smug asshole come waltzing out from the back of the line of barely moving vehicles. The look on the Caddie driver's face, the way he was driving, his entire body language, infuriated Vic. And as the Cadillac began to pass him on the road's shoulder, he pulled out and blocked it.

Vic wasn't aware of the honking and hooting and the indignant look on the Caddie driver's face as he leapt out of his Porsche. He saw only the red mist, and as the strength flowed through his body he felt himself yanking open the driver's door and pulling out the smug bastard. He was huge and fat and smoking an enormous cigar. Vic began ripping punches into the man's face and body. The man's glasses shattered, and Vic felt the bone and tissue in the man's nose break. The bright red blood made him angrier still. He punched him some more, until he felt the man's jawbone break, saw his lips rip and tear and become a bloody red pulp. The other car drivers were honking their horns and cheering him on.

When Vic stopped, the man was lifeless and slumped

across the steering wheel, and he felt the tightness in himself ebb away, beautifully, almost in slow motion. He heard the other drivers saying, "Way to go, man."

He got back into his car and drove away, feeling good and better than before. He was large, strong, and in control of his life. He didn't care about the police or about what would happen to him. He cared only about the pure and unexpected release of something deep within him. He cherished the sensation, feeling it surge through his veins and swell his heart.

The incident wasn't even reported on the newscasts. He'd watched for it. It was many weeks ago now, and he knew he'd gotten away with it, and he was glad, because it was only the beginning for him.

Fridays was always busy, but today it seemed busier. Andrea Reynolds had seen Vic come into the bar and knew by the expression on his face that his precious Raiders had lost. *Men*, she thought. They take things so damn personally. Why can't they just enjoy a game for the sake of enjoying it? They have to work themselves into that primeval frenzy, that fanaticism, that always frightened and disgusted her. Still, he was a nice guy, if you ignored the typical man stuff. And he was a good friend who treated her well.

He always tipped her, too, no matter how the Raiders did, win or lose. He looks pretty peeved right now, though, she thought. It was a shame, too, because when his face had that pinched, tight look he wasn't as attractive as usual and she felt less in the mood to flirt.

She had concluded long ago that they would never ac-

tually date. It seemed that their relationship was destined
to be one of mutual affinity and flirtation. Which wasn't
so bad, really, when you considered that the other men
who jockeyed for her attention had even less to offer.

She checked herself in the mirror behind the bar.
Not too shabby, she thought. She'd kept herself in good
shape, afraid what physical laxness might do to her
naturally voluptuous figure. And her blond hair and green
eyes never failed to turn heads. She reapplied her lipstick
and smiled at her reflection as behind her Vic took a seat
at the bar.

"Hi, Vic. How are you today?" she said, turning and
smiling at him. She brought out a bowl of nuts from behind
the bar.

"Great, Andy, and how's the most beautiful bargirl in
Southern California?"

The corners of his lips turned up in a broad smile, and
it transformed his face; he looked vulnerable, boyish,
happy, interested in her, and she could tell that he really
did like her. That he was interested in how she was doing.
God, he is gorgeous, she thought, feeling the warmth of
his smile wash over her. Her heart beat faster and her
trembling hands grew moist. She was helpless in his gaze,
caught like a rabbit in the headlights of an oncoming car.
And just before the vehicle slammed into her, crushing
the life out of her, she felt his hand touching her hand,
and it broke the spell. He was talking to her, and he seemed
a long way away, and she hadn't heard the words.

"You okay, Andy? Is there something wrong?"

She shook her head, embarrassed. "No, I'm fine. It's
this place, I guess. It gets to me sometimes and, well, I

wish I wasn't here and . . . You know how it is. A girl
has to make a living.''

He watched her carefully, pleased that she was opening
up to him. She was usually so damn tough; this fragility
was taking him by surprise. He found himself wondering
for the thousandth time, Why not ask her out?

Maybe he would. He would have last year, he knew
that, so why not now? That was a tough one. He hadn't
been dating anyone lately. Not for the best part of this
year, and it was December. It never seemed to work, that's
why. It should have with Jackie, he knew that. It hadn't,
and it'd hurt the most. Not the leaving, but the emptiness:
the loneliness of waking up at night and finding the room
full of nothingness, the walls pressing in on him so hard
that sleep was impossible. If she'd been there asleep,
curled up, breathing softly and contentedly, warm and full
of that smell of her, he would have snuggled up to her.
Breathed her into him, felt her warmth, her softness, and
the sleep thing would have come. Well, screw that, he
thought, it still wouldn't have made it work, would it?
None of the relationships worked.

Well, that wasn't true. They worked at first. They
worked well. Made him happy, and the women too. Then
they grew, and grew, and finally . . . came apart, and the
drifting away was on them sooner than they'd expected.
And then they knew, and blamed each other, and him. He
blamed *them* mostly, and it was easy because all his friends
said that it wouldn't have worked anyway, that the women
just didn't have what it took.

One day, back in February, he was shaving and he saw
his reflection in the mirror, and it said:

"Hey, asshole, I've been here a long time, and finally you're looking at me."

What he saw didn't really please him. The mileage was there—in the lines of his forehead, the folds of skin under his jaw. The reflection spoke to him, challenged him:

"Why are you alone, if you're so handsome, so successful, so together, such a good person? Why are you alone?"

He replied that it wasn't he who was to blame. It was the girls he was meeting. They were the wrong ones. Everyone said so, and everyone couldn't be wrong, could they? But his reflection didn't smile back at him as it always had before.

"It isn't the girls, asshole, it's you."

Deep down he really couldn't argue. Most of the women he'd known were good people, special and precious. The love had been good, and yet he'd scared them all away. That was the truth of it. Now it was out, in the open and said.

He'd thought about it long and hard, and there were no real answers. So he spent his time alone; not even with the friends he had, who weren't much as friends anyway. He'd started to look deep within himself, and he wasn't altogether happy at what he saw. That's when the anger started, intensifying as time wore on.

At first it wasn't really directed. At least not specifically. But slowly it was coming into focus. . . .

The girl was waiting for him. She'd returned from the other table and was waiting, and before he could think too long about it, it was said.

"Listen, Andy, I've had a pretty lousy day too. What with the Raiders losing, the parking, the traffic . . . What time do you get off?"

She responded without too much hesitation.

"Actually, I'll be off in about an hour. Why?"

"Well, you said you were feeling a little down. I can relate to that. I just wondered if maybe you'd want to have dinner with me later. We can talk, share a few laughs. What do you say?"

"All right," she said, her eyes glowing. "I'd like to go home and shower first. Why don't you pick me up at eight-thirty."

"Great," he said, and asked her to write down her address and phone number. As she did, he felt the pain at the back of his temples recede.

He left the bar then, planning to go home and change. But first he would go buy some champagne and cigarettes. It was very dark as he drove into Venice. It had started to rain, too, which irritated him, because the liquor store was on the main street and the parking lot was full. It looked as if he'd have to park up on a side street and walk back a couple of blocks.

Venice was really pathetic, he thought to himself, feeling angry again. There was nowhere to park, and traffic cops were everywhere, ready to summon a tow truck if you stayed too long in the wrong spot. Damn police, he thought. Worthless for stopping crime. Good only at terrorizing drivers. He felt it then, the smoky swirling mist, starting in the corners of his eyes, slowly blinding him, enraging him, filling him with violence. "Stupid asshole cops," he screamed at the misting windshield as he pounded the dashboard of his Porsche.

He was convinced that the police and the tow-truck companies were working together, that the cops were making a small fortune in kickbacks. He'd even written to the police commissioner after several incidents this past summer, but to no avail. They stick together pretty well, he thought bitterly, struggling to shake the hazy red mist that was consuming him.

He finally found a spot to park near the Rose Café, and after locking his car he started to walk briskly toward the main street and the liquor store. It was very dark, and the rain was coming down in sheets. The wind blowing off the ocean was cold and bitter, and soon he was very wet. His anger was growing larger, filling him, bloating his insides. And his nails dug into his hands as he clenched and unclenched them, fighting back the images of his father.

Ahead he saw a movement. Blinking through the redness, shrouding his eyes, he saw the two black youths and recognized their intent immediately. They'd cut off the road and were leaning against the alleyway, waiting for him to walk close enough so that they could push him into the alley and mug him, or worse. He patted the hard metallic object he'd taken to hiding in his jacket and smiled. He felt the excitement coursing through his veins and pleaded with them, silently, to try it—try and take him if they could. Then he would show them he wasn't the coward his father was.

Come on, try it, he chanted to himself over and over.

He slowed his pace a little as ahead of him the two blacks scanned the area and confirmed that no one else was about. He was very close now and could see them stiffen and nod to each other.

"Got a cigarette, man?" the taller of the youths asked, grinning at him.

Vic ignored him and was now parallel with the alley. He checked around: still no one was visible. Suddenly he swerved and went into the alley. It was narrow, very dark. He smelled the garbage, and the rain. Perfect. He could see that the blacks had chosen their killing ground very well. The buildings closest to the entrance of the alley were shops that were closed up for the night, and there were no lights burning anywhere. Okay, he thought, this is as good a place as any.

"What's your problem, friend?" he asked the kid who had spoken to him.

"Who you calling friend, mister?" the second youth said. "With your fancy car and clothes, you no friend of ours." The second youth spit down at the ground and curled back his lips contemptuously.

The two blacks had moved swiftly and with practiced ease. Vic was surrounded. There was only one way out of the alley, and that was through one of them. He smiled at the feeling he had. The redness that covered his eyes was a joyous thing, strong, vibrant, and full of clarity. He could smell them, see that there was fear in their eyes, and he knew it would end here for them—that it would be over very suddenly. He wanted to prolong the moment, savor it, place it in his mind for his eyes to play over and over at his leisure.

And then the gun was in his hand. He put it into the face of the nearest youth and pulled the trigger. The noise of the gun's explosion was more a whimper than a bang; it disappointed him that the violence was so subtle. He'd expected, hoped for, a rush, a cacophony of sound and anger all rolled into one. Like the ending of the *1812 Overture* he'd always thought it would be. It wasn't. The youth's head seemed to collapse outwardly, and he crashed against the wall. The blood and parts of his head and brain and hair were splattered against the pavement. When he crumpled he looked like a broken scarecrow, and then the rain washed away the blood and he looked small and frail, not at all threatening. The second youth was watching all of this with a look of sick dread on his face. Then his brain seemed to catch up with his limbs, and he made as if to run. His legs were moving as the bullet entered the back of his head and exited where his nose had been. His last thought was: *I didn't mean it, man. I didn't mean it.*

He ran a few more steps, then staggered and fell face-down onto the pavement. Vic cocked his head and listened. Nothing. Only the wind, and the rain, and the cars on the main street whizzing by. He looked at the two fallen youths, feeling a huge gratitude toward them. They'd freed him, deliciously and exquisitely, and he wanted to touch them. Then the moment was gone and his brain started working and he moved quietly and quickly. Down the alley, around, and back toward his car. As he put the gun back into his jacket pocket, he reflected on it and smiled. He was glad that he hadn't shot someone at the ballgame or on the freeway, as he'd thought he might someday. This was a much cleaner act, and well deserved.

The police were so useless, so inept, that they, too, would secretly be grateful to him. Two more creeps off the street. And this way had been good, almost sacred. He had felt that moment when life becomes death. He'd smelled them, felt their life ebb away and into him, and the pleasure and the joy was greater than anything he'd ever felt before. He wanted to sing, to scream, and to cry all at once. He remembered the girl and felt a curious upwelling of feeling for her. He started his car, and lighter of heart than he could remember in years, drove over to the marina, deciding to stop at a store closer to home.

She answered the phone on the second ring, and her voice pleased him. Also, he felt she was pleased that it was he.

"Listen, Andy, this rain is in for the night. How about I send over a cab, then make dinner for you here at my place? I've lit a fire and we can watch the ocean as we—"

"Sounds great," she interrupted. "Only, don't bother about the cab. Give me your address, and I'll drive over."

He was pleased. This was going to be a great evening. He got the fire going and tidied up the apartment. Not that it was messy. He hated messy places. Always had, since he'd lived alone.

The view was truly spectacular. He lived on the tip of the peninsula, and on nights like this with the elements raging, battering the beach, he felt alive, cleansed. Now, after the other part, he felt more alive than ever. It was so perfect.

He thought of the girl as he showered. He'd been going

to Fridays each Sunday and Wednesday for months, and he always looked forward to seeing her. She was different from most of the others—beautiful, yes, but quiet and unpretentious. More intelligent than anyone he'd met in a long time, male or female. He liked her humor, and the subtle sadness behind her eyes. It was a strange thing, he thought, that he'd never asked her out. He was glad now, though, that he hadn't, that he'd waited until the time was right.

He decided to cook pepper steaks and baked potatoes, and mix a salad. He spent the most time on the salad, cutting everything into small pieces, then tossing it all together and putting it in the freezer for a few minutes. He put champagne glasses in the freezer and chilled the vintage Moët Chandon. Everything was set. Almost as if on cue, he heard the doorbell.

When he opened the door, she smiled and waved a bottle of wine and a bunch of roses at him. He kissed her lightly on the lips and hugged her, glad that they'd negotiated that part in such good spirits and with such ease.

"Wow, what a terrific place," Andy said, obviously impressed. "The fire's great. Where shall I put these?" She held up the wine and the roses.

"I'll take them," he said, "though it's me who should be offering flowers. Go sit by the fireplace over there," he instructed. "You'll be able to look into the fire and see the ocean at the same time. I designed it that way. It's sort of like hot and cold at the same time, and the contrasts are, well . . ."

"Like fire and ice?" she offered.

He smiled and nodded, then looked around for a vase.

"Something smells good, Vic. What's for dinner?"

"Well, I thought steak, baked potatoes, and a salad. I hope you eat meat?" He wondered about that. Most people he knew these days didn't. Especially people in the shape she was in.

"Sounds fine to me," she said, smiling. "Can I ask you a personal question?"

"Sure, but first let me get you a glass of wine and put the flowers in a vase. Why don't you put a record on."

He watched her get up from the chair by the fireplace and move gracefully to the stereo. As she did he noted with admiration the look she affected: everything was contrasted to show off her magnificent body. He reminded himself to tell her how beautiful she looked.

"So you're a Van Morrison fan?" he heard her call out a minute later. "Let's listen to this."

He smiled, pleased at her selection. "Yes, I've been into Van the Man for, well, actually ever since I heard that record by Them. You know the one, 'Here Comes the Night.' I'm surprised you like his music. It's a little before your time." He returned to the living room in time to see her settling back into the chair.

"Well, actually, I was introduced to his music by an old boyfriend, an Irish guy."

"He has good taste—both in music and in women," Vic said, handing her a long-stemmed glass filled to the brim. The power of his gaze made her self-conscious, and a moment later she watched him wander over to the kitchen. That was what he did, wander. He looks so much happier than he did before, she thought, and he looks so handsome. So few men had the ability to dress like that.

He was the most elegant man she'd ever seen, and so together. God, this place was palatial. The wine was terrific, and created a warm glow in her belly. She let her thoughts drift and remembered the way they'd kissed.

She hadn't expected that he would kiss her on the mouth, and she'd been too surprised to offer her cheek. Besides, it felt wonderful. His lips were soft and gentle, and his body felt good when she held him. Firm and toned and strong. *Stop those thoughts, Andy.* How long had she known him? Six, seven months, since he'd first started coming into the bar and they'd struck up a rapport. At first she'd wanted to be here like this and longed for him to ask her out and almost asked him to take her to dinner. But she never found the courage or the right moment. Today had been the absolute right moment. She'd concentrated and sent out her best signals and followed her instincts, and he'd picked up the signals and now the two of them were here. It felt good. He was so nice. Just as she'd thought he'd be. And so good looking. He was everything she'd hoped.

She had wondered if he was gay, and then if he was married, or worse—maybe even bisexual. *Ugh.* The terror word of the eighties. Leave that one alone. She thought of how she'd turned many a conversation around and argued against her beliefs to find out the details of this man, and how he'd always responded in a sensitive way. That comment she'd made about her old lover had been pretty dumb; she'd almost bitten her tongue when the words came tumbling out. But he'd picked up on her nervousness and made it okay. He had class all over him.

The dinner smelled wonderful, and she was famished.

The rain had increased its pounding against the window-panes, and as she watched the flames flicker and curl around the log in the fireplace, she felt drawn into a warm cocoon, knew with sudden certainty that she wouldn't go home tonight.

"That was the best dinner I've had in years. The salad was superb. Thank you, Vic." Andy looked happy and contented. She'd kicked off her shoes and was sitting back on the sofa.

"My pleasure," Vic said. "Say, what was the personal question you wanted to ask me?" He poured them both more champagne.

"Well, it sounds silly, but, you know, you don't look like a Vic or a Victor, and I wondered about that. About your name?"

He smiled. What the hell, why not tell her? It didn't matter anymore. It was all part of the past. Gone, buried, dead and deep.

"That's a good question, although I'm not sure what you mean. Well, actually, I guess I do," he said, sitting close beside her, letting his hand rest against her hand and feeling her soft, silky skin next to his.

"All the Vics that I know of, or have known, have been older guys," he said. "It's interesting, really. When I was born my parents thought I was going to be a girl. So much so that they bought girls' clothes and did my bedroom up in girls' colors. Remember that in those days people couldn't tell the sex of a child before it was born. Anyway, my grandmother on my father's side was called Victoria. And that was the name that they'd chosen for me. I suppose

I was such a surprise to them that they just settled on the first thing that came to mind, and so I was called Victorio, Victorio Perry. As often happens, the name got shortened to Vic, and Vic it is. I must admit I can't imagine going through my life as Victorio.'' What he didn't mention was that his parents had treated him the first few years of his life as if he were a girl. Sometimes even dressed him like one. *Forget that one, Vic, it's gone now . . . forever.*

"Did they—your parents—eventually have a girl? Do you have a sister?"

"No," he said, bored with the way the conversation was going. Who really gives a damn about a name, anyway? He sighed. *Relax, Vic, it's all a part of the mating game. Go with the flow.*

"I ended up as the only child. There were complications at the end of my mother's pregnancy, when I was being born. They were unable to have other kids. It was a shame. But that's life, I guess."

They talked for hours, late into the night, and neither one of them seemed to want to be the first to say good night. He had massaged her shoulders and taken out most of the stress of the day at the bar, and she'd smiled at him and moved closer. Now she was lying with her head in his lap.

He kissed her then as she lay there, and her mouth found his. They kissed hungrily and greedily and then slowly and tenderly. They were filled with each other. He ran his tongue over her mouth and bit gently on the top of her lip, feeling her entire body tremble. He parted her lips, running the tip of his tongue over her teeth, and she his, and they were deep within each other's mouths. He held her face in his hands and kissed her eyes, her nose, then the lobes of her ears, making her shiver. She ran her hands through his hair. He kissed her neck and ran his hands, featherlike, over her swelling breasts. They were heavy and firm, and he could feel her heart beat, her legs shiver, and her nipples harden. He moved his hand and she sobbed out loud, pushing his hand back against her chest. When he asked her if she was sure, she murmured yes; and they went to the bedroom. He stood near the bed, holding her, looking into her eyes, large and luminous, filled with moisture and lights reflecting from the lamps.

She was smiling; all the nervousness was out of her. The anticipation ran through them both deliciously like a living thing. Her mouth opened, and she sighed. He could feel the length of her, and she moved against him with great fluidity and strength. As he moved against her she could feel him start to harden, filling her with power. She ran her hands over his back, feeling the bunched muscles, the tapered waist, and the firm, tight buttocks, and she felt herself getting wet.

Her legs started to tremble again, then shook uncontrollably. She wanted to cry out, to squeeze him, pull his hair, hold him even closer and make him an extension of her. Slowly he pushed her away from him, without force and only a small distance, but he wanted to look at her once more, deep into her eyes, and burn the image into his memory.

Then her hand reached out and touched his face, and her fingers ran over his cheeks and nose and mouth. They spoke without words, an ancient language, transmitted between them. She undressed him, and he undressed her, and it was without urgency.

Then they were naked, and the first touch of their flesh was wondrous and electric. It illuminated the room, and the warmth from them was great. Slowly he laid her on the bed. She cried out to him and he gentled her and ran his hands through her hair, stroking her head, her face, and her long slim neck. He kissed her there, and she lay back and her body was stilled. He ran his hands over her pendulous breasts. The nipples were hard and rough against his hands. He kissed them and felt them harden still more, reaching out to him. And he sucked them between his teeth, and gently ran his teeth over the ends of them, and she cried out and he did it more, and with less pressure, and then harder, and he could feel her moving and moaning under him. Her hands gripped his head and guided him down her body. Over her flat, round, muscled stomach, over her pelvis. He could feel her short, silky hair against his mouth, and he could smell and taste the sweet fragrance of her.

Then he was between her legs, and they parted and her inner thigh muscles tightened and gripped his head. He parted her and ran his tongue in and around her, in and around, and he found the part she wanted him to touch with his tongue. She was writhing and crying, and she was wet, then wetter, and soft and warm. And he was astonished at how quickly she came. And he tried to slow her and hold her back, but it was too late. He heard her cry out and felt her rising and falling and rising again and again, and the spasms went on and on, and she came and came, and she thought it would never end, and it was good

and better than she had ever dared hope and she wanted
more of him and wanted him inside her. He must have
felt that because he had raised his body up, and was moving
toward her. She could see him—large, throbbing, and
swollen. She wanted this huge thing inside her, filling her.
But she wanted also to make him wait. So she grasped
him, kissing his mouth, and made him lie on his back.
Then she kissed him on his mouth more. Then on his neck
and his chest. She explored his muscles; they were large
and hard, not huge, but perfect. His stomach was so incredibly flat and hard, too. Then she kissed his thighs,
running her tongue down to his knee and up the inside of
his thigh to where the large part was waiting for her. She
smiled, kissing his balls, feeling him stiffen and then relax.
She had him now in her hands. She was running her hands
from the top to the bottom of him. He was huge, hot and
throbbing, and she ran her tongue from the tip to the bottom
and then put a part of him inside her mouth, closing her
lips on him, trapping him inside her, and ran her tongue
around and over him. Then with hands and mouth took
him deep into her, then deeper still. Then faster, and faster,
then slower, and faster again. He tasted so good she wanted
all of him and could feel it start in him deep and far away,
so she increased her pressure, feeling him fighting her.
She pushed him back and was pleased that he thought of
her and then she wanted him to come, faster and faster
and she felt it start and then explode deep within her, hot
and salty and more and more and she was filled with him
and still more and she drank him down and more and then
she felt his body relaxing. She kept him there, in her
mouth. She was gentle, very slow and patient. He was

hard again, as before. Their eyes met and she smiled, holding him, kissing his mouth, and guided him inside her. He was gentle and slow and took an eternity to fill her. A fraction at a time. She wanted more and then he filled her and she was gasping, writhing, urging him to go harder, faster. He did, pistoning forward, and she came more slowly and more intensely than before, the liquid issuing in sudden jets. Then she felt him collapse on her and she held him and gentled him, stroking him and giving him back his strength. She took his head in her hands, looked into his eyes, and saw his happiness, and they kissed and moved slightly. Then they wrapped their bodies around each other and slept. Pure slumber now. No plaintive dreams.

Tony Wilson and Frank Morrissey had been eating chili dogs when the call came in, and even though they were both starving, they ran to their vehicle and drove over to the scene of the crime. They'd been partners in Homicide for four years now and knew each other like soldiers sharing a foxhole. It was the only way that you could work together on the force, they'd concluded. Most days were spent sifting through tons of crap, and they depended on each other's highly tuned instincts and experience to make sense of it all. Lately Tony had noticed his partner's agitation. He'd tried to talk to Frank, without success. On the job they shared everything, but Frank was pretty quiet about what went on outside of work. Tony guessed that it was the wife thing again: she hated Frank's job—not only the risks it entailed but the lack of opportunity it offered to make extra money. Who can possibly survive on a detective's salary? she'd said that night Tony had joined her and Frank for dinner. Wasn't it deliberately kept low because everyone knew that the payola supplemented the income?

She'd been drunk that night, and Tony knew that Frank had been deeply hurt and embarrassed by the outburst. It was the last time that they'd all gone out together socially. Frank hadn't said much. The odd comment here and there. Tony knew that he cared deeply for Sue, that the wear and tear on their marriage because of the job was getting him down. He sensed that Frank was at a crossroads: either the wife or the job would be a loser. Which was a damn shame, because no one would be a winner. Frank wouldn't know what to do without police work, and he was good, the best that Tony knew. He never gave up on a case when he had a lead, and his persistence when his instincts told him something wasn't right was legendary. If Frank ever left the force, Tony would miss him badly. Frank was all he had—he and sometimes, rarely, some girl to help pass the lonely nights. There were no *real* women, though. Women here in Tinseltown wanted to hook their wagons to more than a lousy cop. That was the hardest part about leaving Milwaukee. He knew people there. The cops had some status. A girl wouldn't snub you when she found out you were a cop.

Tony laughed then and thought, *Screw it, Frank's problem is his woman and mine's no woman*. Crazy world. When it really came right down to it, everyone was full of problems, lonely and pissed off with life. *Shit*, he thought, *we're the lucky ones, Frank and me. We have the force and we have each other.* More than most, he guessed.

"Frank, you okay, buddy?" Tony asked. "Maybe after we close this one up we can go over to Alice's, have a beer and something to eat. Whatta ya say, partner?"

Frank looked over at him and smiled, feeling a warmth for him. He was a good guy, and the best cop he'd worked with. Never bugged him or stuck his nose in.

"Sounds good, Tony. This one shouldn't take long. The reporting officer said it looks like a drug-related hit. Vice will probably have a handle on it."

Up ahead they saw the red and blue lights, eerie through the rain-misted windshield of their car, and pulled over. The ambulance, the coroner, and the photographer were already there.

"Hi, Doc, what you got?" Frank said to the kneeling man, offering him a smoke and getting a withering look for his trouble.

The coroner turned from the second corpse and stood.

"Nice night for a killing, Frank. The rain's tidied things up. Two blacks, about eighteen or nineteen, I'd guess. Both shot at close range with a high-velocity bullet—point thirty-eight, I'd think. That one over there got it at point-blank range in the face. Died instantly. The other one started to run and took a slug in the back of the head; also killed instantly. Been dead about an hour, maybe two. They were both armed but don't seem to have gone for their weapons. The girl over there called it in. Found the bodies on the way back from the store. As you can see, it's pretty dark here, and what with the storm, it's doubtful anyone heard the shots. Still, you'll check that out, I guess. I'm about all done here. I'll get the report over to you about noon tomorrow. See you later, Frank. 'Bye, Tony.''

Tony walked over to the patrol vehicle and asked the officer, Hank Randle, if the girl in the back of the cruiser was the one who'd called it in. Then he asked the cop to read him his report. It seemed that the girl, Sara Williams, had been working at the grocery store on Main Street. She was on her way home after finishing her shift at seven-thirty P.M. She'd taken the shortcut through the alley because of the rain and had come across the bodies about forty-five minutes ago. She'd run down to the liquor store and called it in, and the black-and-white had responded immediately.

"What's the scoop on the drug angle, Hank?" Tony asked him, ducking his head into the car, out of the rain. "We heard on the radio that drugs might be involved."

The young officer looked uncomfortable and fidgeted with his notepad.

"Listen, Detective, it's just a guess, but a pretty good one, I think. They're both black and young and look like street kids. I've seen them around and, well, you know what this neighborhood's like. What else could it be? By the look of things, they were executed, and you heard what the coroner said. For chrissake, they couldn't be mugging victims, could they?"

Frank had walked over and heard the exchange. It irritated him, and yet the kid was probably right. It did look like a hit, and from what the coroner had said they'd been taken from very close, which would indicate that they were either surprised or that they knew their killers. These kinds of street toughs were unlikely to be surprised by anyone. So perhaps Randle was right.

"Tony, has anyone ID'd these two yet?" he asked, pulling his collar tighter.

Tony had been talking to the girl, who was frightened, tired, and wet. The story that the patrolman had was pretty much it. Better, Frank thought, to get the stiffs over to the morgue and continue everything at the station house. Damn rain. It made police work real hard. Still, this one didn't look like much. If the kids had been hit by a pro, there wouldn't be much to find, if anything. The ground was concrete, so shoe ID's would be hard, if not impossible, and the activity around here was probably considerable. If no one had called in to say that they heard shots, a door-to-door didn't promise to deliver much information.

Still, that was what the job was all about. High-profile crap scoopers we are, he thought, cleaning up someone else's mess, and in cases like this it was unlikely that anyone would really give a goddamn. The captain probably wouldn't expect more than a cursory job, especially if no one was putting pressure on him to bring in the murderer. And besides, he thought, Vice would probably take a look at it first. Then it would end up as just another unsolved murder for the files. Shit, if the public only knew how few murders like this we really solved.

Frank told the ambulance men to take the bodies down to the morgue. The local media had hit the area like an avenging army. This was the worst part, Frank thought, talking to pushy media people who didn't give a goddamn about what had happened, other than it was a juicy piece of news. Next to plane crashes, he figured assassinations came a close second with the TV audiences. Especially gory ones like this: point-blank head shots and drugs. He nodded to Tony and told him to go ahead and talk to the TV people. It was routine. The bare facts and a polite "No comment," then "Please contact the station house for further details."

They drove in silence for a while, each reflecting on what they'd just seen. Tony seemed prepared to accept the most obvious explanation, go through the motions. They'd check out the scene tomorrow and see what could be found, but he was betting it wouldn't be much.

"So what do you figure, Frank? Drug related or not?"

"Sure looks that way, doesn't it. The only thing that I can't figure is why they allowed themselves to be suckered into the alley. And if it was someone they knew, as seems likely, how did he get the drop on them?"

"What do you mean?" Tony asked, a puzzled look on his face. "It looks to me like a pro hit."

"Yeah, I guess. But the fact that neither of the kids pulled his gun bothers me." A pause, then: "Oh, shit, I don't know, you're probably right."

"How about we get this all done nice and fast, then go and have some fun, Frank? I don't know about you, but I'm ready for a drink. We can do most of the paperwork tomorrow. What do you say?"

Frank seemed to be thinking of something. "Huh?" he said finally. "Oh, yeah, sure. Good idea. No rush on this one." Whoever had done this wasn't going to be caught anytime soon. No way.

* * *

It took them a couple of hours to complete the preliminary paperwork. The two murdered men were Lucius Worthy and Alfred Jackson, both Venice residents and both nineteen. Worthy had been arrested seventeen times on suspicion of everything from carrying a concealed weapon to driving under the influence; he was known to the police as dangerous and intelligent. So far he had served time twice: two years as a juvenile and ten months for stealing a car. Jackson's sheet was worse. He'd spent his entire life in correctional facilities since the age of twelve. Mostly armed violence, muggings. Four times he'd been hauled in on suspicion of rape. Each time he'd beaten the charges. He'd been on the streets again in less than two weeks. Which made Frank Morrissey raise his eyebrows a little.

The captain called them into his office and asked for a preliminary. Tony Wilson gave him the scoop and added that it looked like the two murdered men were hit by their own kind. He went on to tell the captain of the arrest records of the two youths, and said so far they had no leads. Captain Weston asked them how the Murphy child murder case was coming and whether they expected any breaks. The press and the commissioner were giving him grief, he said, and they should concentrate all their efforts on that. He'd assign this case to Vice for the preliminary investigation.

They drove over to Alice's place for drinks. Frank loved Westwood. It kept him young, he said; he loved the kids and their bright, expectant faces. Tony hated it; it made him yearn for his youth and feel old and worn out. And besides, the bar people were old enough to be his kids, and flirting with the girls seemed sort of criminal.

Well into their third rounds, Tony figured Frank must be thinking about Susan, since the place wasn't cheering him up as much as it usually did. Frank saw his friend's expression and smiled. He tilted his glass toward the bartender and indicated a refill.

"How long we been cops, Tony?"

"Come on, don't let's start that again. Let's have some fun, or we can just talk. Shit, man, you know how long we've been cops. Longer than most of these kids in here have been alive." He nodded at the other people sitting at the bar and indicated for Frank to do the same. He saw him smile and continued. "Too damn long, I think sometimes."

"Yeah, fifteen years for me and fourteen years for you," Frank said, staring into his beer again, losing the goodwill he felt for the place. His thoughts flickered back to Susan, and he wondered if he should talk to Tony about her, about them.

"Too damn long," Frank said. "Those two that got whacked tonight were only nineteen. Makes you think, doesn't it?"

"Listen, Frank, we're off the case. The captain said so. What's the *real* problem? Come on, talk to me. You and me, we always have a good time in this place. Forget the shit out there and let's have some fun."

"No problem, really. Just overworked, underpaid, understaffed. Overwhelmed, in reality. We go on, though, don't we. I wonder why, sometimes. Maybe Sue has it right and me wrong. Christ, she was the best. She's gone back to her folks' place in Tampa. Did I tell you that? Last weekend it was, just up and left. She loves me, she tells me, and wants me to reevaluate my life and decide what I want to do. She can't go on like things are, she tells me. Never enough money and she's thirty-four and tired of working and wants a kid. Christ, how many kids in your family? There was six in mine and Mom never ever worked and Dad was only a supervisor in the postal services. So where the hell does she come off saying it's my fault that we can't have kids, because I'm only a lousy sergeant and don't make any money? Christ, Tony, I make forty-five grand a year, plus, and she was doing real well making twenty-eight grand. Shit, that's close to seventy-five thousand a year. The house we have is nearly paid for. She has the house fixed up like she always wanted it. It's beautiful, everyone says so, full of beautiful, tasteful things, and she just got a new import car from her job. What the fuck does she want me to do?

"She hates my work. Maybe she even hates me? She wants me to give this up, move to Florida, and work for her father. Man, he's a real cool guy. I like him and her mother. He never pressures or hassles me. But I see it on his face. She's all he has and she's been spoiled and he wants the best for her no matter how much he likes me. It's all messed up, Tony, and the work is getting to be screwed up too. Remember how we used to believe that we really made a difference?" He interrupted his monologue to take a gulp from his drink.

"Remember how proud we were of the force, the city we stood for? It's all changing, isn't it? It's getting so no matter how many bad guys we bust and put off the streets, ten more guys, even worse, come along and take their places. California's gone soft, especially on the criminal. Look at what happened to Martinez. Jesus, that deranged son of a bitch will be on the streets again in twelve years, maybe less, and you and I and everyone else know that the crazy sucker will kill again. Probably many times before we nail him. The way he butchered those women and the two kids, damn, that was one of the worst I've seen, and I've seen plenty. Hell, I almost never have regrets, but I should have shot that bastard. I had the chance: no one would have known he was unarmed.''

"You'd have known," Tony said, lifting his drink and looking at him. "I know you. You couldn't have lived with it."

Frank picked up his glass and drained it. Tony was right. You gotta live with yourself in this life. Christ, what was happening to him? What was happening to them all? It's as if everything was dead or dying and he was mourning it, constantly. He was going to miss Sue; he loved that woman with all of him. He wouldn't give this police stuff up, though, and she knew that when she left. Just had enough, he supposed. He'd miss her friendship the most. She was the best friend he'd ever had. Better even than Tony, and Tony was one in a million. What happened to people? Why hadn't it worked for them? Was it really the money thing? Somehow he thought not.

It was just all messed up, all changed. It was like what had happened on the job. You went in every day, did the best you could, and it was hard. You made all the compromises, but all around you it wasn't working. It was falling apart, and so you dug in and did what you do better than even you thought you could. Still, it eroded and slipped away. . . .

"Hungry?" Tony asked him, throwing a menu.

"Yeah. Say, let me ask you something. Still think the two dudes were drug-related murders?"

That's better, Franky, come back to us, forget all that other stuff, get your mind working.

"Sure I do. Why not? And besides, it's not our problem, is it?"

"If you say so, although I thought our job included solving murders and bringing criminals to justice," he said, laughing and swigging his beer. He saw the look on Tony's face and held up a hand. "Okay, man, only teasing. But listen, you read the rap sheets on those two guys. No mention of drug offenses on either of them. They're small-time hoods. Stickup artists, rapists, muggers. I can't buy that they were hit by the drug lords. Dammit, Tony, the Jackson kid had only been out for a couple of weeks. That's not enough time to make the kind of enemy that would contract-hit you, is it?"

Even as he spoke, Frank wondered if he was just spinning his wheels. What were those guys, anyway? Just a couple of scumbags that got what was coming to them. Maybe he should just forget it and concentrate on the Murphy kid. But if they were scumbags, what did that make the dude who whacked them? Shit, they were low-lifes and all, but they were entitled to the same protection and consideration as any other citizen, weren't they? Tony was gazing at him, waiting for him to finish.

"Let me run a 'what if' scenario by you, Tony. What

if the two dudes, Worthy and Jackson, had been plying a little action themselves? Suppose that they'd fingered someone for a robbery and got the guy into the alley and the guy just pulled out a gun and blasted them? Wait,'' he said, holding up his hand to silence Tony. ''Wouldn't that explain how and why they were in the alley in the first place, and why they never drew their weapons, and how the killer had been able to nail them both? Think, man. He would have surprised the shit out of them. That's it, that's my supposition. What do you think?''

Tony looked like he was giving it some thought too.

''It's possible. It sounds kinda farfetched to me, but maybe you're right. So what do you want to do? Do you want me to talk to the captain?''

''No, let's let Vice run with it. My guess is it will end up on our desk sooner or later. Let's just see what happens. I have a nagging feeling that this is just the beginning, and if I'm right . . .'' He let the thought hang in the air.

Vic had just finished reading the late edition of the *Times.* Gone was the feeling of contentment from the night before, and in its place a slow-boiling anger prompted by the realization that his ''altercation'' had gone unheralded. He raged about his apartment, feeling the anger build, wanting to smash everything—especially the lying, insidious television. He was particularly vexed by that smartass cop and his goddamn ''No comment.''

He slammed open the sliding door to his balcony and gulped in the fresh, salty sea air. But it didn't please him like it usually did. And then he saw the dog. The little mutt was pissing on his alloys and the stupid woman was letting it. Christ, those wheels cost more than most cars; he wished he had his gun. Furious, he grabbed a plant, throwing it with all his force at the dog. It sailed, majestically, through the air, shattering against his windshield. The contents of the plant pot spewed all over his gleaming hood. It seemed to assuage him, and his anger started to subside. Then the woman began to scream and the dog growled menacingly. *Get it together, Vic*, he told himself. *Breathe deep*.

"Sorry, the pot slipped out of my hand," he called down. "Thank God you weren't hurt. I'm sorry." The woman stopped screaming and stared up at him for long moments. She looked up at the balcony and the position of the car, seemed to calculate, and then shrugged.

"That's okay," she said. "I hope you're the owner of the car. It seems quite badly damaged." She yanked at the dog's leash. "Shut up, Dani, for godsake shut up that barking." She looked up at Vic again. "No harm done. 'Bye." Then she was off with her stupid yapping animal and he relaxed.

Now that was stupid, Vic, he thought. You're on a mission pal, don't mess it up. This is your time. Your time for paybacks.

He returned to the den and switched the TV back on. He watched FNN for the next couple of hours, charted the stocks he was interested in, and then called his broker with his buy and sell orders. He loved the market; it was incredibly easy to play. And over the past two years he'd turned his modest fortune into a substantial one. Mostly, though, he loved the hours: getting up at the crack of dawn; the freshly squeezed orange juice; the long, hot showers after a quick run on the beach; then down to business. Usually he was done by eleven A.M. and the rest of the day was his.

Time had become important to him several years ago. He would be forty next year, and time seemed to be moving along at an incredible rate. He smiled at that, remembering how he'd spent most of his early years wishing he was older. When he was a teenager, he wished almost daily that he was twenty-one, so that he could be in control of his own destiny. He didn't realize, of course, that control had little to do with actual years; rather, it was attitude and perspective.

He imagined how his father must have felt watching him screw everything up when his father really did know best. But who would have thought that ridiculous, cowardly, henpecked old fart knew anything? He remembered finally reaching the magical age of twenty-one, and the golden doors of life opening at last. Except that they were only partially opened. Even as the adult world beckoned him forward, it made it clear he would not be taken seriously. He recalled that agonizingly slow wait for the nirvana of thirty. To finally be taken seriously. The time crawled by, excruciatingly slowly. And then, finally, with much cere-mony, he was thirty. Quite suddenly, it was as if he had stepped onto a bobsled and the time was whizzing by so fast that he was unable to glimpse it, let alone savor it. And did the bastards take him seriously? Of course they didn't. So he said screw them and he left IBM and went into his own software business.

After seven years of total dedication, he'd been bought out for 2.5 million. It had seemed like a fortune until he'd asked how much the vacant lot at the end of the Marina Peninsula was. That brought him down to earth.

He thought then of the girl and of how good it was with her last night. He hadn't had to ask her if it was good for her, or if she had come. He knew that it was and that she had. That she would call him, that they'd spend some more time together. It pleased him because she was a beautiful, fun, intelligent woman and he'd need her more in the days ahead.

He started to laugh then, loud and long, wetting his eyes. He was astonished, deliriously happy, that even the rotten, stupid teary part was leaving his body. He remembered all those nights lying, crying for her in his room, for his mother and the shame of him, his father. But mostly he had cried for himself, and now that that layer was gone, too, he could hardly contain himself.

The news had come on the TV, and he was distracted. Shit, he thought, it was a rerun of that smug, wimpy-looking cop again. God help you, L.A., if that's the best you have to protect and serve you, he screamed at the set. Then he listened.

"The identities of the two murdered youths are still unknown," the cop was saying. "However, a complete statement will be issued later."

The channel 4 reporter probed a little more, and Vic saw the cop shift uncomfortably.

"Detective Wilson, do you think the killings are directly connected to the recent outbreak of violence stemming from the realignment of drug territories?"

Wilson shrugged.

"Perhaps. Early indications are that the two dead men

may have been involved in drug distribution in some way. The method of the killings falls into a pattern we've been seeing in this area lately."

"What sort of pattern, Detective?"

Wilson let out an audible sigh and ran his hands through his hair.

"The killer or killer acted swiftly. The site of the killing was well chosen. There appears to have been no witnesses. Although it's early yet, someone might have seen something. At this time I have nothing more to say, thank you."

"One last question, Detective," the reporter said, smiling encouragingly at Tony. "The police commissioner is on record as saying the drug task force assigned three months ago to clean up the Venice/Palms area would put an end to these types of brutal murders. It would appear that the violence is escalating. Do you have any comment?"

Tony snapped. He'd had it with these stupid fucking questions. He should never have let the reporter sucker him into this kind of dialogue. Christ, he should have let Frank handle it.

"We are making progress. In the past three months we have arrested thirty-seven drug pushers and confiscated drugs with a street value in excess of three million dollars. The stakes are very high, and everyone involved"—except you assholes, he thought bitterly—"realizes that it's a long-term project. We have a police commissioner who is committed to making the streets drug free. Eventually we will put these gangs out of commission and end these mindless, cowardly killings. I have nothing more to add."

Vic snapped off the set, watching the last flicker of light

disappear in a red haze. Well, wasn't that typical of the cops? Steal my thunder will you? He cursed. What was that smug cop's name? Tony Wilson. Well, Tony goddamn Wilson, we'll see what your buddies think when you're planted six feet under like those other two scumbags I wasted. What had the cop said? A "cowardly" act? Oh, he'd pay for that. Vic would see to it. He slammed his hand into the wall again and again as around him the red mist continued to swirl, intoxicating him with its vapors.

Later that day Vic drove over to the Porsche dealer and asked the mechanic to repair his car. He arranged for a loaner car, surprising the sales manager by asking for a Volvo wagon.

Then he drove over to the station house. It was going to be easy, he thought, and laughed. What wasn't? The place was swarming with cops who were so damn sure of themselves they didn't see any danger. He thought of blasting the whole building to smithereens. But what would that do? Maybe he'd do it later, when they knew they had an enemy out there they couldn't stop and were scared as hell. Later, blue boys, later. He laughed. He saw Wilson come out a little after one P.M. Off to lunch, no doubt. He was an easy mark, tall and skinny with a mop of curly black hair.

Vic fingered the gun, feeling the cool metal. He imagined the bullet smashing into Wilson, tearing a bloody, gaping hole through his head. No, he said softly to himself, no guns. He would take the cop out slowly, at close quarters. Then Mr. Wilson would find out who the true coward was. *Soon, Wilson, soon.*

* * *

Tony Wilson had the look of a typical cop in his wrinkled and worn suit. He had that weary, seen-it-all look, and his great height was lessened by the stoop in his shoulders. His partner—Vic assumed the man with him was his partner—was different. Tall also, but large and powerful, he, too, wore a suit, well pressed and modern. His hair was cut short and fashionable with the wet look. A cigarette dangled from his lip, and Vic could make out the powerful, determined jaw, the strutting walk. The man's eyes were unusual. Washed out, almost. A faded tattered blue that occasionally paled to gray. He hadn't shaved for a couple of days and looked unlike any cop that Vic had ever seen. More like a goddamn mobster, he thought. Italian or Irish, to be sure. *Well, Mr. whatever your name is, pretty soon you're going to have another partner.* He felt excited.

The two policemen crossed the street and went into the Sizzler restaurant. He thought about that, then decided to hell with it, he'd go see what the creeps were all about.

He parked the car in the resturant lot and went in after them. They'd been seated in the smoking section near the window, and there were plenty of empty tables nearby. The hostess smiled at him and asked: "Smoking or non-smoking?" He said: "Smoking," and asked for a window seat, explaining that he was expecting someone else. He also asked if there was someplace he could get a newspaper. The girl smiled at him again, this time a bit more provocatively, and pointed him toward the cigarette machine at the rear of the restaurant. As Vic walked away, he could feel her eyes follow him.

When he returned he gave the hostess a nod, then took

a seat with his back to Wilson. Separated by a scant two feet, he'd be able to hear what the two cops were saying without being spotted.

"So, what do you think about the latest from the captain on the Murphy thing?" Tony asked. "The press and the commissioner are sure giving him shit."

Frank put down the menu and sniffed the air. Someone was smoking English cigarettes. Must be the guy at the next table. He smiled sadly. While he and Susie had honeymooned in Europe, she'd taken a liking to British smokes. They were damn difficult to get over here in those days. Not now, though. The world was getting smaller. That was the best vacation they'd ever had, he thought. The art, the buildings, and the theater; she loved those things, and he, too, appreciated them when she'd introduced them to him. It was too bad he'd never found time for that stuff after he made detective.

"Earth to Frank," Tony coaxed.

"Sorry, Tony, what did you say?"

"Boy, are you tired or what? I asked you three times what you wanted to eat, and you never answered me about the Murphy case."

"Ah, I guess I was daydreaming. I haven't slept very good these last few days. Fucking dog keeps me awake. He misses her too, I suppose." Frank took another quick glance at the menu. "I'm gonna have the usual, I guess. Salad and some coffee. Not really hungry. As for the Murphy thing, I don't know. It's a weird case. Last month I would have bet on kidnapping, but there's been no ransom note. Her folks are squeaky clean. No mystery there. Shit, he'll probably be the governor of the state sometime soon, and she's everyone's favorite soap star. Even like her myself. Anyway, I'm beginning to think that it was a random, spur-of-the-moment thing,'' he said absently, offering Tony a smoke. Tony shook his head, indicating for Frank to continue.

"Shit, you know the facts as well as I do," Frank said. "The kid was walking home from school. It wasn't dark or anything. No one remembers seeing her, or seeing anyone with her. She looked older than fourteen. My guess is some guy stopped and offered her a ride. He put the moves on her, figuring she was older, and then panicked and killed her. The mutilation and the other shit was probably done to cover up the situation, make it look like another psycho sex killer on the loose. The doc's report seems pretty conclusive: she was choked to death, not stabbed, or raped, or beaten. It's a tough one, Tony, and we aren't going to solve it unless we get lucky and someone comes forward. Someone who saw a car or a person stop her in the street.''

Tony thought about that and pretty much concurred with him. It was a damn shame. The kid had lots of friends. She didn't take drugs or drink. She was even a virgin, for chrissakes. And Frank was right: the trail was cold. Stone fucking cold. She'd been grabbed off the face of the earth and no one had seen a damn thing. Damn. Someone had to have seen something. . . .

"Maybe the media can help us on this one," Tony ventured. "I know you hate the press, and especially the television people, but Santa Monica and Venice are big tourist spots, and maybe, just maybe, if the TV keeps the hype going, someone, somewhere, will remember seeing something and come forward. The captain told me the appeal will be broadcast nationally again this week, and the new picture should help. That was a break, her boyfriend having taken some shots of her the same day.''

Frank nodded. The mention of the photos caused him to perk up. If he hadn't gone back to question Timmy West, and seen the photos in his room, the task force never would have gotten hold of them. Still, that was what police work was all about. Not glamorous, just taking bits and pieces of something and trying to make them fit together in a sane and actionable way. And never forget the public. So many impossible cases had been solved because someone had seen something. Often something small, insignificant, and unrelated that only made sense when added to the other data available. That is what we need right now, Frank thought to himself. A little help from John Q.

Vic had been listening to this exchange and was smiling to himself. Stupid-ass cops. They'd soon have more than the Sandra Murphy slaying to worry about.

He wished that his father was still alive. That miserable, goddamn coward. He'd see something then, wouldn't he? God, how I hate that man, he thought as he picked up a fork and bent it in his hands. The red mist swirled about him as he recalled that time in Yosemite so many years ago.

It had been so perfect. So incredibly perfect. He had been only twelve then; he and his father had gone camping, just the two of them. Mother never liked the outdoors much, or so she said. Later he found out she was glad to have them away so her lover could spend the nights. Vic and his father had been there in the park for almost a week, having a great time. They had their own campsite, and the fishing and hiking were things he would have always remembered.

One day they spent several hours casting their lines into the lake, and by the end of the afternoon had three large trout to show for their efforts. They were going to clean them and cook them for dinner when they got back to the campsite. Vic had never eaten fresh trout, fresh anything, and he could hardly wait. They returned to the campsite at around seven and stowed their gear, feeling the warm rays of the setting sun on their backs. Everything was perfect, almost.

The two bikers were about thirty yards away, crouched on the grass with two leather-clad women. They were drinking, smoking, and carrying on. His father hadn't seemed to notice them, but Vic was curious because he'd never seen people like this up close. The two men were quite young, with long hair and beards; both had tattoos and wore sunglasses. He was fascinated by the bright patches and logos on their leather jackets. The two seemed harmless enough, and when one of them smiled at him and waved, he smiled and waved back. He saw his father stiffen and start to tell him to ignore them. Vic asked why, and his father sort of shrugged and continued to prepare the fish.

As the aroma from the cooking fish drifted across the clearing, the hikers suddenly approached and offered father a beer. Father explained that he didn't drink. When one of the bikers asked if they could join him, the answer was "no." The biker stood for a long moment, looking at him, but father wouldn't look back. The mood of the bikers changed. The girls said something to the larger of the two men and he swore at father, calling him "a miserable fucking pig." Father asked Vic to go into the tent. Vic didn't want to and instead suggested they share the fish, since there was plenty. "Screw the fucking fish," the large biker said, and kicked the frying pan into the air. Vic was enraged and started screaming for his father to beat them up. Father was much larger and stronger than either of the two bikers, and the boy couldn't believe that he simply sat there. Vic shouted again and looked pleadingly at his father, who seemed to be shrinking before his eyes. Suddenly, Vic saw tears on his father's face, saw his father's body heave as he begged the bikers: "Please go away . . . we don't want any trouble."

The boy couldn't believe it. The shame and hurt wrenched tears from his own eyes, and he ran into the tent. The bikers were laughing now. They had pushed father onto the ground and were standing over him. He could see the bikers unzipping their jeans. The girls were laughing and cheering, and the bikers called to the boy, telling him to watch. Though Vic knew what they were going to do, he couldn't remove his eyes. He ran out of the tent and jumped at the smallest biker. But he was too slow and the biker's boot caught him flush in the face and he fell back into a heap and stared openmouthed and dizzy. His father remained prone on the ground. Then they did it, both of them. Pissed all over father's head, his face and shoulders. And the boy thought it would never end. He smelled their urine, saw the brutal joy on their faces, their large cocks hanging ugly and hairy and limp. And then it was over.

They were gone, and he sat for a long time as his father refused to move. The smell was unbearable. Eventually Vic brought out towels, water, and blankets. He stood over his father and contemplated the awful truth: his father, the hero he had always worshiped, was a coward. The knowledge burned itself into his consciousness, left an impression that would not go away.

The next day they went home. Neither spoke of it again. And it wasn't ever the same for them after that. Not even close.

The two cops had paid their tab and were leaving the restaurant. Vic decided to wait a while; there was no point in getting spotted. He would visit the station house later this afternoon and try to spot the car that Wilson was driving.

"Everything all right?" a voice asked. "You haven't touched your food."

Vic looked up at the waitress, who wore a look of concern.

"Everything's just fine," he said quickly. "Just not hungry, I guess. I will take some coffee, though."

The memory of the camping trip was fresh and open. He was bleeding inside, but he decided to let it bleed until it was dry. Then it would be over and done with.

His mother had hated father too. Why else would she have moved Derek into the house with them later that year? She told Vic that Derek was going to be a lodger, that he'd stay with them for a year and be like an uncle. Okay, he said, and for a while having Derek there wasn't so bad. For two more summers they all got along pretty well, considering. But Derek and his mom were sharing his father's room, and his father was sleeping in Derek's room over the garage. It was all so weird. Finally Vic came right out and asked them all: "What the hell is going on?"

His mother told him to hush and mind his manners, but he persisted, telling her that all the boys at school were talking about it. Was it true? he wanted to know. Was it true what they were saying? His mother had looked down, and Derek had excused himself.

Father's eyes filled with those big wet tears again, and Vic knew then that he hated this man more than he would ever hate anyone, or anything, in his whole life.

"Yes, it's true," his father admitted, going on to say that when Vic was older he'd understand. Father said that he loved Vic and his mother very much—that it was all right, really, because he didn't mind. He understood that he wasn't exactly what mother needed, but they were all together, and that was what was important, "keeping the family together."

Vic hadn't understood then, nor later, when he was older. Jesus, everything was *already* broken. Irreparable. His father was just a goddamn, pathetic cuckold, and what did that make Vic, and his mother? Derek, as it turned out, was just the first of many "uncles" Vic would have. The cycle was only halted when mother's looks finally deserted her, and then she stayed home most nights.

Father, though, kept right on trucking, pretending like he had the perfect family. And then one day he was gone, and Vic was glad the old bastard had popped off. He was amazed to see tears spring from his mother's eyes. He'd asked her what they were for and she'd said that his father was really a "good man," that one day he'd understand it all better. Jesus, what was there to understand?

Vic had been sitting outside the station house for about thirty minutes. He was getting ready to move on when he saw them. He checked his watch—7:05 P.M. *Keep long hours, don't you, boys?* The two cops had stopped and were talking. "Mobster man" was shaking his head at Wilson, looking at his watch. Wilson shrugged, then waved and walked toward a late-model Ford. Dark blue and very dirty. Not the easiest car to tail, Vic thought.

Wilson got into his car and gunned the motor. *Okay, Wilson, come to me*, Vic thought, starting his engine. The cop turned right, then went east as he exited the car park, which was perfect. They were both facing the same direction. Vic smiled. Yes, things were going well.

He slid in behind the Ford, several car lengths behind, hoping that he'd be able to follow without being obvious. He wondered, though, how many people really checked into their rearview mirrors. It wasn't something *he'd* ever done. But then, he wasn't a cop.

As Wilson headed for the freeway, Vic let him pull ahead slightly. Suddenly he noticed that the glass on the Ford's rear left-side was broken and that it was both yellow and red. *Damn, pay attention, man.* That made for easier recognition. He let a dozen or so cars get between them, then changed into the slow lane. Sure enough, Wilson's

Ford was instantly recognizable. The car was indicating a right turn, which meant Wilson was changing onto the San Diego Freeway. Would he go north or south? South it was.

They drove for several miles past the marina exits out toward the airport. Then past the airport and to Rosecrans Boulevard. Vic could see the Ford pull over and signal a right turn. He did the same. A few minutes later, the Ford made another right turn into a small side street. Residential, small, prewar houses. He could see the Ford's brake lights, and once more the right signal indicator. He decided to slow down and pull over.

As Vic crossed the road on foot, he noticed that the lighting was poor and that it had started to rain again. Up ahead Wilson was taking something from the back seat of the Ford, then fumbling with his keys and stretching his back. Vic slowed. What was the bastard doing? Had he seen him after all? Was he waiting till he got closer? *Well, friend, if it's now, it's now. I'm ready.* Then Wilson turned and went toward the only unlit house, near where he'd parked the car. Vic continued to walk. "Move it, asshole," he muttered. Wilson was at the front door now, letting himself in. Vic saw the lights come on and Wilson checking his mailbox, and then he was past the house. He continued up the street, then turned down the next intersection. Okay, he thought, wait a while, have a cigarette then walk back on the other side of the street. You've got to get the address of the house. He did. No one else was out tonight; he was glad about that. 2137 Darcy Avenue. Good. He looked at his watch—7:54 P.M.—and smiled. He was seeing the girl at nine o'clock. Better hurry. He would drive back here tomorrow in the daylight and make his plans.

She was on time, and he decided that they should go see a movie. He didn't much feel like talking. Soon the killing would begin, and he needed to conserve his strength. It thrilled him to think about it. He wanted to make it slow and memorable. Lasting and pure. The images of the ghosts from the past started to unwind slowly before his eyes, and he pushed them away, breathing deeply. It was his time now.

Tony was agitated. He almost hadn't come home. You gotta sometimes, though, he thought, then sighed. Last night had been hard. Too much to drink, and the goddamn cases were getting him down. Frank was feeling it too. Tony wondered sometimes why they even bothered. Things weren't getting any easier, and the lousy media were a big part of the problem. Shit, the department spent more time and energy on public relations than it did on criminal investigation. At least it seemed that way to him.

With the exception of the other night, he hadn't spoken to the media since the child molestations and murders two years ago. Those dumb bastards with their frenzied need for news had depicted the murderer as an inexorable force that could not be stopped, and Tony was convinced that the constant antihero status the Francis guy had been afforded had boosted the body count. Tony had only spoken to the television people on Sunday because Frank had been so down. He'd do anything for Frank. It was that kind of friendship.

He switched on the TV set. The Monday Night Football game was on. Jets and Dolphins. Who really gave a god-damn about either of them outside of Miami and New York? He knew he didn't; until he listened to the com-mentators oohing and aahing over a great play and was hypnotized into thinking it really did matter who won, who might or might not make the playoffs. It was amazing how television reeled you in.

He went to the refrigerator and popped a Bud. He smiled to himself. Enough of these, he thought, and the world won't seem so bad. He needed a vacation, though. He knew that. It had been three years since he'd any quality time off. He kept promising himself that he'd go to Mex-ico, catch some rays, drink some margaritas. Maybe he'd get in some marlin fishing; that had always appealed to him. . . .

Later, after he'd gone to bed, Tony dreamed that he and Frank were in a large boat on the surface of a vast ocean. Again and again they cast their lines into the sea, and as the hours passed they hauled in hundreds of fish. At the end of the day they returned to port, and when they went to the hold to show their friends all the fish they'd caught, they were shocked to find the hold empty. The fish had mysteriously disappeared. Tony dreamed the same dream again and again throughout the night, and when he awoke in the morning he was exhausted.

Vic spent the next few days watching Wilson's routine. He was pretty sure that the cop lived alone. Also, that he had no pets. Or at least none that required attention, like a big snapping, snarling Doberman.

It was close to Christmas now, and Vic figured that this would be the best Christmas present he could give himself. The head of Anthony Wilson. His anger was increasing daily. Nothing more had been said about the two blacks he'd killed; instead, the tabloids and the television stations were full of the Murphy kid slaying. Whoever killed that kid was going to be pretty famous, Vic thought. If the assholes ever caught him. Which he seriously doubted.

Vic pondered the question of how to get into Wilson's house. It might be a problem, especially during the day. He wondered if it would be better to follow Wilson to a bar or restaurant and waste him there as he was returning to his car. That seemed the easiest way to do it. Safer. But then he wouldn't be able to sit with him, watch him die, and get the feeling. He needed that feeling. He could feel the loss of it, empty and hollow in his guts, and he wanted to be filled again and made stronger. He also felt a desperate need to communicate with Wilson, to touch him and talk to him as his life ebbed from his body. It had to be the house, then, and it had to be soon.

Tony and Frank were at the station house, going over the reports for the tenth time. Tony had the phone up to his ear and his feet on the desk. He seemed to be concentrating furiously. Actually, there was no one on the other end of the phone and he was catnapping with his eyes open. He'd learned how to do this over the years and clued Frank into his scam. The telephone, he told Frank, was a prop. If the captain or someone else came in, they'd see the phone in his hand and not think twice about what he was doing. Frank had said he was full of shit, but he'd watched over the years and no one had ever called Tony on it. So he guessed that it worked. His phone rang.

"Is this Frank Morrissey?"

"Yeah, who's this?" Frank asked.

"Joe Harrison. I'm with the FBI's Denver office. Listen, I was told you were the guy heading up the Murphy investigation. That right?"

"Sure is," Frank said. He nodded for Tony to pick up the line.

"The local television station ran a piece on the Murphy girl last night and showed the two new photos. . . ."

Frank and Tony both sat upright then, completely alert. Tony gave Frank a thumbs-up.

". . . We got a call about ten minutes after the show aired. That is, the local police did. Seems this guy was on vacation with his girlfriend in L.A. They remember seeing the girl. At least the guy did. He remembered thinking she was real cute, then getting into a fight with his girlfriend because he'd smiled at her. Well, after that he watched the Murphy kid sit down and wait for a bus. A minute or so later, he sees a late-model red Corvette pull up. The driver starts talking to the girl. Did I say it was a convertible?" Harrison asked. Frank glanced over at Tony and rolled his eyes.

"No? Sorry, it was," Harrison said apologetically. "They talked for about a minute and the Murphy girl got into the car. The guy who saw all this, Jeff Kelly, well, he figured that the guy in the car was the girl's father. He gave us a pretty darn good description. It's on its way to you now over the Fax. But that isn't all. The guy in the

'Vette had a personalized license plate. And get this, Kelly remembers it. It was T-A-N-K. We checked the computer, and the car is licensed to a corporation in Westwood. Are you writing this down? Ayers Financial on Wilshire Boulevard—12222 Wilshire Boulevard, Suite 1200. Looks like we broke your case, guy."

Frank couldn't help noticing the glee in Harrison's voice. What the hell, the guy had the right to gloat.

"Great work, Joe," he said. "Who else knows?"

"We put a call in to your captain, who's unavailable. Seems he's at city hall, know how that goes," Harrison said, laughing. "Our FBI man in L.A. knows. He gave me your name. All the paperwork will be sent over the wires to you. My problem's going to be the press, and keeping this between us until you arrest the suspect. How do you want to handle that?"

Tony had already reached the captain and had him on another line. He filled him in on the details. The captain wanted to speak to Harrison himself. Tony asked him to hold a second and got back onto Frank's line.

"Joe, this is Tony Wilson. Excellent work. We owe you one. Listen, I got the captain out of his meeting. He's on the other line. Wants to have a word with you. And Joe, when we break the story we'll be sure to mention your part in this. Spell me your name."

Tony winked at Frank. A little stroking never hurt. You never knew when you might need a friend. After he'd transferred the call, he put the phone down and let out a whoop. He went over to Frank and gave him a high five.

"Fucking A, Frank. We did it. The old missing-witness

deal comes through again. Jesus, you were right. What a great Christmas present. Let's go," he said, grabbing his jacket.

Frank smiled at him. Good old Tony, he thought. He gets a big bang out of closing a case. It really excites him. It *was* a good Christmas present, though. Maybe they'd get tomorrow off. A dark cloud suddenly passed over his face. Then again, maybe it would be better to work. It sure wasn't much fun on the holidays when you had to spend them alone. He thought of calling her. Maybe . . . Ah, screw it all to hell.

They drove over to Westwood. Weston called them twice and went over the details again. "Do it right, guys," he kept saying. "No guns. No bloodshed." He told them that he'd called a press conference for twelve noon. It was 10:15 A.M. Jesus H. Christ. *The damn press again*, Frank cursed under his breath.

"Listen, what if the dude isn't there or has gone on vacation or something?" Frank said to Tony. "It's Christmas Eve. Tell you what, let's check out the car park before we go blowing into the offices. Jesus, we're reacting like assholes. The driver of the car could have been anyone. Doesn't have to have been someone who works at Ayers Financial, even. Shit, whenever the press is involved, and city hall, all the good, by-the-book police procedures go out the window and we go off half cocked." He thought for a moment. "Screw the captain. Call in some backup, Tony: a black-and-white, no sirens. Have it meet us at the parking structure of 12222 Wilshire."

Tony shrugged but said, "Okay, okay. I'll call for a

black-and-white. Anything for an easy life. You worry too much.''

They drove over to the building and met the two patrol officers. Frank briefed them, telling them to search the car park for the car and radio him when they found it. They weren't to approach the car, but they were supposed to keep it in sight and make sure no one drove off in it.

While the patrolmen entered the parking structure, Frank and Tony entered the lobby and checked the building directory. Ayers Financial was there and was in Suite 1200, as the Fed man had told them it would be. So far so good.

"Let's take the elevator up to the twelfth floor and wait for the patrol guys to give us a call before we go into the office,'' Frank said.

"Sure, but why not grab a coffee in the coffee shop while we're waiting,'' Tony suggested. Frank shrugged his assent.

The patrolman called them ten minutes later.

"We have the car, Sergeant. It's on level P3. Alvin's with the valet-parking guys, making sure they don't call up to the owner. Word is, the guy only just got here in the last thirty minutes or so.''

Frank asked a few follow-up questions, then clicked off the radio. He turned to Tony and said, "Let's go.''

They went up to the twelfth floor. Ayers Financial seemed to take up most of the floor. Frank gestured to Tony, indicating he should stay back a little. He approached the pretty receptionist.

"Excuse me, miss. The guy in the parking lot, P3, told me that the owner of the red 'Vette worked in this office. Is he in?''

"Mr. Ayers, you mean? I believe he's in. May I ask what this concerns?"

Frank pulled out his badge and flipped it on the desk.

"Detective Sergeant Morrissey, miss. Official police business. We'd like to see Mr. Ayers right now."

The girl looked from Frank to Tony, hesitated a moment, then seemed to make up her mind. She rose slowly from the reception desk and led them through the main office area to a large double-doored office suite at the end of the corridor. She pointed at the doors and sort of smiled. Frank nodded, and the men drew their guns and went through the doors. Ayers was sitting behind the largest desk that either of them had ever seen. A beautiful brunette was kneeling at his chair. Frank looked at Tony, embarrassed as hell. Damn, she was blowing him. Christ almighty. No wonder the girl from the reception desk had smiled.

The brunette rose and replaced her blouse. Jesus, what a pair of tits, Tony thought, staring at her. She didn't even seem embarrassed. Ayers was red-faced and struggling to zip up his pants. He looked so small behind the huge desk. A strange thought flashed into Frank's mind. He understood now why the Vietcong sometimes stripped off the clothes of the people they were interrogating. It destroyed their self-confidence, made them vulnerable. Jesus, look at him with his limp dick hanging out, Frank thought. He looks about ready to cry.

Ayers had negotiated his zipper, finally. He was standing now and starting to bluster.

"Who let you in here? What is this? Who are you?" He turned to the girl. "Molly, call the police."

"Stay where you are, Molly," Frank told the girl. He

turned to Ayers. "What a coincidence, Mr. Ayers. You wanted police? Well, you've *got* police. My name is Frank Morrissey. Detective Sergeant, L.A. Police, Homicide. This is Detective Sergeant Wilson. Now, is there anything you want to tell us?"

Ayers sat and crumpled into his chair. He sure doesn't look like a child killer, Frank thought. Then again, most of them didn't. Ayers was stuttering, and his face had that waxy look.

"I guess I've been expecting you," he said. All the energy and bluster was gone from his voice.

"Read him his rights, Tony, and cuff him."

They took him out of the office, and the girl on the reception desk winked at them and smiled. Huge and mischievously. Tony handed her one of his cards. Typical, Frank thought. Typical. He was glad he had Susan. He sure would hate to be out there in this city in the eighties and be single. He shuddered. Christ, if Susan gets her way, that's gonna happen. Shit.

The tears were rolling down Ayers's face, and he couldn't wait to talk. As they drove to the station house Tony called the captain, telling him they had their man. The captain congratulated them and asked that they use the rear entrance to the station house since the press was already on its way.

Vic had parked several blocks away and was walking toward Tony's house. He saw a car pull out of 2125 Darcy, next door, and it surprised him. The people shouldn't even have been home yet. Then it occurred to him that it was

Christmas Eve and perhaps everyone would be home early. Dammit, he was too close now to change his plans. No sign of Wilson's car. That was good. He looked at his watch—5:05 P.M. He had hoped that it would rain. It hadn't. All the houses were dark and quiet. He could hear his shoes, and they sounded unnaturally loud. He even thought he could feel his heart, and hear it, thudding in his chest. It felt powerful. He smiled and fingered the nine-inch knife he had in his jacket. It would be like cleaning the trout, he thought.

The houses across the street were also in darkness, and he hurried now, up the driveway and through the fence leading to the backyard. So far, so good. He'd been worried about the place being wired. Well, he'd soon find out. He couldn't believe his luck when he spotted a kitchen window that was slightly open. "Cops," he said, and sniggered, tugging at the fly screen as it came away in his hands. Inserting his fingers into the partly open window, he tugged and it came open easily with a loud screech. He waited, cocking his head, listening. No signs of life anywhere. He threw the screen into the bushes and went in through the window. It let him into the kitchen next to the sink. No problems so far. He took out the towel he had in his pocket and wiped away the marks that his feet had left on the sink and counter. He closed up the window, then walked around the kitchen, feeling for and finding a chair. He would wait a few minutes for his eyes to adjust to the dark. It wasn't pitch black, but it was dark enough for him to want to wait a few moments. Christ, he wanted a cigarette. He looked at his watch. It was 5:36 P.M. Good. If everything went to plan, he'd be out of here soon.

He could see much better now. Okay, better check out the place, he thought. The kitchen let onto the living room. The den was to his right, and a small passageway led to the front door. The bedrooms were off the living room at the back of the house. He thought about it for a while. The first thing Wilson would do would be to put on the light. That was bad. Bad for him. He went into the den and looked around. There was no overhead lighting. Good. So when Wilson came into the house, through the front door, the only lights he'd be able to switch on would be the hallway and the lamp in the den. He checked the hallway. No lights. Then he saw it—a small spotlight, attached to the trellis that ran from the door down the right-hand sidewall and separated the hallway from the den. Good. He went over to the lamp in the den and removed the light bulb. If he sat down behind the half wall that supported the trellis, he'd be in perfect position to take Wilson. The light wouldn't show him and the shadows cast by the spotlight would keep him in darkness for that brief moment it took Wilson to enter the house and walk toward the living room or the den. About two strides, three at most, and he'd be behind him. He settled back to wait.

They were in Alice's again, on their fourth Bud. The good feelings of before, the euphoria of closing a case that had seemed unsolvable, were slowly evaporating, and Frank was becoming reticent and melancholy. Tony was losing his battle to be jovial and wondered if maybe they shouldn't just take off and go home. He'd been certain that Alice's would cheer Frank up; when all else had failed before, this place always worked. Susan hadn't left him before. That made a helluva difference. Tony glanced at the clock over the bar—6:05 P.M. Christmas Eve. All dressed up and no place to go.

He'd hated Christmas ever since he could remember. It was the worst time of the year for him. He wondered if there was something wrong with him. He looked around the bar and noticed that everyone else seemed to be having a good time. Except, of course, Frank. Still, he had a reason, didn't he? Tony tried to remember the last time that he'd been really happy, having a blast with a bunch of people. People he'd chosen to be with, wanted to be with. He couldn't. Sure he could remember occasions, rare, one-on-one things with girls. Good times, for sure. But so damn fleeting.

It seemed to him that everything was anticlimactic. You let your anticipation build for some big event and couldn't wait for its arrival, but then it happened and left you indifferent and you couldn't remember why you'd gotten so excited about it. He frowned into his beer. Jesus, he was a sad case, feeling sorry for himself like this.

Then he brightened. He had a theory. Especially on nights like this when he'd been drinking. When it wasn't making him festive, when everyone else seemed to be festive. He figured that it was all a con. That the media and the corporations had mass-hypnotized the entire planet and that no one was really happy or contented, except those few who called the shots. It was all a stinking scam. Everyone was as miserable as he. Except that, somehow, he'd been asleep or out of things when the big hypnosis thing had happened, and they hadn't nailed him—damning him to eternal misery and the alienation it brought. He looked into the bar and saw his reflection and raised his glass. So what if you're right, asshole? The knowledge does you no good at all, does it? Stop feeling sorry for yourself. Cheer Frank up.

He supposed that they *had* to hypnotize everyone, though, or else the whole world would grind to a screeching halt. After all, how would people get out of bed each morning if they realized just how goddamn hopeless the situation was? Truth was, they wouldn't. Would they? It stood to reason that they wouldn't. And if they didn't all get out of bed every morning, then how could the corporations exist and make money? Screw it, maybe all that wasn't true and he was just a fucking manic-depressive. Yeah, that was probably it. He felt something tugging at his arm.

"So what you thinking about, big guy?" Frank said, looking over at him.

Tony thought for a second of really telling him, but decided not to.

"Not much, just reflecting on another year in the life of one Anthony Wilson. That's what this time of the year is all about, isn't it? Reflecting on things. Making plans for the next chapter."

Frank was smiling and looking at a spot above Tony's nose. Yeah, you lying bastard. I know what you need. He smiled deeper then and thought about the surprise Tony would be receiving this evening. He'd done it on the spur of the moment yesterday. He had seen the advertisement and thought that it would be the perfect gift. A strippergram. She'd be arriving at Tony's house at eight P.M. He had to make sure that he got him home on time.

"Yeah, it was a good way to end the year. Say, Tony, did I ever tell you how much I truly enjoy your worthless company?"

Tony smiled. "You're not half-bad company yourself, Frank. What do you say we have another round?"

It was a little after seven P.M. when Frank got Tony out of the bar. He briefly considered driving over to his house with him, but decided not to. He expected that Susie might call this evening, and he didn't want to miss her call. Besides, they were spending Christmas day together, he and Tony. They had volunteered to dress up as Santas and do the children's hospital thing for the department. He was looking forward to it. That's what Christmas was all about: the kids. It had been Tony's idea. They said good night then, and drove away, guiltily. Both of them were over the limit. Great advertisment for law enforcement, he thought. To hell with it, it's Christmas and neither of us is legless. Not even close to it.

Vic was beside himself. The rage was a living thing, and it was all he could do to sit still. He wanted to smash the stinking place up, slash and rip the walls, break everything in sight. It was 7:25 P.M. He'd been sitting for close to two hours. He wanted to stretch his legs but figured the second that he moved the damn cop would be there. Come on, you bastard, he thought. The phone rang, and he gave a start. So he's expected? That calmed him a little.

He held the knife, feeling the blade's serrated edge. He had sharpened it yesterday, and the day before. It was like a razor. He imagined it ripping through Wilson's flesh, and he smiled.

He heard a car outside and breathed deep. It had stopped, and he heard the door slam. He looked at his watch. It was 7:38 P.M. He heard the footsteps on the concrete, then the jangle of keys. He got himself ready and was surprised at how calm he felt. *Come on, Wilson, get the goddamn door open.* He heard the keys rattle and then a clatter. The idiot had dropped them. Vic was getting antsy now and could feel the perspiration on his forehead. *Come on, cop. Come on.* Finally the door creaked open and he heard the light switch. Then Wilson's grunt as the lamp in the den didn't go on. The door closed and he could feel him, smell him, the beer and the cigarettes. Damn, he wanted a cigarette at that moment.

Wilson moved inside slowly, grunting to himself. Vic moved swiftly, silently. Then he was behind him, and the knife gleamed in the lamplight. He felt it go in, and it went in so deep, so far, so incredibly easily. He laughed out loud, hearing Wilson cry out and try to turn around and grab him. Vic put all his weight behind him and pulled upward. He felt the flesh ripping and could feel the hot blood flowing, gushing in a stream, down his hand and wrist. It had an odor, too, and it excited him. He pulled out the knife and pushed Wilson to the floor. Their eyes met, and he was astonished to see that Wilson's were defiant, filled with anger, not fear. He rested the dripping blade against Wilson's throat, pulled out the cop's gun, and threw it into the den. Next came Wilson's handcuffs. He snapped them onto the dying cop's wrist, kicking and prodding him.

"Up, asshole, get up," Vic said, baring his teeth.

Wilson struggled and found his feet.

"Into the bedroom. Now. Move."

Vic kicked out at Wilson's back. The cop staggered forward a few steps, almost falling. Then the knife went in again, not as deep this time, into the fleshy part of his belly. Just then the doorbell rang.

Who the hell is ringing the doorbell? Vic thought. He was really angry now, and the rage was making him lose focus; he shook his head to clear it. The stupid, goddamn doorbell rang again, insistent, needing to be answered. Deprive me of this moment, will you? he screamed to himself. He turned and thrust the blade into Wilson's throat, releasing another torrent of blood. The cop's eyes suddenly went glassy, and Vic knew it had ended far sooner than he'd wanted it to. *Damn.*

He was at the door now, and he looked through the sentry, seeing that it was a girl and that she was alone and pretty. He wondered at his great fortune. The redness was still there, swirling smokily before his eyes, and he wondered about the girl and if he should let her in. Hell, yes, he thought; this could be very pleasurable. He grabbed a scatter rug from the den and covered the dark, bloody carpet. He hid the knife in the back of his belt, then opened the door, putting his hands into his pockets.

The girl smiled.

"Tony Wilson? I'm your Christmas surprise from Frank. Well, are you going to let me in?" she asked, smiling impishly.

"Uh . . . yeah, sure, come in. Sorry it's so dark. The

light bulb just went out, I guess. Go on into the living room. So Frank sent you, did he?''

The girl was alone and carrying a ghetto-blaster. She smiled and went into the living room. He followed her, put on the kitchen light, and sat on the bar stool. This was going to be fun, he thought. Damn, she sure was cute. The girl had slipped off her coat. She was dressed as a French maid. Suspenders, the works. She knelt down and put on her music machine. Jesus, her tits were huge, and what a great ass, he thought, watching her intently. She started to dance to the music, and he felt himself getting hard.

"Don't sit so far away, Tony. Come on, come over here. Come closer," she said, smiling and pouting seductively.

He went over toward her and saw her eyes reflect the horror as she saw the blood dripping from his hands. Even in the dim light it was unmistakable. He moved quickly and had his hand over her mouth before she could scream. He pulled out the knife and showed it to her. Huge and menacing, dripping blood. He saw the color drain from her face and wondered if she was going to faint. She didn't. He loosened his hand and whispered to her.

"See this knife, pretty lady? One murmur out of you and it's yours. All nine inches of it. Understand?"

The girl nodded. He could see the tears, large and wet, filling her eyes and running down her face. She wasn't pretty anymore. Just pathetic. He hated tears. God, how he hated all they reflected. The image of his father and the goddamn bikers floated eerily through his mind. The redness began to choke him and surge through his body, making him want to hack and slash and be rid of her and her damn, pathetic, cowardly tears. He stepped back, seeing her pleading look, and he slipped the knife into her. The terror on her face was a thing to behold. He pushed gently, feeling it enter her, and then viciously he pulled upward, feeling her body stiffen, then go slack. He pulled out the knife and let the body crumple to the floor. He listened for her heartbeat, but she was dead. And he was alive, very alive. He felt jubilant. He looked down at the girl, then used the knife to cut off her bra and panties. She had shit herself, and he was disgusted. Her tits were soft and slack. He kicked her body and walked into the bedroom.

Back to Wilson. He was dead, of course. Dead and lying in his own excrement. The stench reminded him of an abattoir. It was done, but he was reluctant to leave because he wanted to feel the parting, life passing into death. He wanted to see if they came into him, as the black kids had. He lit a cigarette. It tasted wonderful. Then it was time to leave. He put the knife back into his inside pocket and went out the back door.

Everything was still, quiet and peaceful. His feet felt light and he wanted to sing out. He peeled off the blood-soaked cotton surgical gloves and put them into his pocket. Quickly he walked back to his car. He opened the rear hatch and took the knife and the gloves and placed them in the blanket he had brought, then removed his jacket and did the same. He put on some other leather gloves and another jacket, then pushed Tony's gun into his waistband.

It was a risk, but he had plans for this gun. Big plans. He drove slowly toward home.

Once home, he showered, rinsing the blood off his arms and singing softly to himself, smiling as he watched the pink residue trickle down the drain.

The telephone woke him. Frank was still dressed, and his mouth tasted as though he'd been licking lint all night. He looked over at the clock. Christ, it was 10:26. Had he slept through? He was supposed to be at the station house at nine A.M. Jesus, what a way to live. He shook his head, groping for the telephone.

"Yeah, Morrissey here," he croaked, barely recognizing his own voice.

It was a woman's voice on the other end, a pleasant voice. *Susan*? No, it wasn't her. That's why he had been sitting there. Waiting for her call. She hadn't called. Shit, that depressed him.

"Frank? Is that you? This is Connie Fink from the Arbour agency," the woman said. He heard the concern in her voice.

He shook his head to clear it. It dawned on him that it wasn't morning after all. What the hell did Connie want? Tony? Then it came back to him.

"Hi, Connie. Sorry, I must have dozed off. Had a few drinks earlier. Merry Christmas. What can I do for you?"

"Well, it's weird. Lisa—you know, the girl I sent to Sergeant Wilson's house? Well, she had another party to go to at ten, and so far she hasn't shown up. It's unusual because the next place is not too far from the sergeant's house. I called Sergeant Wilson and the phone rang and rang; there was no answer. I was wondering if you'd heard from him. You know, since it was your gift to him. Have you?'' she asked, hope in her voice.

He was fully alert now. She was right; it didn't figure. He felt his stomach constricting. Maybe the girl never showed and Tony was out partying? That must be it.

"No, Connie, I haven't heard from him. Are you sure that this girl even showed? Where was she before? Maybe she decided to take the night off."

Connie was indignant.

"What kind of a place do you think this is? She went to Sergeant Wilson's from an office party in El Segundo. She called to say she was on her way. I just know she went there. Dammit, usually we send a guy with the girls. But with this being Christmas Eve and all . . . and the client being a police officer . . . who'd have thought there would be any problem? What should I do? Do you have another number for him, one that he might answer?"

He'd started to sweat now, and his heart was thumping in his chest. Something's wrong, old buddy, he told himself. Very damn wrong. He shook his head again, lighting a smoke.

"Relax," he said. "Take it easy. I'm sure there's nothing wrong. I do have another number. Hang on to the line a minute. I'll be right back."

He put her on hold and called the hot-line number. His hands were shaking; he misdialed it, twice. *Answer the fucking thing, Tony.* It rang over and over again, but no one answered. Finally he took several deep breaths and stubbed out the cigarette. He hung up and got back on the line with Connie.

"Listen," he said, "I just called, and there's no answer. Maybe they went out for a drink or something. Tony can be a real persuasive guy. . . ." He thought for a moment. "Look, I know you're worried. How about if I take a drive down there and see if I can find out where they might be. Okay?"

"If you would. I just have a bad feeling. Nothing like this has ever happened before, Frank. Ever. Give me a call when you get there, will you? Thanks a lot."

They hung up, and he checked his gun and grabbed his jacket. Damn, he needed coffee. His eyes felt like they were glued together and under the glue some goddamn pervert had placed sandpaper. Oh, well, nothing he could do about it now.

He got to Tony's in twelve minutes. He saw Tony's car and another one in the driveway. Must be the girl's, he thought. He'd look like a horse's ass, barging in on them. Something told him, though, that that wouldn't be the case. He approached the house cautiously, gun drawn.

The front door was locked and there were lights on. He rang the doorbell and waited. Then waited some more. He was getting very edgy now; it was goddamn freezing out here, and he could feel the perspiration forming on his brow. *Answer the damn door, Tony.* He went around the back and saw right away that there was a screen missing on the kitchen window. Oh, Christ. He cocked his gun, looked carefully through the window. He saw the girl. A part of her. Her legs and bare ass. She was lying down

and was still, and the body angle was all wrong. *Jesus*.
He hesitated, then quickly ran back to his car. He requested
a backup and an ambulance. The dispatcher told him to
wait till the black-and-whites arrived, but he said he was
going in. That was his buddy in there.

He ran back to the house. The kitchen door was unlocked, and he went in fast and low. The house sounded
and felt lifeless. Then the smell hit him; he gagged on the
stench of human shit and blood, and something worse—
the stink of death. He threw himself into the living room
and saw everything. And nothing. The girl was there and
dead. Very dead. She had bled all her blood and she had
died badly. He saw her guts hanging out, and it made his
legs weaken. You never get used to it, he thought. Never.

He got a towel from the kitchen, wet it, and put it over
his nose and mouth. Why was he stalling? He knew Tony
was in there and that he was dead. Was he afraid he
wouldn't be able to handle seeing him like that? Like what?
He both did and didn't want to know. He wiped his face
and felt a little better. Well, not worse. He didn't bother
checking the girl's vital signs. She was as dead as dead
gets. Then he saw the blood, and it went from the living
room to the bedroom. Slowly and agonizingly he followed
the thin red line, until he could smell it again and something
else. Something familiar? What was it? Then he was in
the room, and he saw him and the badness of the death.
Something horribly evil had been at work in his friend's
home. Why? He felt his legs weaken, and he tasted the
rancid bile in his throat and mouth. He felt, and couldn't
move. His mouth moved and the words were stuck somewhere. No sound came out. Then the hot, fiery tears were

running down his face into his mouth, and he was propelled back through time and space, a child again. He wanted his mother and felt so alone, so goddamn afraid.

Tony had gone, just as his mother had gone. He missed them both. He knew that it was going to be bad, never the same again, and a part of him was with Tony, wherever he was. Then it came out, a huge roar leaving his mouth like a child from a woman during a difficult pregnancy. It was out and the pain was less but still fresh, etched and burned into the memory. He screamed and screamed as he held his friend, seeing the handcuffs and so much blood. He realized that his friend hadn't been killed but massacred. It was inhuman. Who could have done this?

They found him there, holding his friend in his arms and rocking him. The patrolmen were afraid of him; they recognized that look he had on his face and didn't envy the bastard that had done this thing. They couldn't get Frank away from the body.

He traveled with the bodies in the ambulance downtown. The medic driving called ahead and was patched through to Captain Weston. Weston was good, and had it figured: "Take him to the hospital," he told them. "Unload the bodies and take them over to the morgue. They were friends, and about all that the other had. This is a bad day for us. Real, fucking bad."

Frank woke up later, much later, in a hospital bed. He saw Tony's body in front of his eyes. It all came back to him, surging and crashing through his subconscious, numbing him, debilitating him. The crying part was done;

the mourning was still to come. But now it was the cold, icy anger that he needed, and he had it. He rang for the nurse. . . .

He had checked out of the hospital and bummed a ride back to the station house. He hardly heard the sympathetic greetings of his associates. He wanted only to talk to Roy Weston.

They were sitting in the captain's office.

"Look, Frank, I want you to take a few days off," Weston started. He saw Frank was about to protest and held up one of his huge hands.

"Wait. Hear me out, will you? I haven't said anything before, figured it was none of my business, that you'd talk to me if you wanted to. Well, I know that you and Susan are having some problems. . . ."

"What the fuck does—"

"Frank, just hear me out," Weston said. "I know how it was with you and Tony. I do know, believe me. I've been there, remember that. But for now I want you home and resting for a couple of days. You're no use to me as you are. You and Tony were the best that I have. We all want to get the fucking maniacs who did this, believe me. But for now, Ramirez and Cooper will start the preliminary investigation."

Frank jumped up from his seat, rage and indignation written on his face, his mouth working furiously. The captain stood, raising his hands.

"Wait, I haven't finished. Next week, when you're ready, come on back. If you're feeling better, you can head up the case. That's it. I'm sorry, Frank. You know that. But that's the way I'm calling this one. Go home and get some rest. Okay?"

Frank didn't like it. Not one goddamn bit. But the captain wouldn't be swayed. Reluctantly, he went home, and it was weird. Nothing seemed the same. He realized that he was depressed. Upset. Angry. But it wasn't just what had happened. There was something else. Something that had been building inexorably over the years.

The whole of his life he'd been a goddamn "toe the line" kind of guy. Didn't even cheat on his income taxes, for chrissake. And nothing good had come to him. What was that malarkey his long-dead mother had preached? About reaping what you sowed and the meek inheriting the earth. It was a goddamn crock of shit. All of it. The whole fucking system was eroding. Once there had been a few bad cops, a few guys on the take, greedy men who took advantage of the trust that they'd been given. Now it was real hard to find any good cops. Well, at least committed cops. Shit, any good anybodys. Really good, straight-shooting, salt-of-the-earth types. Guys like Tony. And what had Tony's good nature brought him? The worst kind of death: Tied up and slaughtered, cruelly and slowly. No death by natural causes or a quick bullet in the brain, but a brutal, slow-motion, agonizing death. It wasn't right and it wasn't goddamn fair. It was all beyond him. The whole thing was falling apart. And sure, he'd find Tony's murderer. He had to. Then what?

He didn't have a goddamn clue.

Frank didn't know what woke him. It was a presence in the house. He could feel it. It wasn't a threatening one, either. He licked his lips. Christ, they felt cracked and parched. But he felt stronger, focused, and the anger was there. Peripherally. He welcomed it and invited it in. It was good, it made him want to get up. Want to get on with the living. Then he realized that it was the warmth of the house that he felt, the smell of something cooking. *Christ, she was home.* He jumped from the bed and felt the room start to spin.

"Susan. Susan, is that you?" he yelled, running out of the room, feeling the wobbliness of his legs, the wooziness surging through his body.

He heard her call out. Then she was there at the bottom of the stairs. She looked wonderful. Christ, he was happy to see her. She'd been crying and wasn't wearing any makeup. She looked just like the little girl he'd met sixteen years ago, fallen madly in love with. His heart lurched.

"Frank, oh Frank, I'm so sorry about Tony. I loved him too. It's so damn unfair. I came as soon as I heard. The captain called me last night. I took the first flight this morning, got here a couple of hours ago. I didn't want to wake you. . . . I—I've been looking at the pictures we took at Thanksgiving and remembering him and how you were so much more alive when you were around him . . . and . . . and I was jealous of him. . . . I'm so sorry, Frank, for some of the things that I thought and said. Oh, Frank . . . I missed you so much."

She ran up the stairs as he staggered down to meet her, feeling his heart hammering in his chest. They held each other for a long time. He rocked her and her breath came out in long sobs, her body heaving. She felt so small and frail to him. He realized that it was the first time in years that they'd held each other unconditionally. Somehow it seemed to bring things into focus. Damn, he was glad that she was there.

"What happened, Frank?" she said at last, lifting her eyes to meet his. "Or don't you want to talk about it. . . . The captain told me just that Tony was dead, and that you were taking it badly and I should hurry home. From my vacation, as he put it."

They were holding hands. Something they always used to do. In the old days. The days when he thought that the world was theirs for the taking. Lifetimes ago. He wanted to talk about it with her; tell her how he really felt inside. It was tough, because they'd been fencing and dancing with each other so long. He sighed. Everyone always said it was never too late when two people really cared. Perhaps. He leaned toward her and kissed her on the tip of her nose. He saw her face soften. But her eyes still had that questioning look.

He began haltingly. "We . . . we were out . . . drinking together, celebrating the closing of the Murphy case. Did you hear about that?" She shook her head. "Well, someone came forward. Some guy in Denver. We nailed the killer here in L.A. Some hotshot, girl-crazy investment guy. He hadn't meant to kill her. Then when he did he tried to make it look like a psycho had done it. We couldn't figure how he had the stomach to cut her up like he did. Turned out he was high on cocaine and vodka when he did it. He says he can't remember the actual details." He held her more tightly.

"Anyway, Tony wanted me to have dinner with him. *Now*, of course, I wish I had. I didn't because I wanted to be home if you called. I was . . . well, I was missing you a lot. I'd arranged a strippergram for him. For a Christmas gift. Sounds kinda silly, I guess. But he'd been down a lot these past weeks and he was busting his tail trying to cheer me up. And you know Tony, how shy he is with girls.'' Frank went on, not realizing he'd used the present tense. "Well, I figured why not do this for him. Then maybe his Christmas wouldn't be a total bust, maybe he'd feel less lonely. Did you ever notice over the years how he kind of shied away from Christmas?'' he said, pausing to light a smoke. She glanced at him and nodded.

"The girl and he were both murdered. I don't know who yet, or why. But someone got into his place and did a real butch—'' He corrected himself. "They did a real job on them. Tony's big, strong, and it couldn't have been easy for someone to get the drop on him. I think Tony was killed or being killed when the girl arrived. He'd been . . . well, he'd been cuffed, slashed, and stabbed many times. Then the . . . the maniac who did it slit his throat, let him drown in his own blood.''

She heard the anger in his voice—the pure, white-hot rage. It frightened her.

He continued. "I think that the girl was taken down quicker, there only seemed to be one wound . . . and . . . Christ, it was the worst I've ever seen.'' At that he ended abruptly, and for a long moment there was nothing but silence.

She was quiet for a while; then she, too, lit a cigarette. She offered him one. It was one of those British ones; he passed. He preferred his own Camel Lights.

"And you have no idea who it could have been? Might

it have been someone they just let out of prison—someone who had a grudge against Tony?''

He hadn't had time to really think about the motive. Not yet. She had a point, though, a good one. He'd follow that up with the department. He sat up, suddenly sniffing the air. Jesus, he thought, that was the other smell in Tony's house. He leapt from the sofa and ran to the telephone.

''What is it, Frank? What's wrong?'' she said.

He motioned for her to wait. The phone was ringing and ringing. Christmas Day. Come on, you lazy bastards. He hung up, and on a hunch called his own extension. His and Tony's. It was answered on the second ring.

''Ramirez. Homicide.''

''Glen, hi. It's Frank. Better, thanks. Susan's here. Listen, have the lab boys finished at Tony's place yet?''

''Probably. Why?''

He thought about that for a second. Glen and Jim Cooper were good men. Glen had been close to Tony. They'd played softball together. He decided he wouldn't hold anything back. They wanted the bastard caught as badly as he did. Almost as badly.

''Listen,'' Frank said, ''I got one of those feelings. When I went into Tony's house, there was this awful smell. You remember it. You were there. It was the pits. I used a towel and wiped off my face and blew my nose. When I was moving toward the bedroom, I started to smell the same odor, and I knew that Tony was gone. At the same time my nose caught something else, something else that I recognized. I'd forgotten about it. Until just now. Susie smokes British cigarettes. She just finished one, and that

was the smell I caught. Cigarette smoke,'' he said, and
waited, wondering what Ramirez was thinking. Wishing
he could see his face.

"Listen, Frank, I realize that you're upset and want to
nail this guy. But what are you trying to tell me? Cigarette
smoke, shit. That narrows it down to maybe fifty-six million people.''

Frank bit back his impatience. It was the learning-curve
thing; Tony knew him and how he worked, and wouldn't
have questioned him. Ramirez didn't.

"Just listen, Glen. Do you smoke? Okay. What kind of
smokes? Marlboros. So the smell of them would really be
noticeable to you, because you're used to it, right? Bear
with me. Tony didn't smoke. Well, not much, anyway.
If he'd been smoking or if the murderer had been smoking
and it was American, I wouldn't have noticed the smell.
Trust me, I wouldn't. British smokes smell different. No,
I'm not shitting you. The tobacco is different.''

"Okay,'' Ramirez said, "so let's assume I believe you,
just for a second. What's your point?''

Jesus H. Christ, what's my point? he screamed silently.
Susan had seen his agitation, and came over and hugged
him. He smiled at her. And spoke very slowly into the
phone.

"Well, maybe the one who'd smoked the British cigarette was the murderer. So, why not ask the lab boys to
double-check for butt ends—not just in the house but out
on the street. I figure that the place must have been scoped
out pretty well by the killer, don't you?''

He heard Ramirez exhale.

"All right, Frank, I'll get the boys out there if you think

it will help, though I don't know that linking the killer to a lousy British cigarette will get us anywhere fast.'' He sighed, apparently reconciled to indulging Frank on this point. ''Listen, buddy, give Susie my best.'' Frank heard the phone click and looked over at Susan. She was smiling at him, her head slightly cocked to one side.

''The cigarette, Frank. It's a place to start, isn't it? What was it you used to say when you started out? Give me one piece of the puzzle, no matter how small, and one day it will get solved. Do you remember those days, Frankie?'' she said, and smiled at him, stroking his hair as she always used to.

They were sitting in the squad room—Ramirez, Cooper, the captain, and Frank. The reports were placed on each man's desk. There was something about it that seemed unreal.

Captain Weston broke the silence.

''Look, guys, we all miss Tony. I mean no disrespect to any of you. Especially you, Frank. But we gotta shake this one off, get on with things. Let's go through what we have again. Okay?'' he said, nodding at Cooper.

Jim Cooper picked up the file and stood. He was a pacer and couldn't stand to be seated for any length of time.

''You all read the coroner's report. Tony was stabbed three times—once in the back, which may have been enough to kill him. The murder weapon was a blade, maybe eight or nine inches long, sharpened to a razor's edge. The killer was right-handed, probably very strong. The wound that the girl received showed that he was very close to her when he inserted the knife. She appeared to put up no kind of a fight. He didn't rape her, which is odd, considering that he sliced off her bra and panties. It may be that he was going to and then panicked. We don't know. The perpetrator entered the house through an open kitchen window. Left through the back door. So far Forensics has nothing. The place was clean, nothing missing, so I figure we can forget the robbery angle. All indications are that a lot of planning went into this. The girl was just unlucky. In the wrong place, at the wrong time. We're—''

Frank had been listening to this with mounting irritation, not at Cooper, not really at anyone. Just the matter-of-factness of it all. He interrupted.

''What about the ashtrays? Did you guys have Forensics check out the ashtray angle?''

Ramirez, who had been sitting doodling, looked up.

''We did check it out,'' Cooper said. ''There was a cigarette butt in the toilet. They're doing testing on it right now. We expect to get the preliminary report this morning.'' He turned to Ramirez. ''Glen, why don't you call over, speak to Joe Grayston, see what he has.'' Then Cooper went back to addressing Frank. ''We found plenty of butts on the street, too, but I wouldn't hold your breath. The rain fucked up what real chance we had of finding anything conclus—''

Frank interrupted. ''Listen, it may sound stupid to you guys. I understand that. But I have a feeling on this one. Just hang in with me. Sorry, Coop, go on.''

Weston had been watching this exchange closely. It was bothering him the way the men were reacting toward each other. "Mind telling me, Frank, what this is all about?" the captain asked.

"Not at all," Frank said. "When I went into the house I smelled something. Something more than the usual death smell. Not right away but after, when I went into Tony's bedroom. I couldn't place it until Susan and me were talking. She lit up one of her smokes—the British type—and I knew that's what I'd smelled before. I called Glen and told him to have the lab boys keep their eyes open for any butt ends. Also, now that I've had a chance to think about it, I figure that whoever killed Tony was in the room; watched him die, then made sure that he did die. The killer smoked a fucking cigarette while he was waiting. That tells me a lot. It tells me he's a cool customer and isn't the sort that's bothered by a guilty conscience. Shit, I think the bastard enjoyed what he was doing."

Weston nodded. It was a pretty slim lead. Still, it might be something, and right now, anything was better than nothing. "All right," the captain said, "we'll see what the lab boys come up with. What else do we have? What's the plan?"

Everyone looked toward Frank.

"We'll start with door-to-doors in the immediate area, see if anyone saw or heard anything, or if anyone spotted a strange vehicle or a stranger in the area around Tony's house the last week or so. Someone might have seen something. I think the department should issue an appeal on television. Also, I want to review Tony's arrest record to see if anyone who'd fit the m.o. was released in the past three months. Later today, I'm going to go over Tony's house and have a look around. That's it for now. The lab boys will maybe have something. Glen, what do you think?'' he said, looking over at Ramirez, trying to get a measure of him.

Ramirez was thinking dark thoughts at the moment. There were no leads, no motive. He had a bad feeling about this one. Still, Frank's plan was sound. It was about all they could do under the circumstances. A week had gone by, almost, and the trail was stone cold.

''Sounds great. Jim and me will start the house-to-houses if you want.''

Weston nodded. ''Okay, guys. I'll handle the press. Keep me apprised. Frank, let's talk.''

The two men went into Roy Weston's office, Frank following behind, realizing he was about to get a pep talk. He means well, Frank thought as he lowered himself into a chair. Roy's a good guy. One of the few who aspired to the commissioner's job who was worth a damn. Frank looked at Weston now as he settled behind his desk, smiling that huge smile of his. Frank had known him long enough to see under the smile, to recognize the steel-hard glint in his eyes. It was a warning that he'd better not ignore.

''Have a good Christmas, Roy? By the way, thanks for calling Susan. I owe you one.''

Weston visibly relaxed, and his eyes lost their icy glint.

''Glad that Susan came home. She's a good girl.'' He paused. ''Listen . . . I know it's none of my business, but Cindy and me have gone through the same kinda shit. If it wasn't for the kids . . .'' he said, shrugging. ''Well, I think that I wouldn't have been able to make it work. It's hard on the women. Harder than most realize. This job, if you give a good goddamn, is sometimes all there is. The womenfolk have to take a back seat, and it gets frustrating, sharing their men with the department." Frank started to speak, but Weston raised his hands. "Wait, let me have this at bat. There aren't many jobs out there that take this kind of toll on the women. It's not just the time spent on the job, either. It's the constant threat of death or injury that preys on their minds. Imagined or real. Some can handle it. Others . . . well, it's like rust on a car. It wears out the parts and then one day the damn engine just won't kick over. We don't see it happening, and as we get more into the job we need the women more, and they're drifting away, feeling second best. That's a hard thing to deal with, always being second fiddle." He stopped, apparently considering what to say next. "Frank, this thing with Tony is bad. Bad for the whole department. If I thought I could make you, I'd take you off the case. Send you on vacation. But I know you. You wouldn't go, would you?"

"No, Roy, I wouldn't," Frank said. It was that simple.

Weston nodded. "Just do me one thing, then, Frank. Try to spend some time with Susan in the next month or so. It will take the edge off. Make you a better cop. And it'll help you two to stay together."

Frank said he would. What else could he say? What the captain had said made sense. Right now, though, he wanted to do his job, which was to find a killer.

"If that's all, Roy . . ." Frank said, starting to get up.

Weston nodded, then called him back. "Frank, there was just one small thing. Tony's gun was missing. We haven't been able to locate it yet. I hope it doesn't mean what I think it might mean.''

Frank stared at him for a long moment. Dammit, he thought, that's a pretty big item to have forgotten to tell me. Had it been kept quiet for fear of a leak to the media?

"Who else knows?" Frank asked.

"No one other than special affairs. We only just finished looking in his locker, his car, his home. I'd hoped that it would turn up. It didn't. What can I tell you, except it's not for general release."

"What about Cooper and Ramirez?" Frank asked, staring hard at Weston and trying to see his eyes.

"I suppose. That's up to you. For now we need to keep it as quiet as possible, though. Maybe there's an explanation," the captain said, and shrugged his shoulders. He'd finished.

And maybe there wasn't. Frank was angry. It was goddamn obvious that the murderer had Tony's gun. But why would a killer risk stealing the gun of his victim? Unless he intended to do more killing . . .

Frank returned to his office deep in thought. There was a message for him to call Grayson at the lab. Screw it, he'd drive over. It'd be good to get out of there for a while. The walls were starting to press in on him. He walked out into the warm, sunny California day and got in his car. He wondered what Susan was doing as he drove over to the lab. Less than ten minutes later he'd parked and entered Grayson's office.

"Hi, Joe. Got something for me?"

Grayson was sitting behind a desk that looked as if it

had the entire paperwork of the department on it. He was staring at his computer screen and scratching his head.

"Hi, Frank. Sorry to hear about Tony. Yeah, I have something. Don't know what it'll mean, but I just finished running a make on the butt we found in the toilet. You're right about it being British. It's a Dunhill. Also, we've matched it up to several others we found in and around Tony's street. I hope it helps," he said, looking over at him.

Frank felt the first stir of excitement, vindication. He'd been right.

"Great work. Let me have your report as soon as you can. Anything else turn up? Anything at all?"

"Nothing else. The guy was in and out and very careful. No prints or footsteps. I wish we could give you something to work on."

Frank sighed. "Well, thanks for the info on the cigarette butt." He was standing toward the door when suddenly he did an about-face. "Say, any word on the murder weapon?"

Grayson foraged amid a pile of papers on his desk and came up with a printout. "As a matter of fact, yes. I just got the word in a couple of hours ago. Let's see. It was probably a hunting knife—one with a nine-inch serrated blade, very sharpened. Single edged and with a curved tip. From the printout I'd guess that it's a standard type, found in any gunsmith's or sporting-goods store. Nothing special. What can I tell you?" He shrugged, gazing at the sheet of paper.

Frank nodded. He hadn't expected much. But this was bad. Police work was as efficient as the items or leads the detectives had to go on. Still, it was early yet. *Don't worry, Tony. Something will come up. It has to.*

Vic was sitting on his balcony, deep in thought. The killing urge was strong. It had been weeks since the last one, and the stupid stripper girl had spoiled everything. Almost. He'd still nailed that lying cop. But it wasn't like he'd planned it. He wanted to feel the dead man's soul pass into him, as the black kids' had. He needed the strength. It made things better with him and the girl, physically better. He could feel the tension in his body. The tightness in his head. He fingered the gun and put it up close to his face and rubbed it against his temple. It felt good in his hand, cool and friendly, an extension of himself. He squeezed the trigger. It clicked, and he smiled. He felt good, strong and invincible. The images of all those people who'd called him weak over the years drifted past his eyes. He smiled. He wished they could see him now. Wished they were all lined up against the wall, every single one of them. They'd be terrified as he put the gun against each of their temples. He felt his finger tighten on the trigger of the gun. They'd see the strength in his eyes, the power flowing through him. They'd sob and scream for mercy. There would be none, of course. Not for them. Not for those losers. Then their sphincters would release, as the cop's and stripper's had, and they'd all know that it was *they* who were weak and cowardly, not him. He felt his loins stir, and he thought of Andy. The lovemaking with the girl had been incredible. She couldn't get enough of him. This morning had been especially intense.

They had both gotten out of the shower. He was drying

her back and butt. Then her breasts and between her legs. She smelled so damn good. They'd been talking about her job. About whether or not she should continue at the bar. He wondered about that. He liked the times he had to himself, and her working there was fine as far as he was concerned. She'd been drying him off, and he'd started to get hard. Christ, he'd thought, after last night's experience, I didn't think I could get it up again for days. She was smiling, and she told him to go into the bedroom. He was wondering what she'd planned, and then she returned.

She had something in her mouth. He'd started to ask her what she was doing, when she smiled and put her finger to her mouth, telling him to be quiet. He relaxed and lay back. She was over him now and had him in her hands. Slowly she rubbed him, and amazingly he started to respond immediately. Shit, she was something, this one. He could feel his body shudder; his cock throbbed, and he wanted her. She smiled, pulling her hair back and taking him with her mouth. He jumped, startled. The feeling was incredibly intense. Hot and cold all at once. Damn, she'd put ice in her mouth. He started moving his hips in time with her mouth. She moved her hands and let him push inside her farther and soon all the way into her. He was incredibly excited. They moved together, slowly, and he could see her large, beautiful lips devouring him. He heard her murmuring and the slip-slap of himself in her mouth. He could feel her tongue, her teeth, the roof of her mouth, the tightness of the back of her throat. He wanted to touch her and feel her breasts and the soft warmness between her legs, and the anticipation only made him harder. He was helpless, and she was his master. He couldn't hold it, and he started to come. She swallowed him deep and then cried out, sucking at him harder. He seemed to be coming forever, and then she was gone, laughing and smiling as she went into the bathroom. He laid back and absorbed the moment. He could still feel her mouth around him and pulling him into her. He was astonished at her, wanting her, calling her name softly. He heard her laugh somewhere, off in the other room.

He must have dozed for a few moments. He was still thinking of her, being in her, the hot-cold feeling that was incredibly intense. He opened his eyes and she was there before him, kneeling over him. She had him again, inside her mouth. He was hard, responding to her, and she was laughing and squeezing him, playing with his balls, running her tongue and fingers between his legs and rubbing his buttocks. He tried to make her stop, to take off her clothes, join him in the bed, but she laughed and sucked harder and longer. He was with her again, rising, falling, and coming. He felt it deep within him, the first great spasms, and he let it go. The hot jets hit the back of her mouth as she gulped him down. Then an incredible fatigue shot through his legs, and his body could hardly move. She was laughing at him, calling him a "horn dog." She said she had to go and that he wouldn't "feel the urge to screw someone else now, would he?" He was perplexed and didn't know what she meant. It was good with her, and he wanted her and couldn't figure it out. Christ, that was hours ago, and he thought his cock had died and gone to heaven. Yet, just thinking about her, he felt a stirring again. That girl. Jesus, something else . . .

Vic had been driving around for hours, letting the redness consume him, absorb him, fill his eyes and his body. He'd decided that he'd park and see if the pushers he'd spotted would try and sell him some dope. He was walking down the side street and checking the area for a good killing ground. He was concerned that it was taking so long. Too much exposure. Someone might remember seeing him. Screw it, why worry, they wouldn't catch him anyway: he was invincible. He saw the three men ahead of him, leather jackets and long hair. He felt his body tighten. He blinked. The red mist flowed over his eyes. He became focused, powerful. He caressed the .38 Smith & Wesson in his pocket. He'd decided against the cop's gun; it was too big, too bulky. He would use that for something special. Later. He'd taken special care loading the gun, making sure that each of the rounds was carefully prepared. Soft hollow-point shells, maximum firepower. He grinned. The gun in his hand felt good.

They'd seen him approaching them. They'd appraised him. Typical West Side yuppie, they thought. Too much money, too little sense. Probably a damn fag, too, judging from his clothes and pretty face. They figured this one would be good for $175 a gram, two, maybe three grams. They'd decided to give him the lowest-quality shit they had. Good way to start the evening.

"Hi, guys. Got anything that I might want to buy?" Vic asked quietly, directing his questions at the tallest of the three men.

The man shrugged, looked around warily.

Vic smiled. "How about some coke?"

The three men looked at each other, an unspoken dialogue passing among them.

"Maybe we do, maybe we don't. Let's see the color of your money, friend."

Vic was getting the rage feeling now. He almost wanted to do it then and there. These three smug assholes were smiling at him. They were like the ones at school. Always pushing, always smiling. Always the same goddamn, condescending sneer. He felt his hand gripping the gun tighter in his jacket pocket, and its closeness calmed him a little. He took a deep breath, kept it there, red and powerful, controlled. He reached into his pocket, pulling out the wad of hundred-dollar bills he had.

"This look like enough? So show me what you've got. Only, not here on the street."

The leader of the three men looked around, then smiled, showing large, predatory, yellow teeth. He nodded at the others.

"Follow me, friend," he said, clapping him on the shoulders. "We got all you could wish or want for: reds, yellows, whites, and of course the best nose candy around."

They walked to the end of the block, into the nearby alley. It was dark, silent, and empty. Vic felt a rush of pleasure. It was the most perfect spot on earth. He felt the cold metal of the gun and gripped it in his hand tightly. Okay, half-wits. Let's party.

The three men had stopped. One of them was taking out a bag from his pocket. They were all close to each other. Vic felt the rush. It filled him, and he seemed to grow taller, wider. The gun was out, and he pointed it at the head of the nearest man. The terror in the man's eyes was beautiful. Vic smiled at him, wanting to touch him. He pulled the trigger, and the bang was louder than he remembered it from before. It made him jump a little. The man's face seemed to fly into a hundred pieces as the force of the bullet entering his flesh, impacting against bone and muscle, threw the already dead body violently against the wall. Vic moved his hand slightly, shooting the next man in the throat. The hot red blood spurted out of the gaping wound, spraying the third man, who was sobbing and pleading for his life. Vic stared at him, feeling nothing but contempt. The sobbing man dropped to his knees and pissed his pants. Vic knelt down and told him to open his mouth. The man screamed for mercy, and Vic laughed, a loud, primitive laugh that echoed back from the alley's dirty walls, filling his victim with dread as Vic put the barrel of the gun into his mouth.

"How does death taste, motherfucker?" he said, twisting the gun savagely in the terrified man's mouth, feeling his teeth on the barrel.

Then he waited, and at the precise moment that the red mist started to lift from his eyes, he pulled the trigger. He felt the man's body go limp, shudder, and twitch, and as life passed out of it, it seemed to Vic that it was flowing into him. He smiled. After a moment, he returned his gun to his pocket and looked around. Nothing. He walked quickly away.

Frank was feeling depressed. They'd been on the case almost three weeks with no sign of a lead. They'd visited every house in Tony's neighborhood and learned nothing. No one had seen or heard a damn thing. No one had noticed any strangers or strange vehicles in the area, which was not really surprising since it was winter and it had been raining on and off for a month. People in Southern California tended to hibernate during this kind of weather. He sighed. Dammit all to hell. There had to be something that one of them had missed. There had to be. Yet, if it was there, it was eluding him too.

The "bust list" he'd reviewed had also turned up nothing. There had been no one released in the past three months who had probable cause. He'd spoken to the three ex-cons, and it was obvious they hadn't a clue what they were being questioned about.

Frank had requested records for the three months prior to the list he already had, but he felt in his bones that it was a waste of time. Shit, even his cigarette theory had drawn a blank. He didn't know what he'd expected, but the list of stores in the West Side area that sold Dunhills was just too long. And that was assuming that the murderer even lived in the West Side. He needed more. Needed to build on this one thing. More pieces needed to fit into the missing holes to develop a case. *Screw it all to hell*.

The other guys were getting pissed off too. No one had suggested that they stop what they were doing, but he expected that they'd soon get reassigned. The homicides were getting out of hand and the pressure to make arrests was enormous. *Don't worry, Tony, nothing, no one, will make me drop this case*. He wanted to catch this killer badly, see him at the end of his gun sight and . . . That thought shook him. *Sweet Jesus, Frank, what's happening to you?*

* * *

The dinner had been perfect, one of Susan's specialties, duck l'orange with all the trimmings, plus a cold bottle of Chardonnay. They'd lingered at the dining table talking small talk. Frank was preoccupied with the case, with the problems it was starting to create within him.

"What's the matter, Francis?" she asked him, looking into his eyes.

She almost never called him that anymore, he thought. Years ago she had, after good love when they'd held each other and were smiling or laughing and smoking. She would look into his eyes and say, "Francis, damn, you're good." That part had been special; he'd liked the way the "Francis" sounded.

She wants to talk, he thought. He did too, but was afraid. Afraid of the old wounds' reopening.

It had been good since Christmas. Since Tony had died. He felt close to her, and the truce that they'd both tacitly agreed to was better than the fighting, the accusations that had been flung back and forth before she'd gone away. He decided to try and find the right words. There'd never be a better time than now.

"Times like this, Susan, they're good. But there's something just below the surface, isn't there? We have to handle the problems we have. I just don't know how. I realize that you want more from me. More from us. And there's the money thing. It seems—"

"Frank, it's not the money," she interrupted. "Don't you see that? It's never been the money, dammit. I wonder sometimes how you make your living. Being a cop, I mean. You don't see the obvious, do you? Take a look around you. Go on, take a look around.''

He looked at her then, eye to eye. She saw his confusion, the hurt filling his face. She felt an overwhelming urge to hold him, to stroke his head. She straightened out in the chair, shaking her head. *Finish this, Susan. Get it out. Talk it through.*

"Frank, look around the room. Tell me what you see.''

He did, and was perplexed and hurt; he loved this house, it was important to him—to her too, he'd thought. He saw all the things that they'd accumulated over the years. Damn, she'd put it all together so well. The crystal. The furniture. Beautiful pieces that had appeared over the years. He'd let her do the house as she'd wanted, and now . . .

"I don't understand you, Susan. I love it here. It's always been a place that I loved coming home to. What do you want me to see? To say?''

That surprised her. He'd never said much one way or the other about the way the house looked. This wasn't going to be easy. She smiled at him, speaking softly.

"Frank, how much do you think the rug over there cost? The desk in the library?''

Her tone deceived him. What was she getting at? he thought. Who the hell knows what things cost? All he knew was that they had a great home, one all their friends admired.

"I don't know, Susan. I never thought about it. What's this all about?''

"The rug is Persian, it's silk, it cost twenty-three thousand dollars. The desk, half that much. Want me to go on? Where do you think the money came from to buy all of these things? My car, in case you didn't notice, is a Mercedes. It cost thirty-two thousand dollars. The house is paid for, has been for years. Damn, you haven't a clue, have you, Frank?''

He was astonished, unsure of how to answer.

"I thought the car came with your job. The other stuff . . .'' He shrugged helplessly. ''The house. How can it all be so expensive and paid for?''

"Money's not the point, Frank. What it can buy, or having it, or not having it, are not the reason you and I are having problems. I know that I said it was all about money. I don't know why I said that, exactly. Maybe because at the time, when I said it, I was looking for an excuse that you would understand, or maybe it was because I felt guilty about not telling you that we had no money problems. I don't know. All I do know for certain is that I had to do something, say something. To make it easy to leave, to go home to Florida. I love you, Frank. I always will. I wonder if you really love me, or if you can love anyone.''

"I still don't understand what you're trying to say, Susan.''

She had started to tidy up the dishes, then dropped them all back onto the table. He could see the tears in her eyes, the hurt, something else. She was afraid.

"Frank, ever since I was twenty-five, well, we've had enough money for ten lifetimes. I always knew that you'd have difficulty accepting that. I've wanted to tell you. Almost have. So many, many times. Then, as time went by, it became harder, especially with that temper of yours,

that pride, the way you felt about my father." He started
to object, but she plunged forward. "No, wait, Frank. Let
me finish, please. I've been receiving five thousand dollars
a month from my trust account for the past nine years.
That's how come the house is so full of beautiful, expensive things. But that's not the point. The point, Frank, is
that your job is destroying us. It's killing you by inches.
I'm so afraid of what you're becoming because of it. Dammit, you hardly talk anymore. We don't talk. You haven't
slept a decent night's sleep in years. Tossing, turning,
sweating, your whole body shaking, trembling. Like some-
body was squeezing the life out of you, reducing you and
incapacitating you. When was the last time you laughed?
I mean, *really* laughed? Or, for that matter, *we* laughed?
I'm afraid, Frank. That's the truth of it. Scared out of my
mind that someone, someday, will call, and I'll be asked
to go to the morgue to identify your dead body. I almost
died when Roy Weston called. I tell you, Frank, my heart
stopped beating, my legs went to jelly. I was sure that it
was you, that you were wounded, hurt somehow, or worse,
dead.''

"Honey, I—"

"Please, Frank, let me get this done and said. You have
no idea what it's been like for me, have you? I hoped that
you would take a desk job or something. You were always
the best at what you did; everyone said so. But I hoped
that someday the dangerous part of it would end. I pictured
us happy, with kids. Maybe a boy, a girl, and a dog, with
you doing what Roy Weston or Jason Withers is doing.
Wearing a nice suit, being on the TV . . . Christ, Frank,
I only ever wanted us to be happy, together, safe."

He was stunned. She hadn't talked to him that way before. He regretted taking her so much for granted. She'd always been there for him, hadn't she? And the money. Damn, she could have told him. He would have understood. But would he? It was easy to understand now that it was out in the open and less important than losing her. But would he have truly understood if she'd told him before? He sighed, knowing the answer. He wouldn't. She was right to have kept it from him. *But what does she want from me?*

"Look, honey, I appreciate all you've said. I even understand most of it. I'm not good with words, not like you. A lifetime of keeping thoughts to myself, I suppose. But I can see that I've hurt you. I never meant that. Truly I didn't. I know that I love you more than anything in the world. More than the job, even. But it's a different love from the work. I need the work. As much, almost, as I need you. I know that I would do anything for you. Tell me what you want me to do."

Christ, Frank, don't do this to me. Don't ask me what I want you to do. Be you. I love you for all your strength and single-mindedness. Don't weaken on me now. Not now. Can't you see I'm jockeying for position? For my rights. I don't want to be in competition with you. I don't even really want you to change. I loved you before for all the qualities that make you so damn good at your lousy, stinking job. All I really want is for you to make me feel like I'm the most important thing in your life. That's all, Frank. Just to change positions from second most important to first. She smiled at him then. *The great detective who couldn't figure out women.*

"Frank, all I want is that you take me to bed and make love to me."

He came to her then, and the words became unimportant.

Years seemed to have fallen from him, Susan thought happily the next morning as she watched Frank reading the newspaper. He must have slept well. *Must not exhaust the poor baby.* She smiled over at him and he looked up, flashing his real Frank Morrissey smile. It warmed her, making her feel that it would be better for them. Yes, it was definitely going to be better.

The headline in the Metro section caught Frank's eye. Susan saw him frown.

"Problem, darling?"

He handed her the paper.

"Three drug pushers killed last night. Nothing unusual, but read the last part," he said.

She read: "Police found hundreds of dollars of cash, cocaine, and pills on the dead men. So?"

"Think about it, Sue. Who knocks off three pushers and doesn't take their drugs?"

She thought about that and continued to read the story. Three whites, ages undetermined, mid to late twenties, had been shot to death the previous night in the Palms area.

"I see what you mean," she said. "If they were killed for drugs, then they should have been robbed. But maybe the killer just shot them and ran off. Killed them for something that they'd done before." She grimaced. "It's all horrid anyway. It sounds terrible, but it's hard to care about those types getting killed. They almost deserve it. For what they do to others, I mean.''

Frank listened to her, aware that her point of view was typical of most people here in L.A. The tendency was to shrug off these kinds of deaths. But why was this the case? Some sort of bell began ringing in his head. He made a mental note to check it out when he got to the office.

"I suppose," Frank said. "It just seems sort of weird, that's all. Hey, honey, I gotta go. Let's go out to dinner tonight. Maybe to the Indian restaurant in the marina that you like so much. Okay?"

Susan smiled. "Sounds fine by me, but if you're running late, let me know, and I'll pick up something. Maybe we can watch a movie or even have an early night." She gave him a mischievous wink.

Frank had been reading through the file again, hoping, he supposed, to find something they'd missed. So far, nothing. The one guy Tony had collared who seemed vicious enough to try to get revenge was Jarvis King, and he was doing forty years in San Quentin. King had promised to ax Tony one day. Damn, it was such a shitting long shot. Frank wondered if somehow King had managed to get someone to do it for him. Worth a call, he supposed. The telephone rang as he was about to pick it up.

"That you, Frank? Lonnie Tobin in Vice. Listen, I got something you may be interested in. The file shows you and Tony—sorry about Tony, Frank—were the officers on the scene."

"What scene would that be?" Frank asked.

"Sorry, the one last December when the two black kids were zapped in Venice. Say, come on over, okay?"

Frank was alerted by the tone, by what was being communicated and not said. "Be right there, Lonnie. Thanks."

This is interesting, he thought. Then it occurred to him: the December killings were drug related. Could there be a connection with last night's hit? He could feel the hairs on the back of his neck start to rise, and he grinned. He got up and walked over to Vice.

"Come in, Frank," Lonnie Tobin said, getting up from his desk and pumping Frank's hand. "Have a seat. You know Alan Berlinni, I'm sure." Berlinni remained seated, noncommittal.

"Hi, Alan," Frank said, smiling. "So what you guys got that Homicide can help you with?"

The two Vice cops looked at each other, then Lonnie threw a file over to him.

"Read the file," Tobin said, glancing at his partner, who nodded.

"Remember in early December when those two black kids got it? Well, we were asked to investigate it as a possible drug killing. The file's been open. To tell you the truth, it's a pretty low-profile deal. Anyway, we just got the ballistics report in on the three who were waxed last night. By the way, they were drug pushers. We'd been building a file on them for a while. Anyway, like I said, we got the ballistics report a little while ago. They were nailed with a thirty-eight, close range. Hollow-pointed slugs. They never had a chance, dead before they hit the ground. Well, when we were going over things, Alan thought that there were similarities to the Worthy and Jackson killings. Why don't you take it, Alan," he said, looking at his partner.

"Yeah, it was odd," Berlinni said. "The three that got it last night were all armed. One with a piece, the other two with knives. None of them drew their weapons. All three knew the area. It was their turf, and yet they went into a dark alley with someone and got topped. Didn't make sense. Canny guys, these three. I still can't figure how someone got the drop on them so easily. Anyway, we asked Ballistics to compare the bullets used in the Worthy and Jackson killings to the bullets used in these killings last night. Bingo, they were fired from the same weapon. The killer was good. Looks like a pro hit, and yet we can't tie the two incidents together at all. I was wondering if you had any thoughts you might want to share with us."

Frank was thinking furiously. He felt the excitement of the chase, and the satisfaction of knowing that he had been right after all. If the same guy had pulled the trigger, then these killings were about something more than drugs. They might even have another whacko out there.

"The three last night weren't relieved of their goodies," Frank said, "so the motive wasn't robbery. What, then, does that leave? Contract hit? Vigilante? Dissatisfied customer?"

"How did you know that the three last night still had the dope on them, Frank?" Berlinni asked him, glancing over at Tobin.

"Read it in the *Times* this morning."

"Fucking press," Tobin said. "Well, as it happens, it's the truth. You're right. It wasn't about robbery or any drug connection with Worthy or Jackson. To tell you the truth, Frank, we don't believe that Worthy or Jackson were even into drugs. We had nothing substantial on them. The file should have gone straight back to Homicide. What Al and I were thinking was that maybe we could overlap with you, work the two cases together for a while." He was watching Frank, trying to read something from his reactions.

"Sounds good to me," Frank said. "Why don't you transfer the Jackson and Worthy file over to Homicide and copy me with everything you get on the killings last night. If my gut is telling the truth, that file will be transferred over to Homicide real soon anyway."

"So tell me what your gut is saying?" Tobin asked him, smiling. Frank's gut feelings were legendary.

"I remember telling Tony at the time that I didn't believe the killings were drug related. I looked at the bust sheets on both of them and neither had been up on drug-related charges. That alone means nothing, but Jackson had only been out of the can for a couple of weeks. Not enough time to begin plying drugs again, unless he was really enterprising. Anyway, they looked to me like a couple of small-time hard cases. Rape. Holdups. The whole nine yards. What struck me as odd was that they were both armed, yet they went into a dark alley with someone. Neither Jackson nor Worthy drew their weapons, or even put up a fight. That suggests two possibilities: one, that they knew their killer and were negotiating some business, or two, that they'd planned a little trouble and picked on the wrong guy. The latter seems more likely."

Lonnie was tapping his fingers on the desk and looking at him. He nodded his head.

"Yeah, that would fit. The guy that nailed them was their target, and that's why he was able to get the drop on them so easily. It also fits last night's situation. All three were armed, and again none of them drew their weapons or attempted to fight back. If this dude had pretended he was making a buy, they might have taken him into the alley, started to show him the goods, and at that point gotten zapped. Sure does fit the information we have so far. Cool sort of creep that could do that. So what you're suggesting is that we have another whacko or vigilante or something?"

"Could be. If so, the press is going to have a field day. But listen, let me talk to Captain Weston. See what he wants to do. As you know, my time is pretty limited."

"How's it coming on Tony's killer, Frank?"

"I hate to admit it, but not real good. We don't have a single damn lead. Nothing. Glen Ramirez and Jim Cooper are working on it with me. Fucking best that Homicide has to offer, and we have no leads. Kind of ironic, isn't it?"

"Look, Frank, that's the way it is sometimes," Tobin said, pouring him some more coffee. "If you push at it, nudge it, nothing will happen. Sometimes you gotta step away from it. Don't get me wrong. I knew Tony. Bowled with him for years. It's hard not to press too hard and be driven by anger when one of our own goes down. Even more so when it's your partner and buddy. Something will turn up. It will. It always does."

"Yeah . . . Well, thanks for calling me over, guys. Keep me informed. I'll be talking to the captain about this." He got up and made his way back to his own office, thinking how glad he was to be out of there. It was nothing personal. He liked Lonnie. Something was happening to him, though. He felt suffocated, and when he sat for too long he wanted to lash out and run. Out into the fresh air. Away from everything. Get on with the solving of the case. Push forward, concentrate, focus. A step at a time. Tobin was right: something would come up. Always did, just had to keep at it.

Frank tried thumbing through Tony's file once again, but grew restless. He decided to see if Captain Weston was in, and discovered he was.

"Got a minute, Roy?" Frank asked as he poked his head in the door.

Weston waved him in.

"I was just talking to the guys in Vice," Frank said. "They've come up with something interesting."

He proceeded to give Weston a rundown of what had been learned and the conclusions that had been drawn, and when he was finished Weston looked considerably less comfortable than when Frank had first entered.

"Damn, if you're right, Frank, and there's a guy out there with a hit list, the press is going to make the commissioner's life miserable. And that's going to make my life miserable." Weston's mind was working. He hated the idea of another serial killer. *Jesus, so soon after the Murphy thing*. On the other hand, he thought, it does take care of the Tony situation. He'd been as depressed about the lack of results as the rest of them. But he also had the responsibility of fully utilizing his men. For weeks now there hadn't been any progress on Tony's case. The trail was cold. He'd been agonizing over when and how to reassign his men. Now the only question was which one to leave on the investigation. Tough choice. The obvious one was Frank. He'd have to let him decide. He hoped that he'd assign either Cooper or Ramirez, because Frank was the best one to handle this new case. His "gut feelings" would be invaluable.

"Captain, I think I know what you're considering," Frank said, using Weston's silence to come to his own decision. "We have damn few leads on Tony's killer. Those few bits and pieces we do have, well, we can handle them in addition to handling this new case. With your permission I'd like to suggest that the three of us—me, Glen, and Coop—start things up on this whacko angle. We need to put together a mini task force to go over everything, then be ready when—that is, if—the guy kills again. My guess is that it will be soon."

Good man, Frank. Once in a while a prayer did get answered.

"Sounds good to me," Weston said. "Let's get on with it."

Vic was watching the news when the girl came in. He was euphoric. Finally the stupid bastards had made the connection. He was glad that he'd used the same gun. He wasn't happy, though, with the woman reading the news report. For a moment he considered shooting her too. All that pretended concern, he thought. I bet she's happy as a pig in shit.

"What're you watching, Vic?" Andy asked, walking over and putting her arm around him. She smelled good. He leaned back, kissing her on the neck.

"Just the news. It looks as if the City of Angles may have another vigilante on the loose."

"I heard that driving over. Why does L.A. seem like a magnet for those kinds of people? It's scary. There's so many crazies out there," she said, looking at him and crinkling her mouth.

And what would you think, Andy, if you knew that the crazy was here, that you were going to screw his brains out soon? Had already, dozens of times. What would you think then? He started to laugh.

"What's so funny?"

"Oh, nothing. It's just that these anchorpeople crack me up. The most insincere bunch I've ever seen. They report a mass murder in the same tone as they do the birth of test-tube babies. I think that they call it impartial broadcasting. Assholes, all of them. So, what did my beautiful girl do today?"

"Worked as usual. Made seventy dollars in tips this afternoon. Pretty good, huh? What about you? How was your day?"

"Quiet," Vic said. He got up and switched off the set, then walked into the kitchen to get some wine. "Played the market for a while. Boring. Ran about ten miles. Had lunch at the Black Whale. Ever tasted their clam chowder? It's the best. Then I came home, wrote a couple of poems. That's it," he said, handing her a glass of Chablis.

"Thanks," she said. "Say, you always tell me about

the Black Whale, but you never take me. Fancy one of the waitresses, do you?'' she said, teasing. He gave her a faraway look and went over and sat on the sofa.

She thought about how intrigued she was by him. She was falling in love like never before. No, she *was* in love. *So he writes poems, does he?* She wondered if they'd be about her. About them and the special relationship that they had. She was sure they would be, wondering if he would read them to her.

"Can I read some of your poems, Vic?''

Shit no, he thought. Should have kept my mouth shut. Look at her face, though. She won't take no for an answer without being hurt.

"Well, they're kind of personal, not even very good. Are you sure you want to?''

"Not if you don't want me to,'' she said, sipping her wine, her eyes never leaving his face, willing him to read them to her.

Liar, he thought. Read them if you want to.

"Sure, it's fine. They're over on the desk. Go ahead.''

"Won't you read them to me? Please. Let me sit here by the fire with my wine and hear you read them.''

"Okay, but just one of them. The others need work.''

"Thanks, Vic. It'd make me happy.''

Sure it will, Andy. How can you say that until you've heard it? Well, you asked for it. He went over to the desk and unlocked the drawer. Okay, he thought, if it's what you want.

"THE EMPTY CROWDS GATHER
IT'S CRUCIFIXION TIME

HUDDLED MASSES UNITE TO PLUNDER THE
   HEART
OF HE WHO STANDS ALONE, UNASHAMED
STARING WITH MALIGNANT WONDER
PONDERING THAT FINE LINE
HEROES OF YESTERDAY
THE FODDER OF TODAY
THE CRY OF MEDIOCRITY IS LEFT
STRANGLED IN HIS THROAT
MAN, YOU TELL THEM WHAT THEY WANT TO
   HEAR
NEED TO HEAR
NOT THAT WHICH MAKES THEM THINK
THEY CANNOT BE YOU
SO THEY HAVE TO KILL YOU
SOLIDIFYING THEIR OMNIPRESENT STATE
YOU VAINGLORIOUS DOER OF DEEDS
THE VERY CORE OF YOUR SOUL LIES
EXPOSED AND VULNERABLE
READY TO BE TORN ASUNDER
THE STRENGTH DISSIPATED, AMORAL
DEGENERATING AS IT LIES
IN THE BAYING CROWD'S MEDIOCRE
   SOLIDARITY
QUIXOTIC OF NATURE
BORN TO WIN

BUT NOT ON THIS EARTH
FOR THE LOSERS
PERPETUATE THE MOTION
LEAVING CREATION THE VOID . . ."

"That's it. Happy now?" he said, moving back toward the desk, feeling his face reddening, wishing the interfering bitch hadn't asked him to read the poem. It was his, and personal. Damn her.

She was staring into the fire looking inconsolably sad. He regretted having read it to her.

"What's the matter, Andy?" he asked, feeling the first hint of anger, small tremors.

"It was so sad, Vic," she said softly, the beginning of tears in her eyes. "I love you so much. You're so sensitive. I never realized that you believed in our Lord. It was about him and how they destroyed him, wasn't it?"

He was stunned. For many moments totally speechless. He stared at her, feeling his hands start to shake, the redness filling his eyes, consuming him. He wanted to feel her neck in his hands as he squeezed the life out of her puny body. *Stupid, pathetic bitch*. She had walked over toward him, and he licked his drying lips trying to shake the redness from his eyes. Somehow she seemed to understand . . . something. She took his silence for an affirmation, then took his hand, leading him to the bedroom.

The girl was sleeping. He was sitting on the balcony, smoking. It was good out here at this time of night. No people. Just the elements. Tonight was beautiful, the sky dark, the moon very bright. He watched as the breakers crashed onto the black sand. So incredibly powerful, endless, eternal. He wanted to be out there. In the night. Feeling the power as he selected his victims. He wished that the girl had gone home. If she hadn't taken his hand, made the physical contact back there earlier, he knew he'd have done it: wasted her then and there. She was cramping his style, staying over so often. He wondered if he could just slip out for a while. Would she wake up and notice he was gone?

They were out there—the losers, the night people. It'd be so easy. So damn easy, he thought to himself. He would have to cool it a little with Andy. She was taking up too much of his time. The valuable night time. He thought about that. Then he started to laugh. Softly at first, then louder until his stomach hurt. Stupid bitch. Believing that poem was about Jesus. He would straighten her out on that later. What an airhead. Who in their right mind believed there was a God?

The squad room looked like a disaster area. Men, equipment, dozens of telecommunication instruments, plus the inevitable mountain of paper. It was late and Frank was pleased with the progress they'd made. He'd decided that Cooper should go back to the first murder scene, talk to the people who'd been interviewed already, ask different questions, then take the sweep a few blocks farther east. Someone might have seen something—a car, a person, something, anything. Glen had been assigned to the second murder scene and given the same instructions.

The coroner's office had finally gotten the paperwork

over to them on the three pushers who'd been wasted the night before. As Frank sifted through it he thought about having to call Susan and cancel their dinner. He was expecting the worst, but she hadn't complained. She surprised him, told him she understood and would see him when she saw him. Maybe they could have breakfast together? she'd asked. He promised himself that he would do that—make her breakfast. He looked at his watch—12:45 A.M.

The coroner's report was straightforward, confirming the earlier report that the three had been hit with .38-caliber, hollow-tipped bullets. The damage to each of the victims had been enormous. Shit, Frank thought, there'd been a time not too long ago when a bullet like that would have been easy to trace. Now you could get them anywhere. Legally or illegally. The pushers had been shot from point-blank range, which suggested that the killer probably had fled with blood all over him. That's something, he thought, underlining that part with a marker pen. One of the victims had had a heart attack, the report said. The coroner didn't know if it was before, during, or after the attack. Frank guessed, however, that it was just before the victim had been killed. He was probably terrified. According to the report, he'd been shot through the mouth.

Frank finished reading the files and decided to go home. It was almost two-thirty A.M. Time flies when you're having fun, he thought. He went out into the cool night and to his car. The heavy fatigue lifted and the breeze seemed to revitalize him. He decided he would drive down to the beach for a few minutes, check out the surf, clear his head. It was only a couple of minutes away. As he drove through

Santa Monica, then down toward the Marina Peninsula, he noticed all the people still awake out on the streets. He'd always wondered about that. Dozens of people all over the city, dicking around when they should be in their beds asleep. Amazing place, Los Angeles. Something for everyone.

He saw no police vehicles and thought how easy it was for a killer to blend into the crowded night, choose his victims, kill them. His mood darkened. He parked his car near the causeway that split the marina from El Segundo. The water was dark and choppy, and he could see the buoys bobbing on the current and the lights on the houseboats in the marina itself. The moon shone brightly, accentuating the darkness of the sky. He walked toward the beach. All the houses were in darkness. At least someone is sleeping, he thought. He could hear the crash of the surf, and he pulled his collar tighter around his neck. He stopped to light a cigarette and noticed a small flicker of light at one of the houses that fronted the beach. So there *was* someone else awake after all, enjoying the same view as he was. "Well, here's to you, fella," he said softly, wondering what the other smoker was thinking.

Vic had seen the person—a man, he thought—stop to light a cigarette. He wondered what the guy was doing down here at this time. He smiled and aimed his gun at the figure, breathed in, and then half released his breath. His hand was steady, so he pulled the trigger . . . click . . . "Got you, sucker," he said aloud. He tossed his dying cigarette over the balcony, then went back to bed.

* * *

Andrea and Karen had finished their workouts. They were sitting across from each other in the sauna, feeling the heat work on their tired muscles.

"You look great, Karen," Andy said, eyeing her friend's tight body as the towel slipped from her. "Really tight and toned. I should start coming more regularly." She felt suddenly guilty, thinking of how she'd lost touch with her friends since meeting Vic.

"I could do this twice a day and never have a body like yours, Andy," Karen said. "But I'm not complaining. It's a little late in life to be worrying about what the good Lord dealt me. I can truthfully say that I've given up envying you."

"Envying me. I didn't know you felt that way."

Karen smiled at her, brushing the sweat from her face and repinning her hair. "It's amazing how naive you beautiful ones are. Don't you remember how you always got the guys' attention when we used to go out? Shit, Andy, you don't know what I'm talking about, do you? Well, it's not important. Tell me about this guy you're seeing."

That brought a smile to her face. Vic. What was there to tell? So much, and yet, well, most of it was the kind of stuff you were embarrassed to talk about.

"Well, I think that I love him," she said, her eyes gleaming. She went over and turned the sauna down a little; it was starting to make her feel sick.

"Does he love *you*?"

"He hasn't said that, not exactly, but I feel that it's different for him. Like it's different for me. We communicate on a level I wasn't even aware of, and, well, the physical part is really incredible.''

"So tell me about it.''

"What?''

"The screwing part, of course,'' Karen said. She never did mince words.

Andrea smiled sheepishly. "Well, we make love a lot. We have from the beginning. Sometimes I can . . . This is going to sound silly, but sometimes I can still feel him inside me the next day, between my legs. And it's sore and exquisite at the same time. You know what I mean?''

Karen didn't. She had been married less than a year, and already the frequency was down to a couple of times a week. She and Stan still loved each other, though, and that's what was important, she told herself.

"Sure, I know what you mean. My Stan, well, he's insatiable sometimes too. But tell me more about Vic.''

"Well, he's handsome, tall, about six-one, in real great shape, brown hair, black almost, big blue, puppy-dog eyes, a soft sweet mouth. He's real sensitive, kind and considerate. He even writes poems.''

"What kind of poems? Poems about the two of you?'' Karen said, smiling. She couldn't imagine her man writing poems. Writing anything.

"Well, sometimes he writes them about us. Mostly, though, they're about all kinds of things. They're deep, sensitive, filled with pain, yearnings. Know what I mean?''

"I'm not sure.''

"Well, it's kind of difficult to talk about. It's probably nothing, really, but a few weeks ago we were sitting by the fire. It was raining, the fire was warm, we were close.

You know, just touching and watching the patterns that the rain leaves on the window. Well, Vic mentioned that he'd written some poems that day, so I asked him to read one of them to me. He did, and it moved me. Made me feel like crying. It was about our Lord. Well, that is, I thought it was. It mentioned crucifixion and all. Anyway, we went to bed early, and the lovemaking was good. I felt real close to him, so I asked him about the poem.''

"And . . ."

"Well, he laughed at me, said if I thought it was about religion I was dreaming."

"And . . ."

"Well, it made me feel weird. Kind of distant."

"Come on, Andy, what are you trying to tell me? Something's worrying you."

"Do you believe in God, Karen?" Andy asked her, looking closely at her, feeling foolish.

"Sure I do. I'm no churchgoer, but I believe. Why do you ask?"

"Well, he said I was deluding myself if I thought there was a God . . . and . . . and that believing in God was for the poor unenlightened masses who have nothing else in life except the fantasy of a better place after they die. He said heaven was the biggest con of all time."

"Listen, honey, didn't you tell me he was a computer man? They're like scientists. I read it somewhere; they all believe in the concept of no God. It's just the type of work he does. It's all intellectual. It doesn't really mean that he doesn't believe. You shouldn't worry. They all believe in the end."

"You don't understand, Karen. He said that Earth was

the black sheep of the solar system and that God had washed His hands of it thousands of years ago. He said that man had screwed it up so royally that even the visitors of other planets didn't bother coming here anymore, that the place had been finished ever since the end of the Minoan Empire. He kept laughing at me, telling me that I'd find out one day that he was right, that this planet was a godless place, full of godless people, that we had to carve our own immortality as best we could. It was all so confusing . . . and so unlike him.''

It did sound strange, Karen thought. The guy sounded like another weirdo. *Dear God, when will this poor kid find someone normal?* Oh, well, may as well put the best face on it. . . . ''Listen, honey, he sounds like an okay guy. My Stan has some strange ideas too, so I wouldn't let it bother you. Even I can see that this Vic is making you happy.''

Andy smiled at her friend's words. She probably was making too much of it.

''Thanks, Karen. I feel better for telling you. I suppose I'm being silly. It's just that everything else is so perfect.'' If everything was so perfect, though, why did she have this sick feeling in her stomach?

Frank arrived at the station house at eight A.M. and was immediately handed a sheaf of papers by Ramirez. He looked through them—the results of the door-to-doors and the neighborhood investigations—but found nothing. Not a thing. All three pushers were well known to the neighborhood, all were connected with crime, all had enemies, according to the reports from family and friends. On the last page was a list of seventeen names. All of the persons on the list had argued with or fought or threatened one of the dead men at some time over the past few months.

"Not good, Glen," he said, tapping the papers. "There's got to be something we haven't considered." He thought for a moment. "Suppose . . . just suppose that Worthy and Jackson were planning to mug someone, as seems likely. What would their 'target' have been doing in that area on a night like that and on foot?"

"What makes you think that they were planning to mug the guy that wasted them?" Ramirez asked. "If it was a whacko, wouldn't the guy who did it have been cruising around, waiting for guys like Worthy and Jackson?"

"I think that's what happened the *second* time. The guy cruised around, spotted the pushers, parked his car, and started to do some business with the three that were killed."

"So? I'm not following you," Ramirez said, looking from Frank to Cooper, who was pretending not to listen, tapping busily on the computer keys.

"Well, I don't think it happened that way the first time. It couldn't have. It was pissing down, and dark as hell. Not the kind of night that you spot someone like Worthy and Jackson just cruising. Also, why would these boys be out in the cold and rain in a dark street if they didn't have trouble on their minds? And why were they near the alley? Doesn't make sense. Listen, let's you and me drive over there and I'll show you what I mean."

Ramirez was staring at him. A second passed, then he shrugged, looking over at Cooper again. No help there, he thought. Go with him. See what he's getting at.

The two men drove over to Venice, to the scene of the first murder. Strange how unfrightening and pleasant the area was in the daytime, Frank thought. As they parked the car, he noticed the No Parking Anytime signs all down the street. Interesting.

"This is the place. Let's walk around a bit. That's the alley there," he said, pointing toward an alley that led back from the main street abutting the shops.

"That's where they were killed," Frank said. "See, it's a couple of blocks from the main street, and there's no lighting. Also, the two shops that back up onto the alleyway here were closed for the night."

The two men walked west, then south, taking note of the area. Frank noticed that about a block and a half up the street, near the Rose Café, the parking became less restrictive. They continued walking around the area. Not really looking for anything, but, at the same time, looking for everything, anything that might click.

"I don't get what we're looking for," Ramirez said tensely. He was irritated, thinking the whole thing was a waste of time.

"Just looking. Let's suppose that the killer was parked up here," he said, pointing back up the street toward the Rose Café, "and was on his way to either the Rose Café or had just returned from the café and was going to his car when the guys spotted him and tried to mug him."

"That doesn't make sense," Ramirez protested. "The alley is west of here about three blocks. Why would the guy have parked so far away in the rain? Besides, there's no parking down by the alley. You mentioned that earlier."

Frank just stared at him and continued to think.

"I do see what you're getting at," Ramirez said finally. "What if the killer had already parked his car here and was going to the liquor store? The guys saw him, then waited by the alley till he approached. It's the only way that someone parking on the street here could get to the liquor store. Only problem is, the liquor store has parking, and what with the rain and all, would someone drive all the way up here, park, then walk back in the rain, when he didn't have to?"

Frank was smiling to himself. *Pretty close, Glen. Good work.*

"Okay, let's look at that. Suppose the killer went to the store and saw the lot was full. He knows the area, realizes he may get towed if he parks illegally. So he drives around. It's pissing down with rain and very dark. He sees a spot, so he decides, screw it. He parks his car, then starts to walk back toward Main Street. Worthy and Jackson are hanging around, looking for some action, or on their way home. Who knows? They're walking up the street, or down it. They see this dude pull up in his car, then park. They watch, then see him start down the street toward them. They decide. Bingo. Some stupid joker on their turf, so they decide to mug him. They walk toward the alley. Remember the conditions—wet and cold, really dark. The guy probably wouldn't have noticed them right off. Or, if they were already in the alley and hiding, he wouldn't have seen them at all. The guy gets near the alley and the two wise guys appear out of nowhere and herd him into their lair. They'd have felt pretty confident. That figures. One guy alone, wet, away from his car going to the liquor store or something. They make their move on the guy, and the killer pulls out a gun and wastes them. Maybe in self-defense. Maybe not. Maybe the first time he's killed. Maybe not. It's wet and dark and windy.. No one hears anything, so the killer goes back to his car and drives away. What do you think?''

"It's good," Ramirez said, feeling for the first time as if all this might lead to something. "Makes sense. Opens up some other possibilities, too. Let's go down to the liquor store and see if we can talk to whoever was working that night. We can talk to the people at the Rose Café, too, maybe post a bulletin there asking for people who were there the night of the killings. One of them may remember something.''

They were both pleased to have something to work on, some direction to head in. Frank noticed for the first time what a pretty day it was. He could smell the sea. They had reached the liquor store, and they went in.

There was a guy, fat and unshaven, in his late thirties with a Grateful Dead beard reading the calendar section of the *Times* and chewing on a red licorice stick.

"Hello. My name's Frank Morrissey—Sergeant Frank Morrissey, Homicide. This is my partner, Glen Ramirez. Is the owner or manager in?"

"Why?"

Typical, Frank thought.

"We wanted to ask him or her a few questions about—"

"What kind of questions?" the guy interrupted, looking away and spitting out a wad of red, oozing licorice into the trash can.

Glen grabbed the guy by the throat, putting his face very

close to the fat man's face, speaking very politely, very quietly.

"Listen, buddy, answer the fucking questions, or if you'd rather, you can come with us down to the station. Your choice, friend."

"Okay, okay, let go of me. Just wondering why two homicide cops are nosin' around. Was it the two blacks that were wasted in December?"

"What makes you think it was about the two black kids?" Ramirez asked, wondering if they'd missed something. The guy's attitude was annoying him. He didn't have as much patience as Frank.

"Stands to reason," the fatso said, putting down the paper and swigging a beer. "I read the papers. No one ever got busted. Plus it did happen just down the street from here. That's all."

"What's your name? You the manager here, or are we wasting our time?" Frank said.

"Dave Becker. No, I own the place. So what do you want to know?"

"Well, you can start by telling us who was working the night of the murders," Frank said. "Was the store busy, and if it was busy, how busy was it?"

"I was working that night. It was a Sunday. My brother-in-law, Fred, was helping, and also my sister, Katie. We were real busy, always are on Sunday nights around six to eight. And, of course, the storm helped too."

"How so?"

"Take it you two don't live at the beach. When the real storms hit, the power is likely to go out. When bad weather's on the way, we always sell a ton of candles, batteries, logs for the fireplace, and champagne. Don't ask me why champagne. But we do.'' Frank thought about that. Interesting.

"So the night of the killings you were very busy?'' Frank said.

"Yeah. The lot was full, and it stayed full till after nine that night. Now, if that's all the questions you have, I got to serve the lady here,'' he said, turning to the girl who had walked in and was staring at them.

"Thanks, Dave. Your help has been real great. Real swell experience meeting you,'' Frank said, smiling and offering his hand. When Becker ignored him and waited on the girl, Frank grinned humorously and nodded at Ramirez to get out of there.

The Rose Café was fairly quiet when they arrived a few minutes later. Glen asked the pretty girl at the door if the manager was in. She said she would check and showed them to a table near the pastry counter. A couple of minutes later they saw a youngish, preppy-looking guy walking briskly toward their table.

"Hi. I'm the manager, Danny Frankel. What can I do for you?'' he said, smiling.

"Hi, Danny. My name's Frank. This is Glen Ramirez. We're both with Homicide. We'd like to ask you a couple of questions. Do you have a few moments?''

"Sure. Would you like some coffee and a pastry, perhaps?''

"Coffee would be great,'' Frank said, looking hungrily over the selection. "Are you the daytime manager, or manager period?''

"There's only me. I have an assistant that generally works the later shift. What's this about?"

"Do you remember the murders that took place a few blocks from here last December?"

"Yeah. It was the talk of the café for weeks, what with it happening so close to here. I wondered if it would impact negatively on the business. It hasn't, though. Two black drug pushers, wasn't it? Was the killer ever apprehended?"

Frank smiled at that. Now, there was a word for you: "apprehended." Usually it was "busted," "caught," "nailed." *We don't usually sit and have French coffee and fresh cream puffs, either.*

"No, we never got the guy that did it. That's why we're here. We have reason to believe that the killer might have been seen in or around the restaurant here on the night of the killing. It may be a long shot, but we'd like to talk to anyone who was entering or leaving the restaurant at approximately the time of the murders. That is, between six-thirty and seven-fifteen on the Sunday night in question."

"How would you go about it?"

"Well, we could post a notice near the hostess desk, asking anyone who was in the café at that time to call us," Ramirez said. "Also, if you'll furnish us with the credit-card slips for that date, we can do some of the contacting ourselves."

The young man shrugged. "Sounds okay to me. I can go through the slips and narrow them down to customers who came in during the early evening. It's just a matter of matching them up with whoever was working the early shift. As far as the sign goes, well, it's not optimum, but for a couple of weeks I don't see why not, so long as it doesn't amount to any of my customers' being hassled. Is that fair?'' he said, beaming at them. The picture of helpfulness. Both cops were relieved.

"More than fair, Danny," Frank told him, meaning it. "You've been a big help. We appreciate it. Thanks again for the refreshments."

The two men sat and finished their coffee. Frank was pleased with the progress they'd made today. So pleased that he decided to treat himself. One pastry wouldn't hurt.

Vic and the girl were listening to music, sipping wine, talking small talk. He still hadn't figured a way to keep her away some of the time without the risk of sending her away permanently. He didn't want that. Not at all. She was the best. But he had to do something and do it quick. The anger had started building in him again. Only yesterday he'd almost punched her for spilling cigarette ash on the leather upholstery in the car. It had been too damn close. He'd only controlled himself because the vehicle had been moving—moving fast. He was doing everything better, faster, stronger these days. He knew he'd have to kill someone else soon. It was like a hunger gnawing away at his gut. *Soon. Got to do it soon, before the press finds another story.*

He'd thought about calling the television station, talking to the pretty blond bimbo who read the news. I'm dedicating my next victim to you, he'd say. *Sanctimonious bitch.*

His mind returned to the problem at hand. How could he stop Andy from cramping his style? He could kill the next one in the early evening while she was at the bar, or later, when she was asleep. But he remembered how the killing of the cop and the fat-breasted stripper had tired him, and how she had gotten home late because it was Christmas Eve. He might not be so lucky the next time. He wouldn't like to have to kill Andy. No, that wouldn't be right. Not yet, anyway. *So how do I persuade her that I need to have some evenings alone?*

"This is nice, Andy. You, me, the fire, the music. Glad you're here," he told her, reaching over and taking her hand.

She squeezed closer to him, looking up from the fire. Her eyes were startling: large and green with a yellowish circle around the iris. They were incredibly beautiful, especially when she looked at him that way. He shivered and felt his resolve start to weaken.

"The stock-market problem is worrying me, Andy," he said abruptly.

"Why?" she said, a bit startled. "What's wrong?"

"The bear market looks like it'll be with us for a while. Believe it or not, it's the best time to make some real money, if you're smart. Anyway, I'm going to have to spend some quality time working these next couple of weeks." He watched her closely. She was real smart, and he didn't think he'd be able to fool her. He saw her body stiffen.

She moved away from him slightly. He saw her eyes darken a little. They always use their bodies to express how they really feel, he thought, remembering the argument about God and her pathetic little beliefs. That night she'd turned her back to him and wouldn't sleep close like she usually did. He pushed the thought from his mind, then pressed on before she had time to respond.

"The New York market opens up at six A.M. our time. It's important for me to be up, alert, ready to make some money. Lately, I haven't been able to do that."

"So what are you saying, Vic?"

"Nothing more than I've said already. It's just—" She sat up, her eyes blazing.

"What you really mean is that I keep you from your fucking work by being here. Isn't it?"

He moved closer to her, looked into her eyes. "Listen, don't take it so damn personally," he said gently. "I love you being here. But I don't get much sleep when you stay over. All I'm suggesting is that on those nights you work late, Wednesdays and Sundays, maybe it would work out better if you went home, slept at your own house. It's not much of a change, is it?"

She looked at him for a long time, feeling the loss. Screw men, she thought, screw them all to hell. When they want you, they want you all the time, orbiting them like a moon around a planet. But when they get tired, they want to escape you completely. She imagined herself dangling in the relationship, choking herself, losing her self-respect. Dammit, she'd promised herself she wouldn't let another man do this to her. Abruptly, she rose from the sofa and swept up her purse, then made it out the door before he could respond.

Vic was dressed and ready to go into the night. He had planned this one carefully. He'd be on foot this time, looking like just another late-night jogger. He put the hood up over his head. It covered his ears and hair, leaving his face in shadows. He went out of the condo and began jogging slowly down Speedway Street toward Washington Boulevard. It was cold, dark, and windy. He could smell the ocean. He felt the sweat crystals beading his brow. Fifty yards ahead of him, two female joggers approached. *Good*. He slowed his step a little, keeping to the shadows.

Stupid bimbos, he thought. They felt safe because they were in twos. *Well, not from me.* The girls had crossed Washington Boulevard and were headed for the bike path that wound snakelike all the way past Santa Monica to the north, then Manhattan Beach to the south. The wind was whipping off the surf, shaking the palm trees. He liked the noise; it comforted him.

They were good runners, and he was having to adjust his step. He could hear his heart, feel the tightness starting to grow in his head, around his eyes. He quickened his step. They were getting close to where the bike path swept away from the ocean, bringing the runners closer to the heartland of Venice. No one else was around. He started to run faster, knowing that he would have to time this perfectly. They were passing the darkened area where entertainers performed during the warm weekends. A sort of grandstand. He cut away from the girls, sprinting a little; then he was past them, running over the sand toward the darkness. They hadn't even seen him. There was no one about—not even a stupid dog, Vic thought. *Perfect*. He was ahead of them now, looking back over his shoulder. He saw he'd timed it well. He ran on another seventy-five yards, then ducked in between two darkened buildings.

Christ, he was breathing hard, he thought. Goddamn

Andy was wearing him out. He'd pulled the gun out of
his waistband and was trying desperately to still his beating
heart. He could hear them; they were close now. *Move,
Vic*.

He stepped out from behind the corner and pointed the
gun. The nearest girl smiled at him, opening her mouth
as if to speak. She was about ten yards from him and
unaware of what he was holding in his hand. Suddenly,
the girls stopped dead in their tracks and started to scream.
He fired, and the first shot smashed into the nearest girl's
face, turning it red and ugly. The bullet must have gone
straight through, because the back of her hat flew into the
air. She crumpled to the ground.

The second girl was transfixed, staring at her friend.
Her jaw worked, but no words passed her lips. Vic saw
the light come on in the third-floor window of a nearby
building, and reflexively he put the gun to the girl's temple,
pulling the trigger. The force of the bullet and the girl's
momentum seemed to make the body fly through the air.
Vic looked up at the building, enraged. It hadn't worked
like he'd wanted; he hadn't had the time to draw strength
from them as they died. Dammit, dammit, dammit, he
screamed to himself as he cut through the alley behind the
building and jogged steadily toward the main street.

He was so angry he'd almost decided that he wouldn't
go home, that he'd find someone else. Then he heard the
police sirens, and he jogged a little faster. He considered
throwing away the gun. No, he thought, if they came near
him he'd blow them away. He crossed the main street,
cutting down another alley that would bring him out behind

Washington Boulevard. His breathing had calmed, and he ran easily, knowing that they wouldn't catch him. No way.

Frank had just received the package from the Rose Café. Jesus, the place is doing great, he thought as he looked at the wad of credit-card receipts. Three piles. American Express. Mastercard/Visa. Discovery card. There was also a list of all the people who'd paid by credit card, and their phone numbers. The manager, Danny, had really come through. Frank totaled the list; there were ninety-three names. The ringing phone disturbed his thoughts.

"Frank Morrissey," he said, reaching for his Camels.

"Yeah, Frank. This's dispatch. We got another two. Shot at close range. Down at the beach. Looks like it could be your guy."

"Who called it in?"

"Some guy who heard the shots. We sent over an ambulance. Listen, you better haul ass. The press will be on this like flies on a fresh turd."

Frank slammed the receiver down and ran over to the lounge. Ramirez saw him and recognized the look. Neither man spoke. They ran out to the car.

They bent a few traffic laws getting to the beach. Christ, who needed an address, Frank thought as he got close to the scene. The whole area was lit up like Disneyland on the Fourth of July. Helicopters, the works. Both men were nervous, feeling the rush.

Frank looked around, realizing that the killer had definitely taken bigger risks this time. The whole area was pretty well built up with apartments. Surely there must have been someone walking a dog or jogging when the thing went down? He turned to Glen.

"What do you think?"

"Same as you. If . . . and I repeat if . . . this was our man, then he was stupid to have done the killing here. Too exposed. Maybe our luck's changing."

"Yeah. Listen, you go talk to the doctor," Frank said. "I'm going to talk to the person who called it in."

Ramirez walked over to the covered bodies. Christ, what a mess. He could see the blood and body parts spattered over a large area.

"Hi, Ian," Ramirez said to the doctor. "What we got?" He pulled his coat closer, fighting the chill.

The doctor looked at him. He seemed weary, disheveled. "Two girls," he began. "Age around twenty-five, I would think. Both shot at close range in the head area by a high-velocity, Teflon-tipped bullet. Died instantly. Both Caucasian. We have IDs on both of them. American Airline flight attendants. Out jogging, by the looks of it. I'd say that the killer came out from behind that corner over there," he said, pointing toward the end of the apartment building. Ramirez nodded as the doctor continued. "Or he was running toward them from the opposite direction. Whoever did this isn't far away from here right now," he said, letting the thought hang in the air. Abruptly, he gathered up his equipment. "Listen, I'm going to take these two down to the morgue," he said, "and start on the autopsy. You'll have my report tomorrow."

Ramirez nodded. "Thanks, Ian. Talk to you then."

He walked over to Frank. The TV crews had begun arriving in force and were clamoring in that high-pitched, frenetic way of theirs for information. Ramirez nodded at the police officer handling the cordon and observed Frank sitting in a squad car, talking to a young guy, maybe twenty years old. He was huge, obviously a bodybuilder, and dressed in a workout suit. Wouldn't do you any good against the type of bullet our friend out there likes to use, Ramirez thought. He shook his head. *Got to get some sleep.*

Frank saw him and walked over.

"Seems the guy over there was just about to start working out," Frank said. He pointed to a nearby building. "There's a gym on the third floor. Around eight P.M., just as he was switching on the lights, he heard what he thought was a shot. He stopped and listened, then about two or three seconds later, he figures, he heard another shot. He looked out of one of the windows and saw what he thought was two bodies. Nothing else. No glimpse of the killer. What's the word from the doc?"

Ramirez told him what he'd learned. He noticed Frank frowning as he examined the two dead girls' IDs.

"Problem?" Ramirez asked.

"No. Not really. Just washes one theory away, though, doesn't it?"

"What theory?"

"The possible vigilante angle. Now we have some real problems starting. The press, the commissioner, the captain—they're all going to go ape shit when they find out about this. These girls will have families and friends who *do* give a shit whether they're alive or dead. Just watch, it's a new ballgame now."

Reluctantly Frank went over to the battery of reporters

standing nearby. A dozen microphones were pushed in his face and the strobe lights hit him.

He parried most of the questions with noncommittal responses, ending by saying that a further statement would be issued later. As he was walking back to the car, a woman in her late twenties—she looked like a lawyer, he thought—stuck out her hand.

"Excuse me, Sergeant," she said. "I'm Tina Robertson of the *Times*. Mind if I ride back to the station with you? I'd like to ask you some questions."

"As a matter of fact, I do mind," he said, irritated at her presumptuous tone. "Call the PR department if you want some information. Good night."

The woman smiled at him. "Are you always so charming to members of the press, Sergeant, or do I particularly offend you?"

He liked that. She had balls.

"Okay," he said, putting up his hands. "Call me tomorrow, early. Maybe we can talk for a few minutes."

She nodded gratefully and walked away.

Ramirez walked over from the black-and-white and glanced back at the woman, then at Frank.

"What was that all about?"

"Just a reporter, that's all."

"Nice-looking reporter," Ramirez said.

"Not bad," Frank admitted.

They both went back to the car. Neither man spoke on the drive back to the station house. Each was lost in his own thoughts. When Ramirez went home shortly after, Frank was left alone with the paperwork.

* * *

As Frank sat in his office, his thoughts turned to Susan. He looked at his watch. It was almost ten P.M. He dialed his house, listening to the purring as his number started to ring. She picked up the phone instantly.

"Hi, hon. Did I wake you?"

"No, Frank, you didn't. Anything wrong?"

"No. Thinking about you, that's all. Wondering if you wanted to meet me at the Velvet Turtle for a late supper."

She hesitated. "Tell you what I'd prefer, darling. Why don't you stop by the store and bring home a fire log or two, maybe a bottle of champagne. Sound like a good idea?"

Yeah. Sounds good to me, he thought. Her suggestion triggered a memory of the liquor-store manager, Dave Brucker. What had he said about logs and champagne? *Forget it, Frank. Go home and enjoy your wife.*

"Sounds great. See you in about thirty minutes," he said, hanging up the phone and smiling. He looked at all the papers on his desk and decided. Screw it.

She opened the door to greet him. The smell of her and the look of her were intoxicating. He held her close, swearing to himself that he'd make it work for them.

"Your day all right?" she asked softly, looking up at him. He smiled at her and kissed her gently on her forehead.

Later they sat by the fire relaxing. He'd finished his supper. Chicken and walnut salad. They were on their second glass of champagne. He felt the tension lifting from his body and the warmth of the wine in his belly. He stretched out, yawning. Christ, it was good to be home.

"He hit again. Two American Airline flight attendants. Out jogging together. Killed them both."

"I saw it on the news. Saw you, too. You don't much like the television cameras, do you?"

"I hate the press," he said. "Not personally. In fact, most of them are okay—regular guys. What ticks me off is the mass hysteria they promote. It just gives these whackos an excuse to keep on killing."

Susan nodded sympathetically. She had heard this all before. "Was it the same killer, do you think?"

"We won't know for certain until we get a ballistics report. But I'm sure it was."

There was a moment of silence, and then Susan asked about Tony's killer. "Any more leads?" she asked.

"None," Frank said, his face wearing a disgusted look. "But something will turn up soon. It always does." He sounded too emphatic, as if he were trying to convince himself.

"Does it bother you, Frank? That the search for Tony's killer has been downgraded?"

He could see she was trying to help him. It warmed him more than any fire or wine could. He moved closer toward her, holding her tightly. The fire was crackling, and he wanted to forget it all, just live life a moment at a time, feeling close to her. He lit a cigarette for himself, then one for her. *So tell her what you feel. Stop thinking it. Talk to her.*

"I miss him, Sue. I want his killer to be caught. But it's hard. There's a part of me that died with Tony. I want revenge, but sometimes I wonder: what's the point? The cesspool remains a cesspool. Put one whacko away and another comes along. I just—'' He stopped, sniffed her cigarette.

"What's the matter, Frank?" she said, alarm in her voice. It'd been going so well between them; he'd looked so relaxed. Now that dark look was on his face again.

He heard her voice in the distance.

"I . . . I just remembered something, Susan. Talking about Tony, I guess. I was this close to the killer, I think!" he said, stretching out his arms.

"How could you—"

"It was a couple of weeks before Tony was killed," he said, the words coming out fast, piling up on each other. "We were having lunch, as usual, at the Sizzler. I remember it because Tony was trying to cheer me up. I was having a bad time with you being gone. Anyway, there was a guy at the table next to us. He was smoking British cigarettes. I remember because when I smelled it I . . . well, I thought about our trip to Europe and . . ."

"And the killer smoked Dunhill cigarettes. I remember you explained that to me."

She was excited now, holding his hand very tightly, looking into his eyes.

"Yeah, I didn't make the connection until just now. Dammit, the killer was watching us all along. And he must have been someone who wasn't known to us to take a chance of being spotted like that." He thought a moment.

"He did know Tony, though. Somehow he knew Tony."

"Do you remember what the guy looked like?" Susan asked.

"No, he had his back to us. Shit, I didn't see him at all, really."

"Do you suppose that the man was watching you both? He could have been, couldn't he, Frank?" She found the thought unsettling. *Was her husband a target too?*

He frowned, deep in thought. There was *something*. He could feel it. What was it that was there, eluding him?

They were in the squad room, going over the pile of credit-card slips and the list of customers from the Rose Café. Frank decided to bring up what he'd remembered about that day Tony had tried to cheer him up at the Sizzler. He took Cooper and Ramirez through the line of thought he'd followed hours earlier.

"Could be coincidence, Frank. Don't you think?" Cooper said, looking like he'd already decided it was.

"I don't think so," Ramirez said before Frank had a chance to respond. "It makes a lot of sense and explains how the killer knew where Tony lived. What day was it when you were at the Sizzler, Frank?"

"Couple of weeks before the killing. Why?"

"Well, it looks as if the guy who killed Tony didn't know him or where he lived much before he killed him."

"Yeah?" Frank said, catching on. "It means it probably wasn't a revenge killing, and yet it wasn't a random killing, either. If the guy was eyeballing us at the restaurant, he might have spent some time in Tony's neighborhood too. Might be worth questioning everyone again, asking them about a couple weeks prior to the murder, not just right before."

"Sounds okay to me," Cooper said, "as long as we

can work it in between this serial-killer case. But what about the motive? If the guy barely knew Tony, what kind of beef could he have with him?''

They thought about that, no one talking for at least a minute.

''Shit, I've racked my brains,'' Frank finally said. ''Nothing clicks. Unless . . .'' He stopped in midthought. *Jesus.*

''Unless what, Frank?'' Cooper asked.

''No, it's stupid.''

''Tell us anyway. We're all stupid sometimes, right?'' Ramirez said, glancing over at Cooper.

''Well, what if the killer saw Tony?'' Frank began, running the thought through his mind, letting it take its own direction. ''On the television. Remember how after the Worthy and Jackson killings Tony went on the TV? I don't know, guys. I feel something. It's just not coming. Listen, call over to channel four. See if they can send over a tape of that newscast. It might help . . .''

They worked on the serial-killer case for the next few hours. Frank was reluctant to admit it, but the media had stirred up a healthy fear in the public. Everyone wanted the killer to be caught, and he was getting more cooperation than he'd expected. The list of Rose Café customers was now down to twenty-seven people that they'd not reached. *Come on. Someone must have seen something. They must have.*

Just after noon the reports from the lab and from the coroner's office arrived. Jesus, Frank thought, everyone was busting a gut to get them information. It turned out

that a bullet that had lodged in the skull of one of the dead
girls matched up with the bullets used in the hit on the
drug pushers and in the Jackson and Worthy killings. No
surprise. The coroner's report told them another thing. The
girls had been shot from close range. No more than five
feet. Something clicked in Frank's mind.

"Glen, Coop, the fact that the killer got as close as
he did indicates that their first reaction to the guy wasn't
fear. I'd bet money the bastard had a jogging outfit on.
Make sure you ask people if they saw someone jogging
around the same time as the murder." He paused. "Any
luck with the telephone calls?" They both shook their
heads.

Frank was getting close to something; he could feel it.
But it wasn't quite ready to reveal itself. Stymied temporarily on the serial-killer case, he made up his mind to
go over to the Sizzler and ask some questions of the waitress and the hostess. Then he'd take the list of people who
lived over in Tony's neighborhood and talk to them again.
He told the guys he was going to lunch and would be back
around five o'clock.

Frank had the date. December 12. The waitress that had
served him and Tony—and, he presumed, the guy at the
other table—was Freida. She knew him and Tony well,
since they'd been eating lunch there regularly three or four
times a week for years now. And she worked most days
at lunchtime. He would start with her, then ask her who
the hostess had been.

"Hello, Frank," Freida said cheerily. "Haven't seen
you in a while. Not since . . ." Her face darkened. "Jesus,

I'm sorry about Tony. He was a good man, always chatting me up.''

"No problem, Freida. I miss the guy too. It's funny, I didn't really think about it before, but I've been staying away from the places we went to together. Anyway, no problem. Really," he said, grabbing at the menu.

"What can I get you? Coffee?"

"Yeah, coffee would be great. Think I'll have a Cobb salad. Blue cheese on the side. Thanks. Listen, Freida, I want to ask you a couple of questions. Can you ask the manager if you can take a break for five minutes?"

"Sure, no problem. Let me get your coffee. Be right back."

She wasn't away long and brought the coffee and the salad, plus a coffee for herself.

"So what you want to ask me, Frank?" she said, pouring heaps of sugar into her coffee. Frank grimaced.

"Can you remember the last time Tony and I were in here, specifically?"

"Sure," she shot back. "It was before Christmas. Couple of weeks before. You sat at this table, like usual."

"Good," Frank said. "Now, listen, that day we were in here, December the twelfth, there was a guy sitting by himself at that table there." He pointed to the table. "He was reading a newspaper. Do you remember? He was smoking British cigarettes," he said, and held his breath.

She thought about it so long that Frank thought at first she wouldn't remember. "Yeah," she said finally. "I do remember. The guy wouldn't eat his food. Left a while after you both did. Seemed sad, upset or something. He destroyed the silverwear. Bent it all to hell. Why?"

Frank felt his heartbeat start to quicken. "Do you remember what he looked like?" he asked.

"Not really."

"Nothing at all?"

"Well . . . he was white . . . tall, I think . . . and well dressed in a casual sort of way. He was wearing tinted glasses. Sorry, Frank, I'm not the best when it comes to describing people. I remember things that happen, that get said. People . . ." She shrugged helplessly. "Damn, I don't even remember what color Tony's eyes were. Is it important?"

He felt deflated. What had he expected? Some shortcut, he supposed. He should have known better.

"That's okay, Freida. No big deal. Just following a hunch. Listen, could you find out who was hostessing that day for me, please?"

"Does it have something to do with what happened to Tony?"

"It might. Right now I'm not sure. Could you find out about the hostess?"

"Sure. Give me a minute and I'll check with the manager."

She left, and he couldn't tell by the look on her face when she returned whether she'd succeeded.

"Like I thought, it was Irene Davis. She's a student somewhere up north. She hasn't worked here for the last month or so. Went back to school." Frank's face fell. "But I do have a number for her," Freida said, handing him a slip of paper.

Frank took the number. "I owe you one, Freida," he said.

"No, Frank," she said. "You don't owe me anything. If it will help find . . ." She shrugged. No more words were necessary. Frank squeezed her gently on the arm and left.

Frank was tired. The afternoon hadn't gone well. He'd talked to most of the people on the block but kept striking out. No one had seen anything.

At five o'clock he found himself walking up Tony's driveway. The house was dark and silent. Sad in a way. Lonely, empty looking. Suddenly, he felt the great weight of guilt enter his body and start to crush him, choke him. His eyes were misting up. He didn't know how but he found himself at the back door. It was locked, but the kitchen window was still open. He remembered that this was how the killer had got in. He went into the house and tried the light. It was working. Strange that no one had turned off the power.

The air felt heavy, and he could smell the disinfectant that someone had used to clean the blood from the carpet. He lit a cigarette, sat in a chair—the only one not covered by a cloth. *Talk to me, Tony. Help me work this out*. He felt bad as he realized that he hadn't done as much as he could. The tears came then. Slow at first, welling up inside of him, filling him. Then the floodgate was open and his body shook uncontrollably. He gave in to it, let the pain have its moment, then much later when the quiet seemed to press in on him he dragged his body up and walked around the house. It was empty, pathetic, sad. Everything had been boxed. Then he saw the photograph in the den, sitting by itself, without a home or a box. He bent down and picked it up, then sighed as he saw Tony laughing, his huge arm around Frank. Frank remembered when it was taken. "For posterity," Tony had said. Frank hated having his picture taken. And Tony had been razzing him. Thoughts were flooding his mind. *I miss you, buddy. Jesus, more than I would have thought, or admitted. You were the best friend I ever had.*

"I'll get the bastard who took you, Tony," Frank said aloud. *I will if it's the last thing I do. It won't bring you back, or make me miss you less. It can only balance the ledger. But I'll get him. I promise you I'll get him.*

Frank had put the photo in his car and called into the office to say he would be back around seven-thirty: he was going to talk to the rest of the neighbors. Cooper told him that some lady from the *Times* had called about a thousand times and would be stopping over to see him at around eight-thirty. Was that okay? Frank had forgotten about her and shrugged. It didn't much matter either way, did it? Ramirez came on the radio and told him that Roy Weston wanted to see him. Frank knew why. The heat was starting to come down.

He walked over to the house next to Tony's. There were lights burning. He was glad. He wanted to get this over.

He knocked on the door, heard someone inside shout. A pretty lady in her early forties appeared. She was wearing a uniform. He guessed she must work at the airport.

"Good evening. Are you Mrs. Davenport?"

"Yes. What can I do for you?" she said, smiling at him.

"I'm Detective Sergeant Frank Morrissey. I wonder if I might ask you a few questions?"

"What about, Sergeant?"

"It has to do with the murder of Tony Wilson and—"

"I spoke to a detective about that twice," she said, cutting him off. "I don't really see how I can be of any more help."

Frank sighed. That had been the response of everyone he'd spoken to. People had short memories where death was concerned.

"I understand that, Mrs. Davenport," he said softly, looking at her eyes. "However, we have reason to believe that the killer might have been watching Sergeant Wilson for a few weeks prior to the murder. We wondered if you could think back. Try to see if you remembered anyone. Anything that was out of the ordinary. Perhaps a car? Or someone hanging around that didn't look familiar?"

She looked at him for a moment, then seemed to make a decision.

"Why don't you come in a moment, Sergeant. It's cold out there."

"Thanks. And you can call me Frank," he said, following her into the house.

She showed him into the den, then sat down on a huge leather sofa. "You were saying, Frank?"

Frank eased into a chair. "I was saying that the killer might have been hanging around the area for more than a few days before the murders, so we're asking everyone we spoke to before to think back even further, a couple of weeks before the murders."

She nodded, leaned back, and closed her eyes. She seemed to concentrate for a few moments, then shook her head. "I can't remember anything out of the ordinary. I saw no one I didn't recognize. You might want to ask my son Alan if he saw anything. Let me give him a call."

"You have a son? There's no mention of him in the report that was filed last December."

"Well, I did tell the detective that I had a son, that he'd been in Aspen since December eighteenth. I don't know why he would have noted it. Alan's upstairs. I'll get him."

The lady was right, Frank thought. The kid had been away a week or more before the killings. No reason why the detective would have followed up.

A few seconds later, Mrs. Davenport returned with her son, who was a surprise. From the way she spoke, Frank had imagined someone much younger. This kid had to be nearly twenty. A tall, good-looking kid with his mother's direct manner.

"Hi, Sergeant," the boy said. "My mother says you'd like to ask me some questions?"

"Yes, Alan. Your mom tells me that you were in Aspen during the holidays. When did you leave exactly, and when did you return?"

"I left in the early evening, December eighteenth. We returned in the late afternoon . . . on January sixth, it was. We have a cabin up there. We—my friends and me—go every year. Well, for the past eight years anyway."

"You know all about the murder of Tony Wilson?"

"Yes."

"I was wondering if you noticed anything unusual in the week or so before you left for your trip."

"What do you mean by unusual?" the boy asked, looking at Frank oddly.

"Well, any people that you didn't recognize hanging around. Any strange cars that you didn't recognize. Anything that wasn't . . . usual."

The boy thought about that for a while.

"I did notice one thing," he said finally. "You see, there's a view of the street from my room. And I remember a certain car. Nothing unusual about it really, except that it was a Volvo wagon, white and new, one of those new turbo-powered ones. Nice car. I wondered whose it was. Although it wasn't ever outside of Mr. Wilson's house."

"Are you sure about the type of car?" Frank asked.

"Yes. Like I said, it was a looker. It's been featured twice in *Road and Track*. Real expensive, costs about thirty thousand. And I know most of the people around here; they're Chevy and Ford people. It didn't belong to anyone I know."

"Are you sure about the color? And how do you know that it was new?" Frank asked, a puzzled look on his face.

"Well, it was light colored. Could have been yellow, I suppose. It was definitely new. It had a third brake light on the back. They only started to do that on the 1987 models. It was one of the 760 turbos. Like I said, I've seen pictures of it in *Road and Track*."

"Mind showing me the view from your window, Alan?"

The boy shrugged, and they went upstairs. Frank saw car models and car magazines all over the room. The kid knew his cars, all right.

"Mind showing me where you saw the car?" Frank asked, looking out of the window at the street below.

"I saw it twice. I don't remember the dates. Once in the late afternoon and another time during the day. Once it was parked over there," he said, pointing, "by the Morgans' house, and the other time farther up, near the Davidsons'."

Frank was puzzled about something. Something didn't quite fit. He needed to talk to the boy alone.

"Could you excuse us a moment, Mrs. Davenport?" Frank asked.

The woman looked at her son, then at him, and shrugged.

"Sure, how about some coffee?" she said, smiling.

"Sounds great. Thank you. White with no sugar, please."

He turned toward the boy, put his arm on his shoulder, smiling. "What I don't understand, Alan, is how you could have recognized the model of the car from here. On a dark night or early evening, that doesn't seem possible. Even in daylight it looks to be too far away. Or does Volvo only make one type of station wagon?"

The boy reddened, then started to say something. He stopped, looked toward the door, and paused a moment. "Between the two of us? Off the record?" Alan asked.

"Off the record," Frank said.

Alan knelt down and rummaged under his bed. He produced a pair of high-powered binoculars. Frank smiled to himself. *Peeping Tom, huh?* Frank put the binoculars to his eyes and swept the area. They were powerful and he could see that the boy wouldn't have had any problem reading the model name on the rear of the vehicle if it had been parked where he said it was. He panned back and forth, sweeping the area. Then he recognized what had attracted the boy's interest. She was cute as a button and sitting on her bed with a Walkman over her head, wearing nothing else and polishing her toenails. A real find, he thought, handing the boy the binoculars.

"Now I want you to think, Alan. Did you ever see the driver of the car?"

"No."

"Are you certain?" he said, hoping that the boy was wrong.

"Yes."

"Did you by any chance see any identifying marks on the car? Did it have a telephone? Did you see the license plate?"

"No, I didn't notice anything except that it had tinted windows. I don't remember anything else. Sorry," he said. He rummaged through a pile of magazines on the table next to his bed and found the issue he was looking for.

"This is one of the issues that featured the car. See," he said, "It's a four-page spread."

Frank glanced at the magazine and made a note. "Thanks, Alan. You've been a big help."

Nice people, Frank thought as he left the Davenports. He felt renewed. Finally a lead. Maybe.

It was 7:40 when he finally got back to the station house. He'd planned to give the captain a wide berth, talk to him in the morning. But he didn't have a chance. Roy was incredible at rooting you out when you wanted to be invisible.

"Got a minute, Frank?" Weston asked him, indicating

his office with a nod of his head. He pretended to not have noticed.

"Sure, be right with you."

"Now, Frank. My office."

Shit, this wasn't going to be fun.

"Where've you been all day?" Weston asked.

"Chasing up some leads. Re-interviewing people. Got some—"

"Cut the shit, Frank," Weston interrupted. "Why didn't you come in when you got my call?" His voice was low and menacing. Tread carefully, Frank thought.

"I didn't realize it meant dropping everything I was doing," he said.

"What *were* you doing?"

"Talking to the people who live near Tony's place. Remember I told you—"

"Yeah, the guy at the Sizzler. Big fucking deal. Listen to me, and listen good. I'm getting a lot of heat from upstairs to get the crazy mother who's killing people. And what's my best detective doing? I'll tell you what he's doing—"

"Listen, Roy, I—"

"Shut the fuck up, Frank. I don't want to hear any more about your wild-goose chases. Now get your ass in gear and find the bastard who's wasted seven people this last couple of weeks. Do you hear me? Get on with your fucking job. Dismissed."

Frank started to say something, then stopped. This was one battle he wasn't going to win. "All right. You're the boss," Frank said finally. He turned on his heels and exited the office.

* * *

He found the guys in the squad room. Glum-looking bunch, he thought. *Wonder why?*

"Hi, guys. What's up?"

"Not enough," Ramirez said, offering him a smoke. "Struck out on the telephone calls. Nothing. No one saw or remembers seeing a damn thing. It's depressing. How about you?"

"I've got a couple of things on Tony's killer," he said quietly. "One, the killer might have been seen near Tony's place. A kid spotted a strange car parked twice in the area. He thinks it was a white Volvo station wagon, 760 turbo, 87 model. Two, I spoke to the waitress in the restaurant, and she remembers the guy at the next table but not what he looked like. I have the phone number of the hostess who was working that day, so we might be able to get a description from her. But all of that is back-burner stuff. The captain wants a full-court press on the serial nut. Has the lab given us any more info on the crime scene, Coop?"

"We've gotten zip," Cooper replied. "The damn place was as clean as a whistle." He shrugged, then seemed to remember something. "Hey, channel four sent over a tape of that newscast if you want to look at it."

"Why not," Frank said. The phone rang, and he picked it up. It was reception telling him that a Tina Robertson from the *Times* had arrived. He looked at his watch—eighty-thirty on the nail. He told reception to bring her through.

"Tina Robertson from the *Times* is on her way in here," Frank said. "I think I'll let her watch the tape too. She might have a slant on it."

Cooper and Ramirez grinned and started to say something when she walked in. Christ, she was something. Tall and slim. Rich brown curly hair, held back with a pearl clasp. Not much makeup, but she didn't need it. This was class goods.

"Put the tape on, Glen, please," Frank said, bringing their attention back to the matter at hand.

They watched as the images of a dead friend flickered on the screen in front of them. Each man sat alone with his thoughts, remembering the good times and the bad. All of them were affected, and the room was quiet for long moments after the piece had ended. It had been a short clip. Tony had looked uncomfortable, cold, wet, and tired. He hadn't said much, just uttered the standard lines. The reporter had asked him if the killings were drug related, and Tony had said that "early indications" suggested they were. Not much else. What had he hoped to see? Frank asked himself. Suddenly he felt the urgent need to get some fresh air.

"Thanks, Glen," he said abruptly. "Miss Robertson and I have to go. Leave the video in the machine, if you don't mind. I think I'll come back and take a look at it later," he added, standing up and indicating to Tina that he was ready to leave. She picked up her purse and followed him out to the car.

They had driven over to the bar in silence. He thought she'd assumed he wanted to be quiet and was giving him some space. He liked that. He asked the host for a quiet booth in the back.

"What would you like to drink, Miss Robertson?" he asked. His voice was a little tight, surprising him.

"White wine, please. And cut the Miss Robertson crap. You know my name, so use it, Frank."

He wondered why he'd even come here with her. He wanted to be home. With Susan. Screw the interview.

"So what do you want?" he said, not even looking at her. He glanced at the menu and tapped his fingers on the table.

She started slowly. "Frank, my paper wants me to do a special piece on this killer. He's captured my editor's fancy. It's news, Frank—hot, juicy news, as you know."

She bit her tongue. Christ, Tina, that was a stupid opening statement, she thought.

He was looking at her, staring right through her. His grayish eyes had a fire in them.

"Yeah, and that's the problem I have being here with you, right now, Tina. It's not exciting, what I do. It's cleaning up shit. We have a deranged son of a bitch out there, and all you media people want to do is turn him into some sort of antihero."

"Look, Frank," she said, her tone apologetic, "what I said just then was flippant, probably very thoughtless under the circumstances. Damn, it's not even representative of how I feel, or of how my newspaper feels. I take it back, okay? Look, can we start again?"

He hesitated a moment, then seemed to come to a decision. "Okay," he said, forcing a smile. "I'll be happy to start over. How long have you been a reporter?"

She liked him better when he smiled. He wasn't quite so damn intimidating.

"I've been reporting on this sort of thing, death and violence, for fourteen years. I was with the *Tribune* back in Chicago for thirteen years. Came out here to L.A. last year. I understand how it sickens you, Frank. It sickens me too. But we have a duty to report these things, and in my experience the newspapers have helped a lot to bring these serial killers into custody."

He sighed, putting up his hands. "Look, I have no problem with the press or the television people, individually. It's just—"

"Then tell me, Frank," she said, trying to win him over with a smile. "Off the record if you wish. What leads are you following?" She lit a cigarette.

"None. We have absolutely no idea who the killer is or what his motive is.

"So what are you doing?"

"Police work."

"Which means?"

"Gathering. Sifting, Sorting. Look, I'm telling you the truth. We don't have much. We know from Ballistics that the same killer committed all seven murders. We know the killer is clever and that he hasn't been seen or shown anything of himself yet. He was less careful last time, and all we can hope for is that he'll be even less careful next time."

"So you're fairly certain that he'll kill again?" she said.

"Absolutely."

"When?"

"Soon. These things usually follow a pattern. Either the killer gets to wanting to do it more frequently, or he just drifts away. Leaves the state and we never catch him.

Until it starts again someplace else, then someone else catches him, and he fesses up to the murders there.''

"Do you think that's likely?"

"What?"

"That he'll leave here and you won't catch him?"

"I doubt it. You get feelings about these guys. Nothing tangible. But I think that this one will kill again and keep on killing until we catch him. What we have to hope for is that we get a break. We need one real bad.''

"Have you received anything from the FBI yet on possible bullet matches with other unsolved crimes in other states?"

"Nothing so far. This would appear to be the killer's first time. It makes sense.''

"What do you mean?"

"Nothing really. Just remembering something.''

"Come on, tell me.''

"Well, my partner, Tony Wilson, and I investigated the first killing. We were doing some dialogue over drinks one night. The word on the first killings was that it was drug connected. I never believed that. Not from the beginning. Tony didn't either, not really. Anyway, I was doing a 'what if' deal, and I figured that the killer was the murdered guys' victim, that he turned it around and shot them both. I wondered then if that was his first time. It probably was, and he probably liked it. That's all.''

She thought about that and had been making notes as he spoke.

"If what you say is true, how do you account for the gun?" she said.

"What do you mean?"

"Frank, regular people don't walk around with point thirty-eights in their pockets, with Teflon-tipped bullets, do they?"

He hadn't thought of that, and she was right. How did she know about the Teflon bullets? That had been withheld from the press.

"Continue, Tina."

"Look, I've covered a half dozen of these things over the years, and the killers always start to go over the edge sometime sooner than they actually start to kill."

"Give me an example of what you mean."

"Well, it could be anything—threatening people, beating people up. Wives. Children. Pets. General violent actions," she said.

"I understand. But what help is that to us?"

"I don't know. Maybe when you fill in a few more of the gaps you can check the records and see if he's on record somewhere for violence."

"I appreciate your input, Tina. No, really, I do. But there are ten million people in the L.A. area. Do you have any idea how many reported acts of violence occur each day, let alone go unreported? With all of the computers in the world working twenty-four hours a day, I doubt we could get a fix."

Tina decided to change the subject. "Frank, why were you watching the old news footage on the video when I arrived?"

He thought about it and decided he would trust her. *Why not?* So he told her everything: about Tony's killing, and the restaurant, and how he'd thought that maybe the killer had seen Tony on the television, followed him, and killed him.

"The only problem is, we still don't have a motive," he said.

She had listened to him with growing excitement and wanted to suggest something, but after the way her last suggestion went down she was reluctant.

"That was good news about the car," she said.

"A place to start. But to tell you the truth, and this is off the record, my captain wants me to forget Tony's killer and concentrate on this other guy. He's right, but it's hard."

She was quiet for a long time, turning over a thought she had. Finally she resolved to bring it up. "Frank, I have an idea. Well, it's more a 'what if' question . . . what if the person who killed Tony is the same one who's killing all these other people?"

Mother of God. Sweet Jesus. That was what had been staring him in the face. *Hold it, Frank. Talk it through. Dammit, she's right.*

"Go on," he said, fighting to keep the excitement out of his voice.

"Well, you said that the killer had been following you and Tony, and that you believed the killer had seen Tony on TV. I saw the video. Tony didn't say much, except that the killings were drug related. I told you I've covered serial killers before. They almost always have huge egos. So if the killer did kill the two black kids and then the newscast invalidated him, saying it was someone else, well, it probably enraged him. And since he couldn't attack the media, he went after Tony."

Christ, the missing piece. She was right. It all fell together now . . . except . . .

"What about the murder weapon?"

"What do you mean?"

"Tony and the girl were killed with a knife."

"Think about it, Frank. Think about the profile of the killer for a moment. If it was the same person and he was watching Tony and wanted to kill him . . . well, I'm sorry, but he probably wanted Tony to suffer. Remember, he probably felt that Tony was deliberately holding back the truth. Listen, I know a psychologist we could talk to—"

"Fuck the doctors," Frank said, his voice rising. "I don't want to hear another word about how it probably wasn't the killer's fault because his mother beat him or his father raped him. It's not goddamn relevant, okay?" His face wore a tortured look.

She said nothing, just kept her eyes focused on the table. Leave him be, she thought. Leave him be.

Frank was out there for a long time, lost in his own world—a world where vengeance was sweet and pure and satisfying. Finally, he came back to his surroundings, raised his hand, asked the waiter for the check.

"Listen," he said to Tina, "I want you to write it. Make the connection. The connection between Tony's death and the other murders. Also, put in your piece that I'm heading up the investigation, that I have several leads, that I expect to make an arrest soon. Can you print it tonight?"

She looked at her watch, nodding, wondering what her editor would say.

"Frank, it's going to get ugly, and my editor will want

to call the commissioner to get the go-ahead. Will you talk to your captain?''

''Yeah. Let's get out of here. We have lots to do.''

Frank picked up the telephone in his office and dialed Roy Weston's number at home.

''Roy, sorry to disturb you. It's Frank.''

''No problem, Frank. What's going on?''

He told him. Everything that he and Tina had discussed and what he wanted to do.

''No damn way, Frank,'' Weston said after he'd finished. ''Everything you're talking about is circumstantial.''

''But Roy, it all makes sense. I've felt that there was something we were missing. Look, if we leak the story, maybe the whacko will be flushed out. Maybe he'll come after me. You've got to—''

''Listen to me, Frank. The D.A.'s office will eat your lunch if we let this story run.''

''Roy, you've known me for years, and you know that when I get this feeling I'm always right. Let me run with it.''

''Sorry, Frank. I think it would be premature to run the story on the basis of what you have. Tell you what, call Tina Robertson and ask her to run it as a nonexclusive. Tell her she can write that 'we believe, based upon recent developments, that the murder of Sergeant Tony Wilson is connected with the serial killings, and that evidence, recently obtained, points to the killer as being the same person.' Nothing about arrests, or spotlighting you.

Okay?'' he said, and Frank heard the finality in his voice. He wasn't going to get him to budge.

"Okay," Frank said, not very enthusiastic.

"Go home and get some sleep. That's an order," Weston said, and hung up.

Frank called over to the *Times* office and Tina came on the line. He could tell that she was disappointed about something. He told her what Weston had said.

"That's good, Frank. Not great, but better than my editor had thought. I've got to go if we want to get this into the late editions. And Frank, let's stay close on this one, okay?"

"Sure thing," he said. There was a slight pause, then, "Hey, Tina . . ."

"Yes?"

"I . . . uh . . . hey, listen, have a good night. And thanks for all your help. I appreciate it."

"We're in this together, right?"

"Right," he said. Somehow, saying that, he felt better than he had in a long time.

Vic was reading the late edition of the *Times*. Tina's story was the lead in the Metro section. Well, well. Finally the idiot cops had made the connection. He wondered how. He'd gone over it many times in his head, and the car part was always what he came back to. Too many times he had gone over to Wilson's neighborhood, been too exposed. Still, it was worth it, and for so long they hadn't made the connection that he doubted it was the car. Anyway, it wasn't *his* car that they'd be looking for. He smiled then. He'd learned a lot. Really learned. It was like anything else, he supposed. Do it enough times, pay attention to details, be prepared, and the chances of hitting, running, and living to fight another day were pretty good. He liked the sound of that and was chuckling to himself when the girl came into the kitchen.

That had worked out just fine too. After she'd stormed out of his place, fury and disappointment on her face, he'd wondered if it was really through with them. But she'd called the next day and told him that he was right and that she shouldn't be crowding him and keeping him from what he had to do. She wanted it to work for them, she'd said. He sent flowers around to the bar, and it had been even better with her since. Last night the sex had been the best ever.

"What's making you so happy this morning, Vic?" Andy asked, sitting down next to him.

"Oh, nothing."

"You must be laughing at something. What's that you're reading?"

He had put the part he was reading down and picked up the sports section.

"Looks like big Al did it again," he observed, watching her out of the corner of his eye.

"Who's big Al? And what did he do that's making you so happy this morning? When I came into the kitchen, you looked as if you'd done something naughty and gotten away with it."

That startled him. She'd better not pry, or he'd get real mean, fast.

"Big Al's the owner of the Raiders," he said, a trace of sarcasm in his voice. "You know, the L.A. Raiders? Football team? Well, he just stole John Elway. It's making me happy, that's all."

She looked at him with a puzzled expression. "I thought you didn't like the Raiders anymore."

"Well, the season's over and . . . shit, they can't be as awful as they were this time last year, can they?" He reached over for the coffeepot, biting back the anger he felt for her prying ways.

"If you say so," she said slowly, thinking that he was acting strange this morning. She looked at the paper again, tried to change the subject. "By the way, what's happening on the serial killer?"

He felt the anger again, and his body was tense. He wanted to end it with her. *Kill her, kill her, kill her.*

"Read the papers yourself. Here. Why're you so interested in it, anyway?"

He could see from the look on her face that he'd hurt her. Her bottom lip was twitching as she took the paper.

"I *wasn't* interested in it, Vic. I was just trying to make conversation. Why are you so mad at me? Last night was wonderful. Now for some reason you're angry at me, and I don't know why."

She was crying now, and he hated her at that moment with all of him. He knew he had to be away from her or he would do it. The mist had engulfed him, was consuming him. He felt his hand reach for the knife on the table, and he knew if she didn't leave he would cut her.

"I'm not angry at you, Andy. Listen, I'm going out to

run. Let's pass on this evening, okay? I have some work
to do.''

He felt his hands shaking as he started to run along the
water's edge. Tonight he would go out. Find some fools.
Recharge himself. The girl was getting to be a real problem. Soon he would take care of her. But not yet. He
needed to finish the other part first. Time for her later. He
ran, very fast, and it calmed him, cleared his head as he
thought again of the newspaper story. He wondered, then
he laughed. Damn assholes. Biggest bunch of half-wits on
the planet. What did they think they were dealing with, a
cretin? He knew then that they had nothing. Maybe a few
inspired guesses. Maybe that silly notice he had seen at
the Rose Café had gotten a response. . . . No, that couldn't
be it. No one had seen or noticed him. Except the black
guys, and they sure as hell weren't talking to anyone, were
they? His mood was getting better as he gulped in the
brackish air. He loved it at the beach. The salty fish smell
beat the hell out of smog. He glanced at his watch—7:43
A.M. He thought of the cop and smiled. Yeah, it's time I
found out where you live, ''Mr. Slick.'' He turned and
ran back to the house, hoping that the girl was gone. She
was.

Susan looked at him as he slept. He looked so vulnerable, so young. She wanted to wake him, talk to him, and
yet she was reluctant. He hadn't slept this long or this late
for as long as she could remember. She bent over him,
kissing his eyelids. He opened his eyes, grinning at her.
She was back in college.

The memory warmed her. Big, handsome Frank Morrissey. She'd been a cheerleader and he'd played nose tackle for the junior college. For them it had been love at first sight. He was the only man she'd ever had in her life or wanted. So strong, so incredibly gentle. They'd spent the whole of that first summer together, learning about each other and making plans. Her mom had adored him from the first meeting, saw the same qualities in Frank that she did. Her father never actually said it, but he'd hoped that she would marry a different kind of man. And when he found out Frank wanted to be a cop, he was disgusted, though he didn't let it show.

"Good morning, darling. You slept well," she said, kissing him softly on the lips.

He was rubbing the sleep out of his eyes, trying to get out of bed.

"Hi, Susie. What time is it?"

"It's seven. Want some breakfast?"

"Jesus, it's that late? Yeah, breakfast sounds great. Feels like I was bitten by a tsetse fly. I'm tired. Give me about fifteen minutes, okay?"

She went down to the kitchen and started cooking his favorite, french toast with maple syrup. The slices of toast were set out on a plate when he rumbled into the kitchen. He looked great, she thought. She could tell, looking at the puffiness around his eyes, that he'd slept well.

"Good," he said. "French toast." He kissed her on the forehead and eased into a chair. "Say, did you see the *Times* this morning?"

She passed him the paper. "The article's in the Metro

section, first page. Doesn't say much. I thought from what you said last night that you had something, well, more specific.''

He skimmed the story. Tina had written it the way they'd agreed. It satisfied him, made him feel as if it would not be long before they got their man. For the first time he found himself brooding about the details of a face-to-face confrontation with the killer. His revenge lasted a few seconds before he brought his attention back to Susan.

''Ah, that's the way the department wanted it to be written,'' he explained.

''Then why were you frowning?''

He hesitated. ''Well, I was just thinking about the politics of this whole thing, reminding myself that we have to do everything by the book so that when we get this guy he won't get off on a technicality or something. Then I started thinking that the case wouldn't get to trial anyway. It sort of made me wonder what's happening to me. That's all.''

She thought about that and looked into his eyes.

''Do you mean what I think you mean, Frank? That you would kill him at the time of arrest?''

''I've never killed anyone, Susan. Never had to. Should have, once. Could have. And didn't. I talked about that with Tony, and he said that it was true, no one would have known. Except me. He was right, and as much as I get frustrated, think these thoughts, deep down I know that it's what makes us different from them. That is, we're not killers. When we have the choice, we don't pull the trigger. But somehow this case is different. I feel like the killer and me, well, we're bound together, and in the end we'll have to resolve this between ourselves." He shrugged. "I don't know, I guess I'm just a little confused."

She took his hand. "You'll do the right thing, Frank, whatever it is. I *know* you will."

He nodded, tried to smile. He wished he was as sure.

Susan had volunteered to bring Frank to work since his car wouldn't start. On the way to the station house they talked idly of going away together, maybe taking a vacation back to Europe. Frank had never seen his wife so happy. He kidded with her about boning up on his knowledge of art museums, and she teased him like a schoolgirl. He was sorry the ride had to end. "Call you later, kid," he said as they parked a half hour later. She blew him a kiss and drove away.

Vic had been watching for Frank to arrive. He was in his car and had been parked for about ten minutes. He'd just decided that he'd been there long enough when he spotted the Mercedes and the beautiful girl driving it. Dammit, the smug cop was with her. He watched as the two kissed, and he smiled. This was going to be fun. He started his car and pulled in behind her. She was driving slowly; he had no problem keeping her in sight. He congratulated himself. This was an unexpected bonus. He hadn't thought of Morrissey as married. He hadn't looked the type.

She was pulling over into the supermarket parking lot. *Dammit. Why hadn't she gone straight home?* She parked, and he watched her as she got gracefully out of the car. Jesus, what a looker. What was she doing with that cop? And the car? Since when did cops make enough to afford a Mercedes-Benz? He watched her walk over to the market. She was tall. Shoulder-length auburn hair. Full mouth with huge, tawny eyes that seemed to fill her face. She walked with a bounce, like a dancer he'd once known.

He decided he'd follow her into the market. As he went in, he realized that it wasn't very busy and he'd have to be careful. He adjusted his sunglasses and grinned. Careful of what? She had a cart and was filling it pretty quickly. He wondered what she was smiling about. Well, beautiful lady, enjoy it, whatever it is. While you can. He grabbed a cart and went down the aisle, parallel to her. If he timed it right, he could get real close, maybe even create a collision. Now, wouldn't that be interesting? As he swung a hard left at the end of the aisle, she was turning right, and the two carts collided. Some of her groceries fell out, so he went to help her pick them up.

"Sorry about that," Vic said. "Still half asleep, I guess. Please let me help you." Vic bent down to pick up the groceries.

"That's okay. It wasn't your fault. My mind was miles away," she said, smiling, showing him a perfect set of teeth. He felt his loins responding to her.

"Where was it?" he asked her, trying to make her look at him.

"Sorry?"

"Your mind. You said it was miles away."

"Oh, that. My husband and I just decided we'd go back

to Europe. Second honeymoon. I was thinking about it. Thanks for helping me pick these things up,'' she said, picking up the last of the spilled packages.

He grinned, thinking: *Not a chance, pretty lady. You're mine now.*

"My pleasure," he said, sticking out his hand. "Alan Mathews. Pleased to meet you. Europe sounds great. He's a lucky man, your husband."

"Susan Morrissey. Thank you."

She was aware of the way he was looking at her. It wasn't threatening or even sexual. Something? She shrugged. *He's just being nice.*

"Well, sorry I was so clumsy," he said. "Have a good day."

He held out his hand again, and she wished that he wasn't wearing those dark glasses. Why does he seem to be laughing at me? she thought. As she saw the man continue down the aisle, her good spirits returned. *Better get a move on, girl. You've got carpet fitters arriving at the house at ten o'clock.*

Vic saw her come out of the market and load her car. She glanced at her watch, frowned.

Vic was surprised at how fast she drove out of the lot. He was hard-pressed to keep her in sight. He wondered if she'd spotted him, then decided she'd been in too much of a hurry to notice anything. He let his thoughts wander, imagining her bloody, and dying in his arms. He tried to picture the look on Morrissey's face when he got home and found her. Damn, he wished he had the dead cop's gun. He saw the Mercedes start to slow down and noticed that the houses in the area were large and well kept. Morrissey lived higher off the hog than Wilson did, Vic thought. He saw Morrissey's wife pull into the nicest-looking house on the block and into the garage, which she'd opened from the car as she drove up. He slowed down and parked as the garage doors closed behind the woman.

The house was maybe fifty yards away, and it looked pretty quiet. He was wondering how to best approach it. Maybe from the back? The gun was in the glove box, and he pulled it out, feeling its power flow through the cool, sleek metal. As he was getting out of his Porsche, a van suddenly came up alongside and almost hit him. He felt the anger starting to surge through him. It was all he could do to refrain from pulling the gun out of his waistband and blasting the damn van. He watched as it screeched to a halt outside the Morrissey house and the front door was flung open. Two men got out, one going toward the house as the other removed several rolls of carpet from the rear. *Goddammit, they're carpet fitters*. Vic couldn't believe it. The anger was boiling out of him as he got back into his car and pulled away, slamming his foot on the accelerator and leaving a trail of rubber in the street.

He almost crashed his car on the way home. His hand clenched the steering wheel so tightly that it was bleeding. Damn her. Damn him. He ran into his house and into the shower. It didn't help. He paced around the room, then went out and ran. It didn't help.

He had to do it. He dressed in jeans and a T-shirt and threw on a zippered Members Only jacket. He took out the gun and carefully unloaded and reloaded the bullets.

This had become almost a ritual. He polished and cleaned each round, rubbed it until it shone. One by one he slid the rounds into the chamber. He felt the power returning to his body. He felt the pain in and around his forehead. He watched the red mist curling smokily before his eyes. Swirling and calling to him. The gun was ready, and he tucked it into his waistband. It was noon.

He drove along Pacific Coast Highway. He was looking for a group of people, anybody who was alone, isolated. He'd expected the beach to be deserted except for the stupid surfers. He hated surfers and all they stood for. Bleach-blond prickheads with their bimbo girlfriends. Gave California a bad name. He thought about the in crowd at school, the ones who'd laughed at him, taunted him. He thought about the surfers again, how he despised them. He imagined them in their stupid wet suits, giving each other high fives as they rode a three-foot wave. He saw them at the end of his gun barrel. He felt himself squeezing the trigger, saw the bleach-blond heads rupturing and turning a misty red. *Where are you, surfer boys?*

He had seen a few of them, but it wasn't safe. Too exposed. He was raging now, and he punched the dash of his car. Glancing into the car's mirror, he saw his face was beaded with a fine film of sweat. His skin was cool to the touch, and inside his guts were churning, bubbling with volcanic rage. He saw the four youths then, in a Volkswagen convertible. He accelerated, downshifted, pulling in behind them. They exited at Topanga. He grinned. Absolutely perfect. He would run the assholes off the road.

The kids were having fun. They'd been surfing and for the past couple of hours smoking a few joints, just kicking back. They were on their way home. Michael, the driver, loved Topanga Canyon. He especially loved it when he had the girls with him. There was little traffic, meaning he could really put the "pedal to the metal." He saw the Porsche pull in behind him, thinking to himself that he'd let it pass. It was one of those big, black, beautiful 930 turbo jobs with the flared fenders, superbig tires, and the scoop on the back and the front. He waved the Porsche past. It stayed behind him. Odd.

He glanced at his speedometer. He was doing seventy-five. Too fast, actually. Better slow down, stop letting the Porsche intimidate him. There was a great spot for passing just behind the first incline. He would pull over and stop. Pretend that they were looking at the view or taking a piss.

Vic was watching the boy; he could see he was driving the VW way too fast. He was getting really excited now and could feel the sensation take hold of him, filling his body. He knew the driver's type. Trying to impress his buddies and the girls. If he stayed on the bastard's tail, he'd pull over, and in all probability, stop. That would give him the chance he needed to get ahead. He had a plan. This kid wouldn't be able to resist.

Michael had his eyes glued to the rearview mirror and the road ahead. The VW was starting to drift badly around the curves, and the passengers, especially Michael's buddy Joey, were yelling at him to "take it easy, man." Christ, Michael thought, the Porsche was tailgating him. He saw a place to pull over ahead and put on his right signal. The

Porsche screamed past in second gear and honked. He saw the driver wave, and he felt better. He pulled the car over and asked if anyone wanted to take a leak.

"I already did, Mikey," Joey said, "in my fucking pants. Jesus, what you trying to do, kill us all?"

"What's the matter, scared?" Michael taunted him, feeling his heart pumping unnaturally fast.

The girls laughed, and Paula, a pretty blonde, told him to stop fooling around. "Get us home in one piece."

Michael had only gone a couple of miles when he saw the Porsche pulled over, mostly off the road. The bastard turned it over, he thought gleefully. He pulled the VW up alongside and stopped.

"Need some help?" he asked the guy, smiling to himself. *Teach you to speed, my man.*

The driver of the Porsche smiled and nodded.

"Went off the road. Sure be grateful if you guys could give me a push."

"No problem. Just let me pull over."

The VW drove around the corner, Michael pulling it off the road and down a side turn. Someone's driveway, Michael thought. Hope they don't plan to leave or arrive just now. The four of them got out and were about to walk back to the Porsche when they saw the driver behind them. . . . Jesus, he had a gun. Christ, he was pointing it at them.

"Okay, guys, let's walk on down here a ways. Move it," Vic said.

"Listen, mister," Joey started, "we don't—"

Vic walked up to the one with the loose lip. He put the

gun in his mouth, smiled, pulled back the hammer. One of the girls fainted and the other one screamed.

"Keep that bitch quiet or you're all fucking dead," Vic said, glaring at Michael. You are anyway, Vic thought as he turned back to the other boy. But not just yet. He cocked his head and listened. He couldn't hear anything. The house that this pathway led to was miles away. No danger there. Unless he got unlucky. He didn't feel unlucky. He smiled at the terrified boy in front of him whose tears were rolling fatly, wetly, down his cheeks. Vic sneered and pulled the trigger. The effect of the boy's mouth and the close range deadened the sound slightly. It was a split second before the other kids realized what Vic had done. The dead boy's head, pieces of it, hit the other boy in the face, and the blond girl was showered with red and gray and bits of yellow. The headless body slid to the ground, twitched a moment, then lay still.

"You three want to end it like this?" Vic said, turning toward the others, eyes piercing.

One of the girls was still out cold. The blonde was shaking, crying and clutching herself. Only the driver was calm. He was looking at Vic, mesmerized, a kind of awe on his face. He saw death, and he wasn't afraid. Or he was too afraid to be afraid.

Vic was pleased that he was able to take his time. *This is the way it should be.* He heard the sound of a car and waited, his ear cocked. It was a truck, and it went past with a groaning, farting sound. It was followed by three cars, and then the quiet descended on them again. He motioned to the blond girl.

"Come here. You. Now," he said, pointing the gun at her.

She looked toward the boy. He shrugged, and she seemed to draw strength from that.

Vic had unzipped his fly and was pointing at the girl.

"This is for you. Come here, bitch, or your friend there dies. I said come here." The girl came, and Vic tore her blouse off. "Now," he said, "take me. Not with your goddamn hands. Blow me. And be careful."

The girl did as she was instructed, in between sobs.

"That's good," Vic said. "Faster. Yes, faster." But it wasn't working. Not even a little bit. He just wasn't getting hard. His fury at the girl's ineptitude made him scream and rage. He saw the tears rolling fat and wet down the girl's cheeks, the mascara lines forming on her face. He placed the gun against her face, pulled back the hammer, and zippered his pants, hating her ineptitude with all of him. The redness made him blink. He breathed deeply, getting it under control. *Don't spoil it now, now, now.* He shot her then in the head and he saw her mouth go slack. He must have hit an artery, because he was covered in blood.

He let out a scream, the ringing sound of his voice echoing back, reverberating through the still forest. He felt the blood pumping through his veins, felt his muscles bunch and tighten. He was invincible. He walked over to the remaining boy slowly, taking his time, watching the last twitching movements of the red and bloodied thing that had been the blond girl. He patted the boy on the head as the boy put his arms around his waist and looked up into his eyes. Vic put the gun against the boy's heart and pulled the trigger. He felt the boy's body jump, then collapse in a bundle at his feet. Kneeling, he stroked the boy's head. He whispered to him, filling himself with the boy's strength. The other girl was still lying on the ground, unconscious. Vic went over and slapped her face. He couldn't revive her. He felt sad. It had been so perfect, so complete, and this stupid bitch was spoiling it for him. He sighed and slapped her again. Her eyes fluttered slightly. He felt her chest, her heartbeat. It was strong, powerful. He let his eyes take in the scene, the trees, the sounds, the smells.

"Come to me, little girl, come to me," he whispered softly.

He shook her then, slapping her face harder. She was out cold. He cocked his head, listening. He heard the sound of vehicles and waited until they'd passed. Then he pushed the gun into her mouth, cradled her shoulders, and, whispering to her, pulled the trigger. He felt her body jump, then go still. A huge ragged hole appeared where her head had been. He smiled, stood, then walked slowly back to his car. As he reached the road, he listened. Nothing. He walked back to where he'd driven his car off the road. He doubted anyone had seen it. And even if they had, he'd removed the license plate, hadn't he? To hell with it; he didn't care. They wouldn't catch him anyway. Not yet.

Vic pulled the car out from behind the trees, backed up, and turned off the engine. He picked up some tree branches and swept the area, then sprinkled a pile of dead leaves over the area where he'd parked. Satisfied, he got in his car, gunned the engine, and drove back over the canyon road toward the beach.

He felt wonderful. The headache, the tightness around his temples, had gone. He hadn't felt this way, well, since the incident with Roger's dog all those years ago. . . .

Roger had loved that stupid dog more than he loved anything. More even than he cared about Vic. It came between them. And in the end Vic couldn't take it anymore. He'd driven over to Roger's house during the day. He remembered the day clearly. It had been sunny, warm, and the sky had been unusually clear. The Santa Ana winds had been blowing. It was as if a giant vacuum cleaner had flown over the city, sucking all the smog and pollution out of the air. He'd felt good and alive.

He knew that Roger always left his gates open, figuring that the stupid dog would scare off any potential thieves. Vic had gone into the yard, and the idiot dog had been pleased to see him, wagging its tail, licking his hand. He'd read somewhere that dogs always knew if you had bad intentions toward them. This one hadn't. He'd brought a piece of rope, and he tied it around the dog's neck, then took it out to his car. No one had seen him.

He drove down to the beach. Out by Zuma. It was the end of February, and the beach bunnies were still not venturing out. He let the dog run around on the sand until it was really tired. Then he walked back toward his car. He tied the dog to a post. He smiled again. The stupid dog had sat there with its tongue hanging out, wagging its tail. He'd checked around. He was fairly certain that the traffic on the highway wouldn't be able to see him, and the few people that were out this day were a distance away. He started his car. In those days he was driving a Trans Am. Then he reversed to where the dog was sitting. As he got closer he hit the gas and heard the dog scream and yelp. He felt the animal being crunched under his wheels. He heard the bones breaking, the bump as his wheels cleared the dog. He put the car in drive and ran over it again, then backed up a final time. He checked around. Nothing. He got out of the car. The pooch was dead, all right. Squashed and bloody with its tongue still hanging out. He took off the rope, threw it into the back seat. He had gotten the dog's blood all over him, but he looked at his hands and shrugged. It'd been easier than he'd thought it would be.

He drove back into Santa Monica and went to work. Roger had called him later that evening, upset and distraught. Vic had gone over to his friend's house, consoled, spent hours with a flashlight and the cookies that the dog liked walking around the neighborhood. But the dog never did turn up. Vic recalled being glad he'd taken the collar off the dog's corpse. That way Roger would never find out what really happened. . . .

Vic was wondering why he'd thought of the dog after so long. He guessed it was because the feeling he'd had that day as he heard the dog yelp and felt its body rip and tear under the wheels was similar to the feeling he'd had as he killed those kids. He liked the sense of being in control—of determining the order of events. He enjoyed being the ringmaster.

Frank had gotten everyone together and was filling them in on the events of last night. He checked his watch. He had to meet with Roy Weston at eleven that morning.

"That's where we're at," Frank said, sitting down and

lighting a Camel. "The car angle looks real promising. I want you to call the Volvo people and get their help. Coop, call the main office. Tell them you need a list of every dealer in the Los Angeles area that had a shipment of white or yellow 1987 Volvo 760 turbo wagons. Find out also if they have any direct sales to car-rental companies or leasing companies."

"Okay," Cooper said, gathering up his papers. "I just hope the killer, if he owns or leases or rented the car, did it here in L.A."

Frank hoped so too. He turned to Ramirez. "Glen, I want you to go talk to the coroner again. Go over everything. See if he has any ideas. Guesses, anything. Also, I have a number here for the hostess who was working at the restaurant the day the killer watched us. Call her; find out what she knows."

Ramirez took the number and followed Cooper out the door.

When Frank stopped by Roy Weston's office ten minutes later and saw the D.A. and the commissioner inside, he knew it wasn't going to be a fun meeting.

"You know everyone in the room, Frank?" Roy said, ushering him in.

"Yes. Hello, Mr. Larsen. Commissioner Daniels," Frank said, seeking refuge in the nearest chair.

"Good to see you, Frank," the D.A., Ron Larsen, said. "How's Susan?"

"She's good," Frank said. "Thanks." He wished that they would just get to the point.

"Look," Larsen said, "this thing is getting out of control—" Frank started to speak. "Wait, Frank, I know your opinions of the media. Let's let that lie, okay? We have a problem. So tell me what you have on this. I want everything.''

Frank went through everything with them. Patiently and unemotionally.

"That's it,'' Frank summed up, looking directly at Larsen. "We're chasing down the leads.'' The D.A.'s face had turned a mottled red and the veins in his forehead stood out. He slammed his fist down on the table and stood.

"That's it, Frank? That's all you have? Fuck, man, it's nothing. What you aren't saying is that you're waiting for the killer to start again. To kill again and make a mistake. Isn't that it?'' He said it in such a way that the words seemed to flow across the room and stick on Frank like a gob of spit, sticky and congealed. Weston saw Frank's shoulders shrug and looked over at the commissioner, who was staring off into the distance, his lips puckered.

Frank sighed and looked over at Roy. Yes, he thought, he'll kill again, and I can only hope that he gets careless. But that's not what you guys want to hear is it? Ever.

"Yes, I guess that's about it,'' Frank admitted. "The leads we have are real and tangible. The killer might go to ground after the article in the paper this morning. Or he might feel brave and kill again, soon. Truth is, we just don't know.''

"Do you need extra men, Frank?''

The commissioner had spoken for the first time. He wasn't much with words, but he was good, and Frank admired him. A tough, honest, and uncompromising cop.

"Yes,'' Frank said, "we could use some help. We're going to have a lot of paper to sift by tomorrow.''

"No problem," Daniels said. "See he gets the men, Roy. Look, this one is a problem. One of the dead girls was well connected. Her father is on the local city council, and he's bringing a lot of pressure down on us through the mayor's office. I know that you're doing all you can. We just want you to know what we're dealing with. The media loves the councilman, and he's been making all kinds of noise. If you need anything, talk to Roy. Also, be sure to keep me informed."

Frank nodded. He recognized the ensuing silence as his cue to leave, and he made his way to the door. Weston walked him out.

"Sorry you have to deal with this stuff, Frank. They're just doing their jobs. Listen, I'll put four more guys on this with you. Talk to me after lunch and we'll see who you can use." Weston paused. "And Frank, I'd like you to do me a favor."

"Sure, what?"

Roy had put one of his huge arms around him and was squeezing hard. They were in the outer office and out of earshot of any curious onlookers.

"I want you to get Susan out of town until this is over."

"Why?" Frank said suddenly, going cold.

"Think about it. Think about what happened to Tony. The killer was watching him. He saw you too. If I read this crazy fucker right, he'll come after you. Especially after the article this morning, as watered down as it was. Under the circumstances, I think you should have Susan go to Florida and you should bunk here until the case is solved. Will you go along with me on this?"

Frank thought about it. What Roy was saying made

sense. And in truth he wanted the killer to be mad at him. To want to come after him. Susan would be better off in Floria. But would she go?

"I agree with you. But you know Susan. I don't honestly know if I can make her leave. Let me work on it," he said, trying to buy some time. Time to think it through.

"No. No ifs and buts. I want her away from this, and if she won't go, then you'll have to take her. Take that smile off your face. I'm serious. Real serious. I have a bad feeling about this. Want me to talk to her?"

"Let me talk to her. If I need you to call her, well, I'll let you know. And thanks," Frank said, noticing the frown on Weston's face.

"Frank, I mean call her now. Not later or tonight. *Now*. Go pick up the fucking phone and call her."

Frank was startled at the captain's insistence. He picked up the phone and dialed.

"Hello, Susan. How are you?"

"Good. Just got back in time for the carpet guys. The carpet's beautiful, Frank. Really nice. It matches the furniture in the den perfectly. I wasn't real sure at first, but now as I see them laying it, well, it couldn't be more perfect. Anything wrong?" she asked, feeling the unspoken words screaming down the phone line. She gripped the phone tighter.

She always knew, didn't she, Frank thought. He turned away from Roy. Never did feel comfortable talking when someone was listening.

"Look, Susan . . . I was . . . well, Roy and me were talking and we think that the killer might come after me. No, nothing definitive. It just follows after what happened

to Tony. The thing is, I . . . we . . . think that you should
go to Florida for a couple of days. Well, until this case is
over. It would be safer,'' he added, not really sounding
too convincing. He wished that Roy had given him time
to talk to her face-to-face. This way, on the phone, stunk.

"No way. You can't make me go. Oh, Frank, things
are so good right now. I want to be here with you. Don't
you want me to be here?''

Shit. Of course he didn't want her to go. Roy was right,
though. She had to. And today.

"Of course I don't want you to go. You know that, but
. . . well, it would make us all breathe easier if you were
safe with your folks. Please, Susan, don't make this harder
than it is already. *Please*.''

He felt the resolve go out of her.

"When do I have to go?'' she said. He wished she was
with him so he could hug her, hold her close.

"Today, as soon as you can.''

The phone was silent for a long time. He could hear his
heart pounding. He looked around at Roy and shrugged.
Roy smiled back, nodding, then put up his thumb. At last
he could hear her voice on the line.

"Okay, if that's what you want. I'll call you when I get
there. Love you.''

"I love you, too, darling. Thanks for understanding.
I'll be at the station house. Probably will sleep here. Have
a safe flight.''

He replaced the receiver and stared at the floor. Roy
was asking him something.

"So? She said yes?''

"Yes.''

"That's great, a relief. Look, I gotta go. Talk to me later. Got to go to lunch with the guys," he said, indicating the men in his office.

Frank waved at him absently as he walked back to the task-force room. He saw the message on his desk from Ramirez. Ramirez had tried the number for the Sizzler hostess and gotten her mother, who'd provided him with a number in San Francisco. He'd tried there but got no answer. *What the hell*, Frank thought. *I'll give it a try.* He dialed ten digits. Bingo. It was answered on the third ring.

"Irene Davis, please."

"Who may I say is calling?" a woman's voice asked him. An older woman, by the sound of it.

"Sergeant Morrissey, Homicide, L.A.P.D. Please don't be alarmed. I just wish to ask Irene a couple of questions. Her mom gave me the number."

The voice on the other end of the telephone seemed reassured.

"I see. Let me get her."

"Hi, this is Irene Davis," a voice said a bit tentatively.

"Hello, Irene. My name is Frank Morrissey. I wanted to ask you a couple of questions about the time you were working at the Sizzler, specifically December twelfth of last year. I was in the restaurant with a fellow police officer. . . ."

"I remember. He was the one who was killed, wasn't he? Freida was really upset; she liked him a lot. I remember you and he came in quite a bit. I usually sat you by the window."

"You have a good memory."

"Well, after your friend was killed, we all talked about it, thought about it. You know how it is. . . ."

He had crossed his fingers and his legs without realizing what he was doing. His mouth was dry. He felt his pulse quicken.

"Think back to that day, Irene. Do you remember some-one else who came into the restaurant after us and was seated at the table next to ours?"

There was a pause. Then: "Yes, I do."

"Can you describe him?" Frank asked. He said a silent prayer.

"Well, I remember he came in after you guys. He asked me if we sold newspapers. That is, if we had a machine."

Frank tapped his fingers impatiently. But what did he look like?

"Do you remember anything about his appearance, his facial features?"

The girl hesitated. "It was a long time ago. I remember, well, generally what he was like. He was nice. Good looking. Tallish. Had on dark glasses and hadn't shaved for a few days. Dark whiskers. Well dressed. I'm sorry, no definite feature comes to mind. Just a general, overall look. I remember thinking at the time he was cute and, well, kind of different. He smiled at me, and I thought he was going to talk to me. He didn't. I watched him, thinking it was really weird that he was sitting at a seat near the window, reading the newspaper with his sunglasses on. I watched because I wanted to see what color his eyes were. Have you asked Freida?" she said.

"Yes. She couldn't remember what he looked like. Do

you think that if we showed you some pictures, you might be able to recognize him?''

"I don't know. The dark glasses kind of made it difficult. I would have remembered him better if I'd seen his eyes.''

Frank thought about it. Should he have her come down and look at the mug shots? It couldn't do any harm, and they were due a break.

"Look, we'd like to have you come down and look at some photos. We'll reimburse you for your out-of-pocket expenses. When do you think we could arrange it?''

"I was coming down on Friday anyway to see my parents. If you like, I'll get an early flight.''

"That would be great,'' he said, and gave her the address of the station house. "See you Friday,'' he said to her, and was about to hang up when he heard her voice again.

"There was one other thing. I don't know if it's important, but I saw his car. When he left the restaurant, I watched him. He was kind of cute and, well, you know . . .''

"What kind of a car was it?''

"I don't know what kind exactly. But it was a wagon, a white one with tinted windows.''

"Irene, you just saved us a heap of work. Thank you. See you Friday.''

That was a break. That placed the vehicle and confirmed the color. He called down to Dispatch to have them find Jim Cooper for him.

He'd just gotten off the phone with Jim Cooper a half hour later when Tina Robertson called.

"Hi, Frank. One of your detectives, Glen Ramirez, said that you wanted to talk to me some more about the profile of the killer."

He'd forgotten he'd told Ramirez to locate her.

"Yes, it would be a big help. Can you come over later?"

"After five, if that's convenient for your people."

"Sounds great. We'll be here till late. Listen, off the record, we got someone else who ID'd the car. Type and color. It's a break. Finally. The same person also remembers seeing the killer. We're going to have her look at some mug shots later." He heard a beep. "Hang on, Tina. Someone's buzzing me."

He put her on hold and punched the other line. "Yes."

"Frank, is that you?"

"Yes."

"Dispatch here. We just got a call from the Malibu police. They just found four kids shot to death in Topanga Canyon. They called over here because of the mess the killer made of them. Looks like it's our boy again."

"Jesus, that was soon. Where in the canyon? Okay, uh-huh. Where's Ramirez?" he asked.

"He's on his way over. He'll meet you downstairs in a couple of minutes. Want me to call Cooper in?"

"Cooper's already on his way over. He can hold the fort here. Call Captain Weston and the commissioner's office. Tell them what we have."

"The commissioner, Frank?"

"Yes, the goddamn commissioner. Talk to you later."

He cut the call and pushed the button back down on the other line.

"Hi, Tina. Sorry about that. Look, the killer hit again.

Can't talk. Get yourself over to Topanga Canyon. Follow the canyon east, and you'll find us.'' He slammed the receiver down, grabbed his jacket, and ran out of the station.

Ramirez was waiting for him with the engine running. They drove down toward the beach and onto Pacific Coast Highway. There wasn't much traffic, and Glen was driving like a madman. Frank looked over at him. His face was grim and set.

They were close now. Ahead they could see the choppers circling. Anytime now they expected to come to the roadblock set up by the black-and-whites. They were starting to descend down the canyon when they saw it. Shit, the boys were out in force. Frank counted seven black-and-whites, two ambulances, and six or seven other cars. Didn't look like the media had arrived yet. That was a relief. A cop was signaling them to stop. Glen flashed his badge and they were let through the cordon. They drove over to where the ambulances were and parked. Frank wished the choppers would leave; the noise gave him a migraine.

They saw the doctor, and Frank walked over toward him. Glen headed for the nearest patrol car to try and locate whoever had found the bodies.

"So what we got, Doc?" Frank asked, looking down at the four partially covered corpses and grinding his cigarette underfoot.

"Take a look, Frank. Not pretty. Four kids. Two boys, sixteen, maybe seventeen. Two girls about the same age, maybe younger. All shot at close range. Three in the head,

one through the heart. Look at the puffiness around the
eyes of the boy there, the girl here. The poor kids were
scared shitless, crying, by the looks of it. As you can
see,'' he said, holding a bullet shell up, ''it was the same
type of slug that was used in the other killings. We'll
probably be able to find the bullets and get you a match
at the lab. That's the kids' car over there,'' he said, pointing toward a small VW. Frank nodded.

''Looks like they stopped and someone was waiting for
them, then blasted them,'' the doctor said. ''The VW
seems to be working, so they hadn't broken down. Been
dead a few hours. Maybe three. The lady who lives back
there found them on her way home. I gave her something;
she was hysterical. Got kids of her own, from what I could
make of it.'' He reached over, pulled the cloth farther back
from one of the corpses. ''Looks like this one was shot in
the top of the head. She might have been kneeling. See,
someone tore her blouse off, but not her panties. Weird.
It looks like she might have just had oral sex. I found what
looks like pubic hairs on her lips and inside of what's left
of her mouth. I'll know better when I get the body down
to the lab and do the autopsy. Come on, Frank, take a
look,'' he said, holding back the sheet and wondering what
was wrong with Morrissey. ''The lab boys are checking
out the area. Bodies have been photographed, and if it's
okay with you, I'll get them down to the lab so we can
get you some real data. Okay?'' he concluded, looking at
him and waiting for his comments. Frank usually had
plenty.

''Sure. Take them,'' Frank said, turning away and
reaching for his cigarettes. He felt sick. It was pretty ob-

vious what the bastard had done. The doctor knew it too. The killer had had the girl give him fellatio, then shot her when he tired of the game. Jesus. What made a person do something like that?

He'd asked himself that question almost every day, and no one yet had given him an answer that he could understand or live with. Christ. He wondered if the killer had made the other kids watch him do that to the girl and then shot her. He probably had. Shit, he had a coolness about him that was scary. He wasn't afraid of being seen or caught, was he? How did he get here? This wasn't an accidental meeting. He had to have followed the kids. Which meant that he had to have parked his car somewhere. Where?

"We aren't going to get much from the lady who found them," Ramirez said, walking up to him. "She's in a pretty bad way. Doc sedated her. You okay?" Ramirez said, looking at him closely and frowning. Jesus, he looked like shit.

"Huh? Uh, yeah . . . sure, fine. What the lab boys come up with?" Frank said, not looking at him.

"Lots of blood. The ground is soft and sandy, and we'll probably get plenty of footprints. Who knows? How do you figure it?"

"Looks like the killer might have assaulted one of the girls," Frank said. It required a determined effort to keep the emotion out of his voice. "He shot them all. Messy. Three through the head, one through the heart. It was our man. I can feel it. Let's take a walk around, Glen. He got here somehow, didn't he?"

They circled the area and couldn't see anything close to

what they were looking for. They followed the path a few yards, then walked back to the main road.

"Looks like the kids were returning from the beach," Ramirez said. "There are two surfboards in the car. Why don't we walk back a ways and see if they had any reason to pull over." Frank shrugged, motioned him forward.

They walked back down the canyon road toward the beach. They'd gone about twenty yards when they both recognized it—a spot where a car had pulled off the road. The ground cover had been removed, then replaced. They nodded at each other, then carefully pulled back the scattered branches.

"See, Glen, where the dirt has been swept over? He parked here, all right. Look . . . no, over there. It looks like oil or transmission fluid. Go back and get the lab guys to come on down and take a look."

As Ramirez trod off, Frank sat and looked. Nothing to see, but he was glad to be alone to think and try to get the measure of the man he was looking for. It took nerve to cover your tracks. Most people run. Get away from the scene as soon as they can. *Have you finally made a mistake, sucker, or maybe you don't give a good goddamn? Is that it? You don't care anymore?* He shuddered then, feeling the hairs on the nape of his neck stand up. When someone stopped caring and had nothing to lose, they were even more dangerous. He stood and started to walk back toward the killing ground. He was wondering, How many more? He saw Tina's car, then Tina herself approaching, but he didn't really want to speak to her. He felt flat, dejected, depressed. She looked at him, and the smile froze on her face. I'm *that* obvious? he thought.

"Listen, Frank, how about if I talk to your buddy Ramirez, then I'll see you later. After five?" Tina suggested. She smiled hopefully, eyebrows raised. He smiled at her, grimaced really, then nodded. He was grateful.

He walked back to the car and sat awhile. Glen was talking to the press, trying not to say anything that was newsworthy. Frank wondered why the TV people even bothered to send someone to the scene. Dramatic effect, he supposed. There was plenty of blood to film this time. Gallons of it. . . .

Frank and Glen drove back to the station house, feeling comfortable with the silence. Frank thought about how well he and Glen had been working together lately. They were beginning to know each other's thoughts, anticipate each other, the way he and Tony always had. As he stared idly out the window, Frank wondered if he'd ever feel as close to Glen as he had to Tony. A part of him didn't want to; a part of him wanted to protect himself from ever again experiencing the pain of losing someone by keeping everybody at a distance. But a part of him also realized that a man needed others to hang on to if he was going to make it through this life. He decided to trust his gut, as he always had.

It was 4:20 P.M. when they returned to the station house.

"Let's hope that Volvo sent over the list today," Frank said as they made their way into the task-force room. "Sure would like to know how many possibilities we're dealing with."

Cooper was waiting for them, and he had a look of sly pleasure on his face. He threw something over to Frank —a sandwich. Frank smiled. *Good guys, these two. Real good.*

"Thanks for the sandwich, buddy," Frank said, opening the wrapper and taking a large bite out of it. He sat down at his desk and reached for the pile of messages that had collected.

"Nothing but the best for you, Frankie boy," Cooper said, shuffling through his pile of computer printouts.

"Got something for us, Jim?" Frank asked, hoping.

"Good news and bad news. Which do you want?" Cooper shot back, grinning.

Glen smiled and gave Frank that "let him have his fun" look. Frank asked Cooper for the bad news.

"The bad news is 231," Cooper said, looking from one man to the other.

"And the good news?" Glen said with a mock sigh.

"It may actually only be 74," he said. Cooper was really grinning now, knowing that Ramirez didn't have a clue to what he was talking about.

Frank was smiling at the two men and went over to Cooper, holding out his hand.

"Give me the list, smartass. Come on, give," he said, holding out his hand and snapping his fingers.

Cooper gave Frank the Fax and he scanned the three sheets. Good, there weren't that many dealers involved. Several leasing companies and no car-rental agencies. That was a break. Then he saw what Coop was referring to. The list was divided into two groups: models 760 and 740.

He read the footnote. It said that the cars had the same body design and shape, and unless you actually saw the model number, it would look like the same car. The number of 740s sold was three time higher than the number of 760s. He smiled. He remembered the binoculars that the boy had used to look at the girl. The others didn't know about that.

"The kid was sure it was a 760. Split the list and get two teams working on the dealers and the leasing people. We want names, addresses, the works. Get the teams started on the dealers tonight. Most are open late. Go over to the D.A.'s office and get warrants to procure records in case you have any problems. Then I want you to go over to the morgue and sit on the doctor. We need the postmortems right away. Also, the lab guys are sifting through some stuff. Call over to Johnny Hector. Tell him we need anything he has, as soon as he can get it."

Cooper nodded and went over to the telephone. Glen and Frank approached the bulletin board and circled the site of the latest killing. They added the four kids to the list and stared at the board for a long time, each with his own thoughts. The phone was ringing, and Glen picked it up. It was the front desk. The reporter from the *Times* had arrived.

Tina entered, looking even more stunning than the first time she'd been at the station. She'd changed from her business suit and wore her hair loose. She was dressed in jeans and a silk shirt, with a sweater tied around her shoulders. Casually elegant.

"Hi, Tina," Frank said. "You know Glen Ramirez.

That one over there is Jim Cooper. Have a seat." Frank shot a look at Cooper, who was staring admiringly at their shapely visitor.

"Hi, guys. I wasn't sure if it would be a good time or not," she said, looking from one man to the other, wondering, after the killings, if she was encroaching or something. The vibes seemed to be okay, she thought. She pulled out her cigarettes and offered them around.

"No problem," Frank said. "I explained to Glen earlier today about the help you provided last night. I was hoping that if we all went over the profile thing together, we might turn up something we hadn't considered before."

"That's what I'm here for," she said, smiling.

"Good, then let's get started. Tina, why don't you acquaint Glen here with your background. Then we'll pick it up at the point we left it at last night."

Glen was only too happy to listen to her expound. He was all ears. And eyes.

Vic had decided to get dressed up and then go over to Fridays. He wanted to patch things up with Andy, see if he could get her to come over later. When he arrived, the lunch-hour crowd had left and the next wave of lonely souls looking for action hadn't arrived. He was sitting at the bar, deep in thought, anticipating her reaction when she saw him. God, he was relaxed. He hadn't felt like this in ages. This good. This strong. Tonight was going to be good with the girl.

She had just come into the bar. She saw him right away. She hesitated, then saw his smile. She came over, and he kissed her on the cheek, hugging her.

"It's nice to see you," she said tentatively. "I didn't expect to . . ."

He smiled, still held her close. It was all he could do to stop himself from grabbing those beautiful tits of hers.

"So, what are you doing here?" she asked. "My manager will kill me if he sees us touching like this."

She was perplexed. He was smiling. He looked happier than he had in a long time. She could feel him hard. She wanted him. She always did. But it was getting ridiculous. They didn't seem to talk much anymore at all. She wanted the talking part back, more than the sex even. She wanted the relationship to go somewhere, dammit. But he wasn't saying anything. He had a faraway look in his eyes.

He still hadn't spoken. He was far away. He was thinking of her naked, her body glistening, as it was when she'd just gotten out of the shower. He was thinking of touching her entire body with his hands, with his tongue, slipping into her, filling her. He shuddered.

"I was miles away. Sorry," he said. He shook his head a little, refocusing.

"Tell me where you were, Vic?" she said, moving away from him, crossing her arms, glancing toward the end of the bar to see if her manager was around.

"Oh, just thinking about you, about me, wishing that we were someplace else. Just the two of us, alone, naked, rubbing each other's—"

"Is that all I mean to you, Vic?" she said abruptly, cutting him off. He felt the color rise in his cheeks. He was surprised at the anger in her, and confused. What the hell was the stupid bitch's problem? He felt the horniness leaving him and saw the redness swirling in front of his eyes. He wanted to do it then and there. Kill the stupid bitch. He tried to speak and couldn't.

She was trembling now and staring at him, wanting him to hold her and deny it, talk to her. But the vicious look in his eyes made her shiver. She turned away then and went to the far end of the bar, thinking, *I'm afraid of him. I really am.*

He felt something pass over him. He looked up, away from Andy. The bitch was driving him crazy. He had to get out of there.

What was her problem now? he thought. Did she know? Suspect? No matter. He would handle her later, slowly. He decided to go back home and get the gun—the dead cop's gun. Dammit, yes, he would go get the gun. Then go visit Morrissey's wife.

Susan was sitting on the bed and staring at the telephone. She looked at her watch. Almost four-thirty. *Should I call Frank and tell him I got hung up with the carpet fitters?* She'd just watched the news, seen the latest work of the "West Side assassin," as the media had dubbed him. Four kids. Jesus, how many was that? Thirteen people in a little over two months.

She felt guilty for not having left for the airport earlier, but the carpet people had been at the house much longer than she'd expected. That morning they'd realized they'd brought the wrong carpet over, so it had been necessary for them to go back to the shop. And then, when they showed up again, one of the guys was moving in slow motion, obviously hung over. She was glad they weren't getting paid by the hour.

From downstairs a voice called to her: "Hey, lady, we're finished." *Good. She'd be able to make the six-thirty flight.*

"All right," she called out. "I'm coming down." She grabbed up the suitcase and clicked off the TV, then went out into the hall. As she descended the stairs, she wondered again about calling Frank. Should she let him know she was leaving late? She decided not to bother him. She'd give him a call from her parents' house.

Tina had relaxed and was explaining to them about the stages that a typical psychopath passes through. From minor rage to blind, killing rage. Frank was feeling a little tense. Why did people always have complicated reasons for why a person kills someone? Wasn't it really very simple? It was to him. A person killed because he was angry, or because he stood to gain by it, or because he genuinely liked it. There was no doubt in Frank's mind why the person they were looking for killed.

"It's been demonstrated that most serial killers start off by committing violent acts that grow in intensity until they actually kill," Tina said. "Then they find that they enjoy the killing. It's never been established that they all feel the same way, but I've sat in court countless times, and the thing that has always struck me is the killers' lack of remorse. The worst ones have said that the act of killing empowers them, makes them potent. It's as if they're using the victims to recharge themselves." She noticed Frank's skeptical look. "I know that to you guys this sounds like a lot of nonsense, but there *are* patterns. Believe me."

"Can you give us some examples?" Ramirez said. For

the moment he'd forgotten about Tina's physical assets and was concentrating on her mental ones.

"Let me see. Well, as I was saying, the killers usually start by doing less violent things than killing people. Like beating up their wives, or children, or pets, or neighbors, or smashing things. They sometimes get involved in a street brawl, and the first time it's very out of character, not what you'd expect. The 'out of character' thing is an important point. Take this guy you're looking for. He's white. You've ID'd the vehicle he's driving as a thirty-thousand-dollar car, right? And you've told me that the waitress and the hostess at the Sizzler both said he was attractive and well dressed. It fits."

"So we know he's not your usual lowlife," Frank said. "What do we do about it?" He realized he was putting her on the spot.

Tina shrugged. "Maybe someone filed a report or complained about something. Something out of the ordinary. I don't know. You guys are the cops. How does the system work?" she asked.

"It doesn't work good enough to do what you're suggesting," Ramirez said. "You want us to pull the records of every call that came into the station here and look through every complaint? That won't work. We have to narrow it down somehow."

Frank had a thought. "Listen, Glen, why don't we order up the records for the month or so before the first killings. Look for something mindless. Maybe an unprovoked assault. It can't do any harm."

Ramirez sighed. "Okay, if you say to. It's worth a shot, I guess."

Frank turned to Tina. "Listen," he said, "you've been a big help, really. Glen and me are going to grab something to eat. Want to join us?" he asked, hoping she'd say yes.

She smiled. "Sounds good. Thanks."

The phone rang, and Glen passed it over to Frank.

"It's the lab," he said.

"Frank Morrissey."

"Hi, Frank. It's Johnny Hector. Fine, thanks. Listen. Got some preliminary stuff from out at Topanga. Just preliminary, but I wanted you to have it. The real data won't be available until late tomorrow, at best."

"That's no problem. What do you have?" Frank asked.

"Couple of things. We checked the area where the killer apparently pulled his car off the road. We were able to take some tire prints. Interesting. Outsize tires. By the looks of them, not real common. We also got some paint from where the spoiler hit a couple of rocks. It's black. It'll take a while to run it down. Also, we took casts of several footprints. As soon as we eliminate the dead boys' prints, we'll know what size shoe the killer wore."

"Good work, Johnny," Frank said. It *was* good, Frank thought, but they'd need a lot more than a shoe size to run this guy down. And he had the sinking feeling that time was running out even more quickly than he thought.

Vic had driven over to his place. He took Tony's gun from behind the false wall in the fireplace and unwrapped it from the denim sheet. He held the gun to his chest and caressed it, then took the six rounds and lovingly cleaned them. He could feel the power surging through his body. He loaded the Magnum carefully and slowly, speaking to each round as he slipped it home. "Soon you'll feel the flesh," he said.

Finally he was finished, and he ran his hand along the gun's large barrel. He pushed it into his waistband, pulling his sweater over it, then carefully buttoned his jacket. He looked at himself in the mirror from the front, then from the side, and he was satisfied. His image smiled at him as he ran his hands through his hair. *Yeah!*

He drove over to Morrissey's house and watched the carpet guys loading their van. He smiled, leaning back in the seat and feeling the redness flow through him as he touched the gun. "Hurry up, you stupid bastards," he said out loud as the fitters dawdled, apparently unconcerned with time. He glanced at the clock on the dash. It was a little after four-thirty.

Finally, the van was packed and the guys got in, waving at Susan Morrissey as they drove off. Then she was gone and Vic wondered again how best to approach the house. Suddenly he saw the garage door open and the Mercedes backing out.

Christ, where was she going? He yelled, feeling the anger surging through his body. He made up his mind to follow her car and do it right then and there, wherever she stopped, wherever she parked. This time the bitch wouldn't escape him. No damn way. He was slipping behind her as she gunned the Mercedes down the street. He wondered about that. The bitch drove like a lunatic. Well, she had no chance against his Porsche. He closed the gap slightly.

He followed her down the street and toward the freeway. The traffic was thick, so he closed the gap until there were only three cars separating them. Where the hell was she going? She was heading south on the San Diego Freeway. Christ, she could be going anywhere. His head was hurting, and he pounded the dashboard, furious that she'd moved and was spoiling things again. He saw her start to move over on the freeway, then use the right indicator to exit. Century Boulevard. He realized with dismay that she was going to the airport. *Why?* He drove faster, closing the gap between them till he was about twenty yards behind her. She wasn't going to the long-term parking. She drove straight past it and toward the arrivals and departures area. Toward the short term-parking? he wondered. The anger had permeated all of him now, alive, surging through every part of his body. He gripped the gun, imagining the bullets tearing through her flesh, ripping her into pieces. Where was the damn bitch going?

He saw the Mercedes slow down, then slip into the left lane, indicating she was pulling into the parking structure. She was taking a ticket from the automatic machine when he decided to pull in and follow her.

Snatching the ticket from the machine, he pulled into the darkened structure, wondering where the hell the bitch was. Had she gone left or right? Over to his right he saw the restricted-parking area for the disabled. He pulled the Porsche over and into the blue-marked space, killing the engine and slipping the Magnum into his waistband under his jacket. He looked around the dimly lit parking structure again. Still no sign of her.

The elevator banks were to his right. He saw cars pulling into and out of the area but very few people in the immediate vicinity. That was good, he thought, taking deep, gulping breaths and trying to rid himself of the tightness gripping his forehead like a steel vise. Where was she? He decided to make his way toward the terminal. Walking over to the elevator, he pushed the button and waited, tapping his foot against the cement, looking around. There was a break in the activity as stillness seemed to descend over the area—no cars, no people, just the faint click-clacking of a woman's shoes. Raising his head slightly, he saw the woman. It was *her*. He couldn't believe it. The stupid bitch was walking toward the elevator, carrying a small suitcase.

Suddenly, out of the corner of his eye he saw her veer left toward the exit sign and the stairwell. He wondered if she had seen him, recognized him. He glanced around again. The place was still temporarily deserted. The elevator still hadn't arrived. His eyes never left her, and as soon as she went through the door he sprinted after her. He felt his heart pounding. Christ, he couldn't believe his luck. Stupid bitch had decided to walk down the stairs.

He moved faster then, closing the distance behind her. She must have heard him, because she stopped and turned. He was taken again by her beauty. And he felt the rage as he saw the defiant look on her face. He pointed the gun at her and smiled. She looked straight back at him. Her eyes were not afraid. The large pistol was pointing at her beautiful face, and she was staring at him like he was a turd on her shoe. She started to speak.

"What do you want?" she said. It enraged him, and the mist flooded his eyes. His lips curled back, his throat constricted. Who did this bitch think she was?

He was standing close to her now. He rammed the gun hard into her stomach. He could see that it had hurt her, but that arrogant look was still on her face. *You don't have*

any idea who you're playing with, do you, bitch? He
pushed the gun into her stomach harder. Then twisted it.

"What do you want?" she said again.

He punched her in the mouth so hard it hurt his hand.
He could see the blood and the way her lip started to twitch.

"Payback time, bitch," he said to her, the spittle flying
from his mouth, hitting her in the face. His face was very
close to hers now, and he could smell her perfume, her
fear. He felt it arousing him.

"No," she cried, the calmness in her voice going, crack-
ing. He smiled at her, then punched again.

"How do you feel about dying, Mrs. Morrissey?" he said,
and Susan saw the sneer on his face. His teeth were bared
behind his lips. She saw the animal then, lurking behind the
well-dressed veneer. She tried to think of what to do.

Frank had told her once that in a situation like this a
woman should keep her nerve, don't scream, whatever
happens. "Try and reason with the attacker," he'd said.
But she knew that this was the killer the police were looking for, knew he was the sort of person who was beyond
reason. The thought deflated her. In a brief instant of time
that seemed to stand still, distended, she saw him raise
the gun and pull the trigger. She didn't really hear the shot
or feel the pain. Then she was sliding down—down into
the blackness.

Vic stood over her. He was furious. She'd spoiled it. It
would have been so damn perfect. He hadn't wanted it to
be like this. He had felt her start to scream, and at that
moment he'd pulled the trigger. The bullet took out a huge
chunk of flesh where her chest had been. The noise was
still ringing in his ears, and the sweet, acrid smell of the

discharged round mingling with her open body infuriated him. He leveled the Magnum at her face. *Goddamn bitch*.

Then he heard the scream. It was a woman. Two of them. He turned, firing twice. The first shot hit one woman in the stomach. She was thrown through the air, then down the stairs, blocking the second woman's retreat. The bullet he fired at the second woman hit her in the ass. Blood was everywhere, and he could hear her screaming. He couldn't decide whether to finish the job on Susan Morrissey or shut the screaming bitch up. He heard all kinds of noise now, people running, screaming, doors being thrown open. *To hell with it*. He fired twice more at the wounded woman, hitting her in the back and again in the ass. Chunks of flesh, blood, and pieces of clothing flew everywhere. He dropped the gun as he began running up the stairs, away from the dead and the dying women. At the fifth floor where he'd parked, he buttoned his jacket and walked slowly toward his car. The floor was either empty or no one had heard the shots this far up. Great. He was smiling as he wiped the sweat from his face. *Keep cool, Vic*. He punched the starter button and drove slowly toward the exit. Still he didn't see anyone.

He handed the cashier his ticket and the dollar bill it cost and drove slowly out of the parking structure onto the main circular roadway. He edged into the slowing traffic and was absorbed into it. Slowly he eased his way through the traffic, then out of the terminal, down Century Boulevard toward the freeway. He watched carefully in his rearview mirror, certain no one had seen him. He heard the police sirens in the distance and then he saw the speeding black-and-whites, seeming to him then as if they were full of righteous anger and pathetic indignation. He laughed at that thought. All that noise and the stupid sirens. They were so useless. He wondered if the cops made all that racket just to reassure the public that they existed. Then he saw the ambulances. Too late, friends. They are all *D-E-A-D*. He switched on his indicator and pulled onto the freeway, feeling deliriously happy in the dense rush-hour traffic.

They had decided to go to Carlos & Pepe's. Tina had said that the Cobb salad was one of the best. Frank thought that kind of strange. Why go to a good Mexican restaurant and order a salad? He realized why as he watched her dispatching her third margarita. She liked the drinks. He smiled. They *were* good. Especially the peach ones. And they were getting two for the price of one each time they ordered because of the happy hour. Tina had loosened up and was telling them captivating, funny stories of her years as a reporter. Glen hadn't taken his eyes off her since they arrived. She knew exactly how to hold a man's attention. A touch here, a throaty laugh there.

Frank sat back, realizing that he was having fun. He looked around. The place was getting packed. The circular bar in the center of the restaurant was doing incredible business. His glance took in most of the customers. They looked young. Probably college kids from UCLA.

As he turned in his seat to look for the waitress, he saw Roy Weston coming over toward their table. Alarm bells began to go off in his head. What was he doing here?

Glen had seen him too. He slipped his jacket back on absently, glancing at Frank. Tina was still in midsentence and hadn't noticed that she'd lost the men's attention. Frank stood, and Roy saw him. He motioned for him to stay where he was.

"Hello, Roy. This is a surprise. Come to slum it with the hired help?" Frank said, attempting levity.

The look on Roy's face made Frank's guts start to lurch even more. He wanted to take a leak, real bad. Something was wrong. *Very* wrong. Even Tina had shut up and was glancing from man to man.

"Hello, Frank, Glen, Ms. Robertson. Need to talk to you, Frank. Alone. Got a minute?" he said, nodding toward the exit.

Frank stood, gripping the table, steadying himself. His legs felt weak. He nodded at Roy and excused himself from the others. The two men walked toward the exit. Tina turned to Glen.

"What was that all about?" she asked him, holding on to his arm, a worried expression flitting over her face.

Glen was watching the men as they left the restaurant. As he lit a cigarette, he noticed that his hand was shaking. What could have brought the captain out here at this time of night? he asked himself. Not at all standard operating procedure. He realized that Tina was talking to him.

"Sorry. What did you say?" he asked her, blinking his eyes, clearing his head. He started to wave over to the waitress, pulling bills from his pocket.

"I asked you what that was all about," she said, staring at him, feeling the annoyance starting. It *was* rude of Frank to just up and leave, she thought.

"I don't know, but it's not good. I can tell you that. Listen, let's get the tab paid. I'd better stick around a while until they come back. I think that it would be best if you left. I'll have Frank call you later," he murmured, dismissing her. The warmth and intimacy they'd all been sharing had evaporated into the night.

She started to protest but saw the intense expression on his face and shrugged. She picked up her purse and jacket and headed for the rear exit, leading to where she'd parked her car. Her instincts told her she should stay. There was a story here. She decided that she would drive over to the station house, see what was going on.

Roy and Frank were walking down Wilshire Boulevard, toward the ocean. Frank had said nothing. He was waiting, dreading whatever it was that the captain wanted to say, and couldn't. Roy stopped, finally, looking at him. Their eyes didn't meet. He was looking at a point over his head and his huge body seemed to be sagging.

"Listen, Frank. There's no easy way to tell you this. She's dead. Shot to death about an hour ago at the airport. She and two other women," he said, watching Frank closely. He wanted to hug him, pull him close, tell him it would be just fine. Words are so feeble sometimes, he thought. So empty and soulless.

Frank grabbed Roy, shaking him. He had heard the words and they had bounced straight off him. He hadn't yet felt the hammer blow of knowing. Really *knowing* that it was Susan. His mind had refused to absorb it, was still thinking, still hoping that it was someone else he was talking about.

"Talk to me. Who's dead, Roy?" Frank screamed at him, pounding his chest with his hands. The force was shocking, and Roy grabbed him in his two huge arms. He held him then, hugged him tightly, saying the words into his ear.

"Susan . . . Susan's dead. I'm sorry."

They held each other then for a long time. Roy could feel his friend's body shaking, found himself searching desperately for something more to say.

Glen had come out of the restaurant and saw them. He looked around for Roy's car, spotted it, and walked over to the driver.

"What the hell is happening?" he asked the patrolman, banging his fist on the door to make his point.

The patrolman looked at him, hesitated. "You his partner?" he asked.

It was a good question, Ramirez thought. No one had said anything. But they *were* partners now, weren't they?

"Yeah, I'm his fucking partner. Now tell me what's going on," he snapped.

"The guy's wife just got wasted. Her and two others, over at the airport," he said . . . just like that, like "two beers, please." Glen wanted to punch his lights out.

"Back up a second. Frank's wife was killed? Are you sure? Who made the ID?" he asked. He hadn't realized it, but he'd grabbed the patrolman and was shaking him. Hard.

"Yeah, I'm sure. I was there. It was a bloodbath. She had her ID in her wallet. She was hit in the parking structure at the airport on her way to a flight, I guess. Hey, give me a break, okay?"

Glen took his hands off the patrolman. He glanced back toward Frank and Roy, saw them coming toward the car. He knew Frank would have to go to the morgue and ID

Susan's body. Glen looked at him as he approached, saw
his eyes staring off somewhere. He nodded at the captain,
deciding he would drive over to the morgue and wait for
Frank there. He might need him then. Dammit, why Susan? Why wasn't she in Florida?

Frank and Roy had gotten into the car, and the captain
was asking the driver to drive over to the morgue.

"Sure you can handle this?" Roy said softly, tapping
him on the shoulder.

Frank didn't answer him at first. Just kept right on staring
out of the window. Roy nodded, and the driver started the
car. After what to Roy seemed an eternity, he heard
Frank's voice. He missed what he said.

"What was that, Frank?" he asked.

"I said I want to see her, Roy. Tell me . . . tell me
what happened."

Weston sighed and nodded, wondering how much one
person could take. First it had been the loss of Tony. And
now Susan. How much could the human spirit take before
it was crushed completely?

"I don't have all the information yet. As far as we can
tell, Susan was in the parking structure, making her way
to the terminal. For some reason she'd decided to take the
stairs. . . . Anyway someone must have followed her. She
was on the third level when she was shot at close range
with a Magnum. We have the weapon. The killer dropped
it. As far as we can see, she wasn't assaulted, and we
think that she died instantly. Whoever did it also shot two
other women who'd just gotten back from Hawaii. Looks
like they just happened by. Anyway, they're both dead.
So far we haven't got any suspects."

As Frank listened he felt the lump in his gut get larger and larger. He was going to puke. He could taste it in his mouth, and he was sweating. A cold sweat.

"Stop the car . . . please . . . now . . ." he gasped, banging Roy in the back.

The driver pulled over and slowed. Frank was out of the car before it had stopped. He staggered forward, bent over, and vomited on the grass. He waited until there was nothing more to come up, then sat down heavily, feeling the rising anger. The anger was cold, icy, and he wanted—wanted so much—to find the person who had taken her. He knew in his heart that it was the man they'd been looking for. Knew it with absolute certainty.

Tina had driven back to the station house and was talking to the man at the reception desk.

"Is Frank Morrissey back yet?" she asked, smiling.

He glanced at her, and she could see from the look in his eye that something was wrong. He was avoiding her eyes.

"No. He'll probably not be back at all this evening. Want to leave a message?" he asked, finally looking up at her.

No, I don't want to leave a goddamn message. I want to know what the hell's going on. She breathed in. Getting aggressive with this guy wasn't going to get her any answers, she knew.

"Is Glen Ramirez expected back?" she asked him, her voice getting harder, more impatient.

"Not as far as I know," he murmured, not bothering

to even look in the book, angering her even more. She counted slowly to ten.

"Can I talk to Jim Cooper, please?" she asked him, smiling that big, wide-eyed smile of hers and leaning over the desk. It was a mistake. She saw the anger flare in his eyes. She wondered what on earth was going on.

Go away, newspaper lady, the desk sergeant said to himself. No one wants to talk to you. Not tonight. He signed, then checked the log. Dammit, Cooper was still in. What should he do?

"Let me check," he said, motioning her to sit down. No way, buddy, she thought, wanting to hear every word he said.

He called the extension, and Cooper answered on the second ring.

"Jim Cooper."

"Hi, Jim. It's Ronnie at the front desk. Listen, we have that lady from the *Times* out here. She wants to talk to you. . . . Yeah, as far as I know. No, she doesn't . . . *okay*, goddammit. Talk to you later," he said, banging the phone down onto the desk.

"Jim says to go right through," the desk sergeant mumbled.

"Thank you for your help," she said, sweetly giving him the smile again.

She walked back through the offices, finding Cooper sitting at his desk talking on the phone. He motioned her to sit. She looked around, trying to feel whatever it was that was making them close her out, but everything seemed as it was before. In less than a minute, Cooper hung up.

"Hi, Tina. What can I do for you?" Cooper said.

That was her breaking point. She felt the color on her cheeks and neck.

"Cut the shit, Jim. A little while ago, I was here and you guys were talking to me. I was trying to help you. For chrissake, not thirty minutes ago I was eating dinner with Frank and Glen. And now I'm getting the big-freeze treatment. Give me a fucking break. Don't treat me like a child, okay? Tell me what's going on."

He shifted uncomfortably in his seat. He hadn't expected her to bore in quite so fast. He thought about it and decided to tell her. Shit, she'd hear about it soon enough anyway.

"Frank's wife, Susan. She was killed a while ago at the airport. Shot to death."

She felt herself go weak. She was unable to respond. *Jesus*. She hadn't expected that. Poor Frank.

"What happened?" she asked.

He stood up, pacing the room, and told her "off the record" what they had.

They arrived at the morgue. Frank was doing better, Roy thought. He had some color back in his cheeks and was breathing more regularly. He would have the doctor give him something, then have Ramirez drive him home and stay the night. He was glad that Ramirez had driven over. Frank was going to need all the help and support they could muster to get him through this.

Roy shivered, imagining all the ghosts this place had in it. All the stories. He shivered again; it was cold. Although he knew that it wasn't *really* cold. It just felt that way. They had reached the end of the corridor and walked through a double-glass swinging door. Along the walls were huge lockups, like giant safe-deposit boxes. The keepers of the dead. Roy saw the doctor and waved. The doctor was standing at the far side of the room. Next to him were five tables. Three were occupied with white-sheeted figures. He saw Frank inhale and square up his shoulders. He let him move ahead of him.

"Hello, Frank, Roy. I'm so sorry about this, Frank," the doctor said.

Frank said nothing, and the doctor looked over at Roy, who nodded. The doctor pointed to one of the tables, then started to move toward it. Frank put out his hand, shaking his head, and motioned them away.

He breathed in and pulled back the sheet on the table. She looked so beautiful. So pale. Someone had tidied her up. He could see that. He felt his stomach lurch as he moved closer. He could see where she'd been shot. The blood was soaking through the wrappings on her chest.

He took her hand, closing his eyes. He held her small, cold hand in his. He had forgotten how to pray, and he told her that, silently. He held her hand for a long time, speaking to her.

And then the words were gone, the moment had passed. He felt someone tugging at his arm, so he pulled the sheet over her, then looked back one last time. He turned then, dry-eyed, and left the place.

They walked back, and he asked Roy if he wanted to get some coffee. Roy looked at him carefully and nodded. They drove over to Francisco's and ordered espressos. Frank was quiet for a long time, then decided what he wanted to say.

"Roy . . . listen to me. No pretty speeches or anything, okay? It hasn't hit me yet. I know that when it does it'll probably crush me. She was my whole life. She really was. And she's gone and I feel emptier than I ever knew a person could feel. Like someone put their hand inside my chest and pulled out my heart. But Roy, it was the *same* killer. I know it. If you check that Magnum you found, you'll find that it's Tony's gun. Listen to me. This is my time now. You owe me that. The deranged fucker that did this was telling us something. *Me* something. That he knows who we are, and where we are, and that we're not safe from him. He's going to continue to toy with us for as long as he's free. We have to catch him, and soon. Taking me off this case, sending me home to mourn my loss and to get over it, will only make it harder to catch this cocksucker. You need me on the case. And I won't get over it . . . over Susan. Not for a long, long time. If ever. I want to stay on this case and find him. Put him away. I want you to back me up on this, Roy. And then, when it's done, when that mindless bastard is out of commission, I want to take a few months and be with her. And figure it out, if I can, and try to understand it. That's all. But I need you to back me on this. Will you do it?"

Roy sat looking at his coffee, trying to answer that question with his head and not with his heart. It was a tug-of-war, and his head didn't have a chance.

"Frank," he said, "I want you to do something for me. I want you to go home tonight and take a couple of these pills the doctor gave me. Have Ramirez stay at your place with you, get some sleep, then come see me in the morn-

ing. If you feel the same as you do now, I'll support you
fully, with one condition.''

''What's the condition?'' Frank asked, watching him
closely.

''That when we find the killer—and I feel it in my bones
that you'll break this case—you not be one of the arresting
officers. That you stay out of that part of it completely.
You have to give me your word on this, Frank.''

''Deal,'' he said, leaning over and clasping Roy's hand.

Frank slept until nine-thirty the next morning. He was
surprised about that. He wondered about the pills and
shrugged. Maybe it was more than the pills. He went down
to the kitchen and saw that Glen was up and ready to leave.
He poured some coffee.

''Thanks for being here last night, Glen. It was appreciated.''

Glen waved him off, looking embarrassed.

''Want something to eat? I make a mean french toast,''
Glen said, holding the pan out to him.

Frank was staring at the pan with a faraway look on his
face. Damn, what did I say? Glen wondered.

Yeah, so did Susan, Frank was thinking sadly. That was
what she made for me yesterday morning. Christ, was
everything going to remind me of her? And would it always
hurt so bad? Well, it wasn't Glen's fault. He'd better get
used to it or stay home. He shook his head at Ramirez.

''Sounds good, but to tell you the truth, I'm not real
hungry. Ready to go?'' he said, sipping the rest of his
coffee.

They got to the station house a little after ten. Roy was at city hall. He'd left a message for him to sit tight; he wanted to talk to him. Frank wondered about that. He got the guys together and a mood of profound melancholy filled the room. No one knew what to say or how to act. He decided he'd make a speech. Not a big one. Or even a very meaningful one. Just a speech. He couldn't stand their sympathy. It was choking him.

"Listen up, guys. Judging by your happy smiling faces, you didn't expect me in today. Am I right?" he said, using his most upbeat voice.

He looked around the room, saw he'd gotten their attention. "What I want to say is, I appreciate your sympathy about Susan. And your concern for me. I feel like shit. That's a fact. But I'm here, and I'll continue to be here until this case is solved. I spoke to Captain Weston about it, and he agrees I should continue, provided that I stay in the office where he can see me and where you guys can bring me chicken soup."

Finally, they were looking at him properly now. He even saw a flicker or two of smiles crossing their faces—ghostly, unsure things that started at the corners of their mouths and didn't quite make the eyes. . . . It was a beginning.

"So let's go through what we have, then get moving on our assignments. I'm going to be right here, waiting, watching, and sifting. Keep close, keep me informed. I've hundreds of reports to read through," he added, and indicated the mountain of paper on his desk.

He gave them their assignments, telling them that he was going to read through a month's call-in log as suggested by Tina Robertson. He wasn't terribly hopeful, but who knew?

The extra men Weston had provided, six in all, were to start going through the reports from last night on Susan's killing. He put some emphasis on the parking structure and the cashiers. Someone must have seen something, he reasoned. He told Ramirez to take charge of it and get the guys moving and then go down to the morgue and talk to the doctor.

Everyone had been galvanized into action, and he was pleased and surprised that his hands hadn't shaken, that his voice hadn't broken. It had been touch and go for a moment, back when he'd mentioned Susan's death. He'd almost lost it. He'd felt the lump in his throat and had struggled to keep it down.

He started to read the reports and was angry that his eyes and mind were not in sync. *Come on, Frank, concentrate*. The phone rang.

He put down the phone. It had been his mother-in-law, whom he'd contacted the night before. She told him that she and her husband would be there late today, and that she'd handle the funeral details if he wanted her to. He thanked her and told her to stay at the house, that he'd be staying at the station for a couple of days. He decided to assign a cop to stay there too, over at the house. Just in case.

He returned to looking at the reports. Glen, Cooper, and the others were out in the field by now and making some progress, he hoped. He'd placed his call to the lab and was waiting for Johnny Hector to call him back. He began to get frustrated, plowing through the pile of complaints. The scope was still too broad. He was hoping that there would be an incident or incidents that would leap out at him. But nothing had.

He walked over to Cooper's computer station, looked

at the list of Volvo dealers and leasing companies. So far, of the seventy-two "leads" they'd originally had, Cooper had made notations against forty-three of them, eliminating them. As he stared at the screen, he felt his irritation growing. One of those cars had to be the killer's car. Had to be. He sighed. Unless Cooper was right and the car had been bought from a dealer in another county. . . .

The phone made him jump. He'd been immersed in what he was doing. He picked it up.

"Morrissey."

"Hi, Frank. It's Johnny Hector. Want to come on over? Got something for you."

"Sure. See you in a couple," he replied, replacing the phone thoughtfully.

He needed a break, and he could tell from the man's voice that he had something. Something good, he hoped. He tidied up his desk and scrawled a note for Cooper, telling him to continue on the Volvo angle.

After getting a car from the motor pool, he drove over to the lab and found Hector. He was smoking and drinking coffee outside the building.

"Hi, Johnny. Waiting for me?" Frank asked, smiling, clasping his hand.

Hector smiled back at him, avoiding direct eye contact, stubbing out his cigarette.

"Yep. Got something real interesting you for, Frank. Let's go inside."

They walked into the lab, then over to Johnny's desk. Frank spotted right away the molding of a tire print and a shoe.

"Sorry about Susan. Real sorry. Jeannie told me to let

you know that she's there, if you need anything, okay?"
he said. Frank nodded, clapped him on the back.

There was a short silence, then Hector began: "Take a
look at this, Frank," he said, pointing at the plaster mold.
"We got a real clear print. It's been made. European
import. Custom job. Very wide tire."

Frank felt his stomach tighten. He lit a cigarette, offering
one to Johnny. He was staring at the tire mold. *Please be
from a Volvo. Please.*

"Would it fit a Volvo?" he asked softly.

Hector scratched his chin, looking at the mold and at
Frank, then back to the mold.

"Not likely," he replied, and shrugged.

Frank felt his heart sink. *Jesus. Don't tell me that,
Johnny. It has to fit a Volvo. Fucking has to.* He pulled
out a chair, sitting down heavily. He didn't want to ask.

"So what type of car would it be from?"

"Like I said, it's a custom job. BMW maybe. Or a
Porsche. It's not a stock tire. We'll be better able to narrow
it down when we get the paint analysis back," he said,
shrugging again. He was an expert shrugger. Guess that's
what happens when you work in a lab and have to wait on
the computers all the time, Frank was thinking.

He was starting to feel sick. How could they have been so
far off base? Was there more than one killer after all? Maybe
the killer had two cars? How could Johnny be so sure?

"Okay, tell me why it couldn't be a Volvo," Frank said,
wanting to run the sequence through again, get it clear in his
head.

He saw the lab man stiffen, then shuffle some more papers.

"I didn't say that it couldn't be a Volvo. I just said it

wasn't likely. Look, this type of tire. See how wide it is. It's made for those little Porsches or the sporty BMW. I never saw a Volvo that had tires this wide. Especially not a wagon. As soon as we get the paint data back, we'll have the type of vehicle and its approximate age. We'll know if its owner parked it outside or inside, at the beach or not at the beach. It's not a Volvo, though. I'd bet money on it."

"Okay. What else do you have?" Frank asked him, his shoulders slumping.

"One more thing. We have shoe prints that don't match either of the two dead boys. A size ten. Based on the preliminary data we have, the guy who wore these shoes is over six feet tall—six-one or six-two. Weighs about 185 pounds. The shoes are very distinctive. Take a look at this," he said, handing him a photo. "You can even see the manufacturer's name."

Frank saw it immediately. Fila. He remembered when Susan had wanted him to buy a pair. Over a hundred bucks. He'd laughed and said he'd stick to his Reeboks. This killer certainly didn't want for money. Drove a Porsche or BMW, smoked Dunhill cigarettes, wore Fila tennis shoes. Frank decided that he'd look at the reports a little more closely. Pay more attention to the marina area and Santa Monica.

"This helps," Frank said thoughtfully. "I think I see the pieces coming together. Anything else?" he asked.

"That's it for now," Hector said. "Like I said, we should have some info on the paint by tomorrow. No need to light a fire under these guys, Frank. They want this fucker as badly as you do."

"I doubt that, Johnny," Frank said softly, his eyes intense. "But I do appreciate them moving on this."

Hector nodded, watched Frank closely as he turned and exited the room. That was a stupid-ass comment to make, Hector chided himself. But Frank had understood what he meant. The boys were up for this. They all wanted to kick some butt. It was getting personal now.

Back at the station house, Frank found himself staring at the bulletin board. It was almost full. Well, he wasn't putting Susan's picture on the wall, that was for sure. He saw Cooper sitting at the computer, tapping at the keys.

"Hi, Coop. Got anything?" Frank asked, wondering what made a guy want to spend all those hours playing with a computer.

Cooper turned in his seat and shrugged. He reached for his coffee and lit a smoke, tossing the packet to him.

"So far the Volvo angle is depressing," Cooper said. "I've covered almost all of the potential suspects. Nothing yet. The Christmas thing really helps, ironically. Most of the people were out of town and had a good recollection of where they were—checkable alibis." He thought for a moment. "There *is* one guy whose story is kind of lame. I don't know, it's probably nothing. Why don't you come and take a look," he said, motioning for Frank to come closer to the terminal. Cooper pointed at the screen as Frank stood behind him. "What you see," he explained, "are license photos of all male drivers who have white Volvo 760 turbos registered. Why don't you take a look, see if any of the photos jog your memory. I realize that you never saw the guy, but that old 'gut' thing of yours . . . Who knows?''

Frank sat down and watched as Cooper ran all the photos past him. Funny how everyone's face reminded you of someone you'd met in your life. Every fourth or fifth photo or so, he thought he felt the stirrings of a vague memory. But the stirrings never coalesced into anything he could articulate. He quickly became frustrated.

"Listen, I spoke to the lab earlier," he said, pulling his seat back from the terminal. "They made the tire print of the vehicle in Topanga."

"A Volvo?" Cooper asked hopefully.

"No, it was a foreign import. Johnny Hector is betting on a BMW or a Porsche. He'll know better when he gets the paint analysis back from the lab," Frank added, trying to sound upbeat.

Cooper smoked for a minute, reflecting on this latest piece of information. It was a disappointment, the car's not being the Volvo. But maybe the killer had two cars. If he did, it could be the break they were looking for. He turned to the computer and started tapping data into it, telling Frank what he was doing as he worked.

"Listen," Cooper said, "that information might help more than you think. We can cross-reference the files to see if we come up with someone who owns both a white Volvo 760 turbo and a BMW or a Porsche. It'll take me a while, but I'll give you a shout if something connects." Frank was amazed at how quickly Cooper's hands flew over the keyboards. He stood and started back toward his desk.

Vic was watching the news. He was still in bed. He'd stayed in bed all day. He'd never done that before. Ever. Not even when the girl was here. He'd just been so goddamn tired.

The newscaster was spouting on about the killer, and the fear was there, all right. Vic had the bastards where he wanted them. Funny, though, they hadn't released the cop's wife's name. He wondered why. Not that it mattered. They hadn't said anything about the gun, either. He regretted dropping it. That had been some heavy-duty weapon. Took the three bitches out easy. He remembered the red splashes and the huge chunks of flesh that the gun tore from the three women. Damn good gun.

He made himself get out of bed. He went over to the fireplace and removed the fake wall, taking out the .38. He checked the ammunition. Only seventeen rounds left. Damn. He wondered where he'd get more.

He'd found the weapon and the two boxes of shells at Roger's house years ago, after Roger had drowned in Mexico. Vic had gone over to his place and looked for the documents he needed to sell Roger's stock. He found the gun wrapped in oily rags along with the ammunition. He realized that they were special bullets, and he wondered what Roger was doing with them. He hadn't even known that his partner knew how to shoot.

He oiled and cleaned the gun, then loaded it carefully. Five rounds. Shit, that left only twelve. He'd have to make sure he didn't waste any.

The phone rang. It was probably Andy, he thought, calling to make up. Should he answer it? Christ, no. She was yesterday's news. Who needed her? He certainly didn't. Jesus, the phone was hurting his head. It rang on and on. "Stop it," he screamed, feeling the tightness in his head and massaging his temples. He reached for the phone and said, "Hello."

"Hello. Is Andy there, please?" a man's voice asked.

Andy? Who knows this number? Why would some guy be calling her at his place?

"Who's this?" he said.

"Sorry. You're Vic, her boyfriend, aren't you? This is Gary Bennett at Fridays. We met a couple of weeks ago. Or months ago. Remember me? I'm the night manager, Andy's boss?

"Yeah, I remember. Why are you calling her here, Gary?" Vic asked, softening his voice a little.

"I take it Andy's not there," Bennett said. "She was supposed to come by yesterday to get her final paycheck. I knew she needed the money, so I had the check prepared, but she never arrived. I thought I might catch her at your place."

"Andy quit her job?" Vic asked, alarmed. What was the bitch doing?

"Yeah, you didn't know? She told me she was going to visit her mother in Seattle or somewhere."

"You say she was going to Seattle?" Vic said, fishing for information. "Any idea of her address or anything?"

"Hey, if I knew that, would I be calling you? I'd just *mail* the check to her," Bennett said.

"Yeah, right," Vic replied. Jesus, this Bennett was a fucking smartass. He pictured himself shoving the muzzle of his .38 into Bennett's face. Now, that would be fun.

"Well, I'm sorry I can't help you out, Gary. All of this is news to me. But I'll certainly have her get in touch if she calls here," Vic said. Hell, I'll do even better than that, he thought to himself. I'll drop her body on your fucking doorstep. Now, how would you like that, Mr. Night Manager?

"Thanks, Vic. Sorry to disturb you," Bennett said, and rang off.

Vic replaced the receiver. He wondered about it all. It didn't sound right. He knew then with absolute certainty that he had to get the girl, and get her fast. She knew something; he'd felt it the last time he saw her. Shit, he should have killed her long before.

He decided to go over to her place to check things out, see if she really was gone. He dressed in his jogging suit and sneakers and was about to leave when he spotted the gun. Should he take it? Hell, yes. You never know when you might need some protection.

She lived over in Mariners Village. Not far at all. He hated that place. So cramped, so full of weird, lonely people. He expected that as soon as anyone saw him they'd pounce on him and try to start a conversation. It had happened before when he'd visited her. They materialized, like ghouls, out of the shadows and threw themselves hungrily at strangers. He hoped that no one would hassle him tonight. He wasn't in the mood.

Jesus, the run had worn him out and his head was pounding. He saw right away as he got close to her unit that the car wasn't there. It didn't mean anything, though. It could be parked anywhere. He walked over to her place and saw it was in darkness, with the drapes drawn.

He went up to the windows and knocked, lightly at first, then a little more loudly. Nothing. It did look like she was gone. Maybe he'd come over early in the morning and double-check. He tapped on the window a final time. The voice startled him.

"She isn't in. Left yesterday morning. Early. Said she'd be back in a couple of weeks. Asked me to take care of her plants. You're Vic, aren't you?" the voice, a man's, was asking him pleasantly.

He knew it. Just knew it. Some stupid interfering bastard. Whoever it was turned on a light on the balcony next door. Vic squinted and moved into the shadows. He saw that it was a young guy, about twenty-five, tall, tanned, and handsome with curly blond hair and a partial beard. The guy was smiling at him, holding out his hand. Vic felt the rage start in him. This smiling bastard was probably spending nights with her when she wasn't over at his house. The bitch was a damn nympho.

He could feel the gun in his hand, and he was holding it tight now, taking the slack up in his finger. He was exhaling and about to fire when he saw the woman. She had joined the man on the balcony. Vic released the trigger and pushed the gun under his top.

"You okay, buddy?" the man asked him, looking at him with a puzzled expression on his face. "I'm Andy's neighbor, Karl Miller. This is my wife, Tammy. Andy told us all about you."

Is that so? Vic thought to himself. The dumb bitch was a regular chatterbox.

"Hi, nice to meet you," Vic said good-naturedly. "Andy asked me to drop by from time to time to make sure she hadn't been burglarized. I'm bushed. I just got through running. Well, nice to meet you. See you in a few days," he said, turning away from them and starting to melt away into the darkness.

The guy was smiling at him again, a shit-eating grin, and Vic could hear the gun calling his name. Shoot the bastard. Shoot him. Splash the grinning bastard's pretty head all over the glass. What did she tell him about me? he asked himself. Damn her, she did know something. He had to get her, stop her before it was too late. What was that girl doing to him? Trying to trick him. Suck him in. They all thought he was a fool. Just like that stupid asshole father of his. That's it, they thought he was like him. Then he heard voices. And behind him a group of people emerged, chugging beer and laughing. He took a last long look at the Millers and smiled a half-smile at them, then turned abruptly and jogged away. *So she knew? The girl knew all the time? He had to kill her. Had to . . .*

He was sitting on his bed, staring at the telephone. She had called and left a message on his service, giving him the number of her mother in Seattle, apologizing for lashing out at him the other night. She told him she was having fun driving up the coast and wished he was there.

He decided he'd call and ask her to come back, tell her he loved her if he had to. He had to fix her. Had to. He dialed the number. It rang and rang, and he put down the receiver. *Think, Vic. Think.* She won't even be at her mother's yet, will she? Leave a message. She's bound to call her mother sometime. Tell her to come back to L.A. Tell her you're desperately ill. Tell her anything. Get the bitch back before she has time to tell her family about you. He dialed the number every fifteen minutes. Eventually someone answered. A woman. She said her daughter was expected in a couple of days and, no, she didn't know where she was. And, yes, she would ask her daughter to call him.

He was shaking with rage, the sweat was pouring off his head. Why did they always do this to him? Spoil everything. Everyone was out to get him. Well, he'd fix her. And then he'd show the whole lousy, stinking world. He'd show them that it didn't pay to underestimate Vic Perry. He hugged the pillow and felt the tears starting. *No, not the tears*. He screamed and threw the pillow at the wall.

They all betrayed him in the end, didn't they? And he'd let her go, given her her life, and the ungrateful bitch was going to betray him. Just like the rest of them. He knew it then, knew he was going to kill her slowly. Bit by bit. His anticipation was like a living thing deep within him, growing and magnifying.

San Luis Obispo. . . .

She was sitting on the bed, staring at the telephone. The drive had been slow. She'd been enjoying herself, liking being with herself. The tang of the sea air as she had driven up the coast with the car top down had cleansed her. She felt happy and alive. And now she was thinking about *him*. Her mother had said he wanted her to call, that he sounded worried and upset. She started to dial the number, then slammed the phone down. What was the point? Why was she continuing with this? The relationship obviously wasn't going to work out. The warning signs were all there. She had to stop kidding herself. *Let it go, Andy. Go home. Be normal. Find yourself. L.A.'s killing you.*

They're all the same, she thought. Takers. Users. God, she'd loved him more than she'd ever loved anyone. He'd made her feel like no other man ever had. *But he never loved me.* It was sad, almost unbearable to face, but it was the truth. She felt the anger then. Toward him, toward all the others who had taken her, used her, given her nothing. She had asked nothing of any of them except that they love her as much as she loved them

Well, she had had it. No more. She wouldn't go back. No matter how much she was tempted. This time she would walk away on her own terms, and to hell with it. She was going home. She turned off the bedside light and closed her eyes. As she drifted off to sleep, she smiled. She was remembering when her mom would take her out into the rolling green hills in Washington, outside of Seattle, when they would walk for hours and smell the fresh, clean air. *Screw you, Vic, and screw L.A.*

Ramirez was pissed. He was on the 405 Freeway and the traffic wasn't moving. Like the case, he thought morosely. How could the killer not have been seen by anyone? He lit a cigarette, exhaling deeply. The carbon monoxide fumes were choking him. *Shit, and we worry about smoking?*

He and his team had interviewed a couple of dozen people, and not a single lead. It was bad, he knew that it was. There was usually something. He didn't doubt that they'd get the killer. No doubt at all. But when? Whoever it was was a cool bastard, all right. He figured the killer had just walked out of the parking structure and driven away. When people were screaming, when chaos was rampant. That took nerve. To not run. He also figured that

the killer had gone up a few floors from where he'd hit
the women. He had to. Probably parked on the same floor
as Susan had. The fifth floor. She was shot on the third
floor. The people who heard the shots were on the scene
fast, swarming from the first and second floors. And none
of them had seen or heard anyone leaving the scene.

It was really hard to believe. He shrugged. The pressure
from the top was starting to strangle them. It had become
so intense that he really believed the press and the public
thought the cops were slouching. They had no idea of the
hours, the manpower that went into cases like this. Dammit. Something had to break soon.

His thoughts shifted to the call he'd gotten from Captain
Weston earlier. A strange call. Weston had told him to
keep an eye on Frank. A real close eye. Not to let him out of
his sight. Jesus, he liked Frank. What was going on? Either Frank was on the case or he wasn't. This spying-on-
his-buddies shit was something he didn't want any part of.

He pushed down on his horn in frustration. Finally the
traffic started to move. A little way along the freeway, he
saw what was causing the backup. Someone had hit the
center divider, and all the drivers were slowing to look at
it. He shook his head in wonderment. Would it ever cease
to amaze him? What was so damn fascinating about a car
that had been in an accident?

He got back to the station house a little before five P.M.
Frank and Cooper were staring at a pile of computer printouts. Ramirez checked Weston's office; Roy was out, not
expected back. He was kind of glad. He shrugged and
made his way over to the guys.

"So, what else do you have?" Ramirez asked, not taking his eyes off Frank. *You gotta know. You can't shit a shitter.*

Clever s.o.b., Frank thought to himself. He'd decided to give Glen only some of the data, hold back on five callins. They kind of fitted the profile that Tina had suggested. Mindless and violent acts. He wanted these for himself. It would give him something to do, alone. Keep him busy and moving. He didn't want to have any down time. Thinking time. He decided to go over to the marina later and talk to the people there. Wasn't going to be easy, though. Glen was bird-dogging him. He could feel it.

"Nothing much. Couple of things I was going to check out later. By the way, Irene Davis, the hostess from the Sizzler, will be in in the morning to look at some mug shots. Coop suggested we let her look through the driver's-license photos we have, see if anything triggers a memory. I don't expect her to recognize the killer, though. I really don't. We're close, guys. Real close. But the bastard's not in focus yet. We need one more piece of ID. Another piece of real data." He lifted a printout. "I noticed this call-in about a guy over in the marina who beats his wife, or girlfriend, on a regular basis. It might be something. The caller said it had started a couple of weeks before she contacted us. She called it in on December oh-two. She was told that no one could do anything unless the woman who was being beaten called in herself, which is bullshit. There was a time when we'd have sent a black-and-white around to see what was happening." He picked up another printout. "Then there's this one. Seems someone down at the beach gets off on killing cats. This guy called in and said he thought he knew who it was. He gave us a name. Seems like it was passed on to the city animal-protection people. Don't know what happened after that, thought that maybe I would check it out. Give the guy a call or drop over there,'' he said, exhaling and holding his breath.

He watched Ramirez out of the corner of his eye and saw that he was uptight. Shit, he hadn't bought a word of it. He could just tell by the way he was looking at him. He also saw the look when he had said he would go and check it out. So Weston told him I was office bound, huh? How to give him the slip? . . . He had an idea.

"So what're you guys doing for dinner?'' he asked them, lightening his voice.

Cooper shrugged and looked at his watch. Glen just stared at him.

"I don't know about you guys,'' said Cooper, "but I want to finish up here, then go see if my wife still recognizes me. I'm bushed. And my eyes hurt after looking at this computer screen all day,'' he added, hoping that the other two wouldn't mind if he cut out. He was tired, and Annie wanted to see a movie tonight.

One down, one to go, Frank thought. But he could see from the determined look in Glen's eyes that Glen wasn't going to buy anything that he said. Well, to hell with it. His idea of slipping away while they were out somewhere sucked anyway. He'd go eat with Glen and then check out the leads in the marina first thing in the morning. Real early, before any of the guys got in.

"I'm kind of hungry. Want to grab something?'' Ramirez asked him.

"Sure. What do you fancy?'' he shot back, glad that

he'd decided against deceiving him. It wouldn't have set well with him; maybe they could talk over dinner, get this thing worked out.

They decided to go to the Hamburger Hamlet in Brentwood. The place hadn't gotten real busy yet, and they'd been served their burgers, fries, and all the trimmings in record time. Frank hadn't felt like eating, but he did anyway, trying to keep up appearances. Shit, he hated this stupid game. He and Glen were both playing, dancing around each other. If Tony had . . . *Give it up, Frank. Tony's dead. Gone.*

Talk to Glen, level with him, Frank thought. The waitress brought them Irish coffees. He was stirring in the whipped cream, remembering how this had been Susan's favorite drink. He recalled how she had got him started on them. Years ago. When was it? Yeah, it was on the European trip. They'd toured in Ireland as part of the package, staying at old inns and farmhouses. That was a beautiful country, so green and peaceful. The people had been wonderful, warm and hospitable. He and Susan had gone to Galway, where his grandfather had been born. Walked those rolling hills, toured the pubs in the evenings, sat close together near the open peat fire, drinking the warm beer, holding hands and smiling.

They were always the last to leave the bar, and she always took an Irish coffee to bed with her and . . . *Dammit, Frank, leave it be.* He shook his head to clear it. Glen noticed.

"You don't like the Irish coffee?" Ramirez asked him, frowning.

Frank shrugged. "The coffee's fine. Just remembering better times, that's all. When all this didn't matter, when things were simple, when we were happy, Susan and me. It seems so long ago. I . . ." He paused, seemed to decide something. "Listen, Glen, remember when you asked me about what else I had? What other little goodies there were? There *was* something. I knew I wasn't fooling you by clamming up." Ramirez started to speak, but Frank bulled ahead. "Not that what I have is earthshaking or even that exciting. It's just a couple of things I figured we should check out. I've separated out about five of the call-ins, and I thought I'd go check them out in the morning. You know, keep myself busy. That's it. Just things that popped out at me. That's all," he said finally, hoping that he'd judged his man right, that they could break down the walls, build some bridges together.

Glen was watching him carefully. Keeping Frank's mind occupied was good, he thought. And anyway, the issue wasn't the call-ins. It was about leveling with each other. He lit a smoke. He noticed that his hand wasn't really steady. He wondered about that.

"Sounds reasonable, Frank," Ramirez said, smiling. "Want me to handle it with you?"

"I want to handle it," Frank said. "You know that. You can come with me if you want," he added, shrugging. He hoped that finally he would go for it. Hitch his wagon for the long haul. He had to know if he could count on him.

Christ, Frank, don't do this to me, Ramirez thought. *Shit*. He took a deep breath and eyeballed him. "Listen, Frank, you know as well as I do that there's no way the captain's going to let you out into the field. He called me earlier, was worried about you. He said you'd agreed to stay at the station. He also said, specifically, that he didn't under any circumstances want you to forget that promise. I'm supposed to watch you. What do you want me to do, blow my career?''

Frank stared intently at Glen. *No, I don't want you to do that. I want you to do what's right. That's all. Come on, man, trust me.*

''No, just do what you think's right, Glen. What works best for you. Let's get out of here. I'm tired,'' Frank said, and started to stand up. He wanted to be out of there. The air had become heavy and the room was suffocating him.

''Wait a fucking minute, Frank. Don't lay that 'do what's right' shit on me. I've spent too many years, worked too hard, to blow it now. You gotta understand that. I've a family and responsibilities too. Come on, Frank, listen to me. Hear the words. I understand your desire to get this bastard. Do you think that we, that I, want to get him any less than you do? But you're making this personal. Real personal. That's bad thinking, man. Real bad. If we do it your way and it goes wrong, we're all screwed. And I don't know about you, Frank, but I've got plenty to lose. Too much. Christ, man, I like you. I was hoping, well, before Susan was killed, that we could end up working together. Permanently. But we gotta do this right, Frank, and by the book. We just gotta,'' he said, and reached over and grabbed Frank's hand.

Frank said nothing. Had he really expected Glen would go along with him? Bend the goddamn rules? Put his job on the line? He decided to sleep on it. Maybe Glen was right. Maybe he *wasn't* being objective. Christ, he was tired. Let Glen check out those five call-ins if he wanted. What did it matter? The end result was all that counted. Ramirez was a good cop. He would handle it okay.

"Let's go, Glen," Frank finally said. "I have no problem with what you just said. None. Who the hell knows, maybe you're right. Listen, I'm sleeping at the station house. Want to drop me off?" he asked, forcing a lightness into his voice that he didn't feel. He just wanted to be alone. They paid the check and walked out to Glen's car, each man alone with his thoughts.

Frank could see the guilt on Glen's face as they drove back to the station house. He supposed that he could make it right. Talk to him. Tell him he understood. But dammit, he didn't. Not really. Tony would have gone to the mountain with him. Had, in fact, several times.

Frank felt tired and alone. The sleep would help, maybe. They'd arrived at the station house, and Glen was sitting and lighting a cigarette, looking as if he wanted to talk.

"Thanks for the ride," Frank said as he got out of the car. He turned and said, "Listen, it's cool. You're probably right. I'm maybe too close to this. Talk to you in the morning, okay?"

Glen looked at him, tried to speak, and couldn't. He nodded, tight-lipped, then drove off.

Vic was sitting in bed staring at the phone. *Call me, bitch. Answer the message I left for you.*

Why was she doing this to him? He had the gun in his hand and he was pushing it against his head, then pushing it harder. Even that wasn't relieving the pain. He wanted to go out into the streets and find some more worthless bums. Shoot them, feel their strength passing into him. God, he needed to be refilled. But if he moved away from the phone, she'd call. He just knew she'd call, and then he'd miss her and she'd be lost to him, back home, betraying him. He had to wait.

He'd called the bitch's mother earlier, and she told him she had given her daughter the message hours ago. He was furious and raged at her, asking her if she'd explained to Andy that it was urgent. She stayed calm, enraging him even more. She said that of course she had. He'd screamed at her, calling her a liar. Then he hung up and had been waiting and waiting . . .

. . . all day and into the night, and the phone hadn't rung. He picked it up again, checking the dial tone. It purred viciously in his ear, and he slammed the receiver down. *Where was she?*

He lay back and lit a cigarette. It tasted like hell. He hadn't eaten since . . . When did he last eat? She wasn't going to call, was she? In the final analysis, she wasn't going to call him. No, the bitch was going to betray him, just like . . . just like his mother had. In the end, when he'd needed her most, his own mother had screwed him over.

He rolled over and stubbed out the cigarette. The memory of his mother flashed before him. It was as if he had a movie camera in his head. He could see her, smell her. It all came flooding back. . . .

She'd promised she would be there at his class graduation. All the other kids' parents had come. He'd sat there at the back of the huge ballroom and waited. Mr. Skolnick, his math teacher, had come over several times and asked him where his mother was, was she coming? The other kids, as they filed past to take their places, were laughing and sniggering. He knew it was him that they were laughing at. He'd heard the snide comments many, many times. Oh sure, they didn't look at him directly, or say anything to him. But he knew, just knew they were all laughing at him, at his humiliation.

Where *was* she? Sitting there among his classmates, he had never felt so worthless. It was worse even than the guys' knowing his father was a coward and a cuckold. So he'd snuck out before they called his name. He ran all the way home, and as soon as he went into the house he knew she was there.

He could smell her. The brandy and something else. Something worse. Acrid and rancid. He'd called her name. Nothing. With despair in his heart, he walked up the stairs to her room. The smell was worsening, and he gagged. What the heck was it? he thought. As soon as he entered the room, he saw her. She was lying on the bed, facedown. She was naked, snoring and grunting like a dying pig. Then he saw the empty brandy bottle and realized what the stink was. She had puked and was lying in her own vomit. It was in her hair, on her face, and it seemed to be coming out of her nose. He was pinching his nose between his fingers, choking and gagging on the smell.

He felt the redness, the rage, and the despair flooding over him. He prodded her with his foot, softly and then harder. She smacked her lips, grunted, and burrowed down farther into the puke and the pillow. He wanted to kick her and punch her. Damn her, why hadn't she come? Slowly he felt a calmness come over him. He took the spare pillow and put it on her head, then sat on it. She struggled feebly, and he responded by pushing down with all his strength. He felt her pathetic resistance, then it lessened. He sat there for a long, long time.

Eventually he got off her and replaced the pillow next to her. Then he bent down and checked to see if she was still breathing. She wasn't. He left the house then. Out of the back. And ran. He ran for a long time.

Then he walked slowly back to the house and called the police. They arrived with a doctor a while later. Vic was told that his mother had suffocated in her own vomit. He'd smiled inside and put on a sad face for them. He knew they wouldn't suspect him.

He hadn't thought about her or her death in years. Purged it from his mind, he supposed. Well, good riddance. She was the worst mother a person could have been stuck with, and she deserved to die. Like Andy deserved to die. He'd get her. In the end, he'd get her. He felt tired. Worn out.

He looked at the clock. It was late, after one A.M. He decided to set his alarm, then go to the gym early in the morning, sit in the sauna a while, see if he could shake the flu bug that was debilitating him. After that, maybe he'd fly up to Seattle and find her. Watch her. Wait for the moment and then rip her into pieces. But he'd screw her first. He felt himself hard and throbbing, and he wanted her. One last time. He would kill her as she lay under him, squirming and moving with him deep inside her. Then he'd run the knife across her throat. She'd be gone, and he'd be safe from her.

Frank heard the phone in the distance, a long way off. He wondered if it was in his dream. He'd been dreaming about

Susan. About them. They were in London. He shook his head, groping for the phone. He dropped it. *Get out of bed, Frank. Get yourself together.* He picked up the receiver, then lit a cigarette. It ripped his throat, and he coughed.

"Morrissey," he croaked into the receiver.

"Sergeant Morrissey. It's the desk. Sorry to wake you so early. We have some guy on the phone. I think you should talk to him. He was in Topanga Canyon around the time the four kids were murdered."

Frank shook his head, trying to clear the cobwebs. He felt like the angel of death had kissed him with her rancid lips. Need some coffee, he thought.

"Sure. What's the guy's name? What time is it, anyway?" he asked, looking around for his watch. Where had he put it last night? He was disoriented. He'd always put his watch on the nightstand at home. Well, he wasn't at home, was he? Where the hell was home anymore? he thought.

"It's a little after six. The guy's name is Ron Golding. Hang on, I'll switch him through," the duty officer said, and went off the line.

Frank waited, then saw the red light on the phone start to blink. He cleared his throat. *Jesus, I'm definitely stopping this smoking shit.* His throat was raw, and his voice raspy and coarse.

"Frank Morrissey here. Nice talking to you, Ron. You got something for me?" he asked. He shook his head again, getting off the bed. That made him feel better, more like a cop at least.

"Yeah," Golding said. "I was telling the officer who answered the phone. I was over in Topanga around the time of the killings. I saw a car pulled off the road. I was going to stop, but, well, you know how that goes. I had deliveries to make, and I was late. Didn't think about it again until I was watching the news last night. Made me remember. My wife said I shouldn't get involved. And, well, it's probably nothing. But I couldn't sleep last night. Got kids of my own and . . ." He let the words trail off, unfinished.

"What were you doing in the canyon, Ron?" Frank asked. He was covering all bases.

"I was making deliveries, like I said. Oh, I see what you mean. I work for UPS. I had some packages to deliver. It's my route. I'm there most every day," he added, wondering if he'd made a mistake in calling. This cop sounded like a tough s.o.b.

"And you're sure of the time, Ron?" Frank asked.

"Yeah, I'd just had my lunch break in Woodland Hills. I do this route every day, and I'm in the canyon around the same time, give or take a half hour, every day."

"What did you see, exactly? Go slow. I'm writing this down."

"Well, like I said, I was driving over the canyon. Not much traffic, I remember that. I'd slowed for a bend, and as I was coming around the corner I saw this Porsche kind of off the road. Well, off the road and in the trees actually. Looked like it had run off the road. I was going to stop, but thought, Screw it, I didn't see anyone, and it's a problem parking around there. I figured it'd probably happened the night before. You see lots of cars that have gone off the road. Not usually the type that this one was, though. Well, I went home and forgot about it until I saw the news last night. Got me thinking. Especially when they said that the suspect had probably parked somewhere close to where

I saw the Porsche. That's about it," he said finally. He wondered if he would have to testify. He hoped not.

Frank was sweating now, and he could feel his pulse quickening. Now for the million-dollar question . . .

"Do you remember what kind of Porsche it was, Ron? What color it was? Anything about it?"

"Sure. Didn't I say? Sorry. It was a 930 turbo. Real beauty. Flared fenders. Wide wheels, the works. It was black."

At frigging last, Frank said to himself. At last a real one-hundred-percent lead. He wanted to jump in the air, give someone a high five. Dammit if the media hadn't come through again. But how could the guy be so damn sure about the car, actually recognizing the model as well as the make? Frank knew *he* wouldn't have.

"Listen, Ron, just one final question," he said, glancing again at his notes. "Are you certain it was a 930 turbo?"

"Sure, that's one car that's easy to spot. It's a dream car, know what I mean?"

Frank didn't. He shrugged, putting the thought behind him.

"Can you find the time to come over later today, sign a statement on this?" Frank asked, not really caring, wanting to get off the phone and on with the chase.

"Uh . . . yeah, sure. What time would be good? Will I have to testify?" Golding asked hesitantly.

"Maybe. No use in me bullshitting you, Ron. More than likely, if it's material evidence. What you told me may help. It may not. But do me a favor. Don't talk to anyone about it. Not yet. Give me your phone number and address . . ."

Frank hung up the phone. Dammit, he wished Cooper was there. He got dressed quickly and went to the task-force room. The computer was over in the corner, staring at him benignly. *Screw it*. He walked over and began tapping the keys. He stared at the screen. The words "Sign in" were flashing in green at him. *Goddamn, stupid machine*. He sat down at Cooper's desk, eyeing the printouts Cooper had run yesterday. Reviewing them again, he saw that Coop had listed all the Porsche and BMW dealers in the city. Jesus, the list was enormous. He continued down the list and saw two much smaller listings at the end of the page. One listed dealers who sold both BMWs and Volvos; the other listed dealers who sold both Porsches and Volvos. He felt the excitement surging through him. *Good work, Coop*. It was a long shot, but maybe there was a link; maybe the killer owned both cars and had bought them from the same place.

Well, he didn't need the BMW listing, did he? Not now. He went over the Porsche/Volvo dealerships again. There were five that sold both vehicles in the Los Angeles area. Walking back toward his office, he decided to call Ramirez. Two of the dealers were on Glen's route into the office.

Ramirez answered the phone on the second ring. Frank heard the kids' laughter in the background.

"Morning, Glen, it's Frank. Listen, we just got a call. A delivery guy was over in the canyon around the time the kids were killed. He remembers seeing a car. A Porsche 930 turbo, black."

"*Great*. That saves us a ton of work. So what do you need?"

"Cooper made a list of dealers that sell both Volvos

and Porsches. It's surprisingly short. Two of the dealers are on your route into work. Want to stop by and see what you can find out?'' he said, listening to Ramirez exhale and hesitate.

"Sure. Give me the addresses. What about the others? *You* going to make a visit to them?''

"Stop worrying. I don't plan on going anywhere. Figured I'd wait till Coop gets here and maybe drive over with him. Shit, you're the guys who know about cars, not me,'' Frank said in a joshing tone. "I just figured since it was on your way in, you might want to stop by. That's all.''

Ramirez laughed, and the tension was gone from his voice.

"Okay, Frank. I guess you *are* something of an idiot when it comes to cars. I'll see what I can find out.''

Frank heard Glen ring off and smiled. Men and cars. Somewhere, somehow he had missed the boat on that. He didn't give a damn what he drove. As long as the car started in the mornings . . . It hit him then in the gut. *Jesus, if the car had started that day, would she still be alive?*

He did his best to squelch the thought, turned his attention to the list of Porsche/Volvo dealers, wondering. Would he and the killer be meeting soon face-to-face? He felt his insides grow cold.

Vic had barely slept. The sweat had drenched the bed, and he couldn't rid his mind of the images of the girl. His anger was squeezing his temples so tight that it hurt to open his eyes. The alarm shrilled. Its high-pitched whine stabbed at his throbbing temples, sending him into a fit of uncontrollable fury. He grabbed the clock radio and smashed it against the wall. The redness was all through him now, filling him and easing the pain in his head.

He remembered why he'd set the alarm, then smiled. The gym was a good idea. It would flush the flu bug out of his system and relax him before he went and found the girl. Seeing images of her flickering before his eyes, the knife entering her body, her blood flowing down his arm, warm and sticky, soothed him, calming him even more. He swung out of bed, grabbed his jogging suit and sneakers, and dressed hurriedly.

He wondered about the gun as he picked up his car keys and glanced over at the fireplace. He should take it with him, he thought, blinking away the red mist that still swirled in front of his eyes. He wanted to feel the gun's power. It relaxed him, calmed him, gave him even more strength. He walked over to the fireplace and removed the false panel. The gun felt good in his hand, cool and powerful. Slowly he released the chamber catch and slotted the five Teflon rounds into the chamber. It transformed the gun, and the rounds gleamed as they smiled back at him. He spun the filled chamber, flicking it with his wrist, and snapped it back into the body of the gun. It was ready. He was ready. Nothing could stop him now.

After tucking the gun under his track-suit top and replacing the panel, he strode toward the door. . . .

A minute later, the car roared into life. He was tapping the steering wheel impatiently as the electronic gate slowly opened. He saw the movement outside the gate and smiled. It was going to be his day. The stupid, pestilent dog was taking a leak against the wall, just outside the garage. *Shouldn't do that, dog. That's a naughty thing to do, taking a leak on other people's property, especially mine*. This time he would nail the little bastard. He smiled gleefully and hit the gas. The Porsche roared and the tires screamed as he accelerated out of the underground parking garage. He felt the power of the car under him and the redness filling him as he gripped the steering wheel tighter. The distance between him and the dog closed. Off to his right he saw the woman lift her arms, horrified. Her screams echoed in his ears. Then he felt the thud as the car hit the dog. He heard the crunch as the wheels went over the animal, dragging it under the car. He accelerated, laughing to himself as he spun the steering wheel hard left, almost hitting the woman before accelerating down the street. Glancing in his rearview mirror, he saw the stupid bitch running toward the white, bloody lump that had been her pet, and he wished he had spun the wheel to the right, crushing the woman under the wheels too. His body felt powerful, strong, as he mashed the gears and slammed his foot harder on the gas pedal, yelling out as the car screamed toward the highway.

Ramirez glanced at his watch. It was seven-thirty. He figured he could be at the first dealership at a little after eight. Frank was right to play it this way, he thought. If they could connect the killer through the dealers in some way, this was the way to play it. Calling was too iffy. Personal visits always worked better. Besides, if they really were able to pinpoint the killer, the last thing they wanted was to have him be tipped off. He wondered what Frank was doing. It wasn't like Frank to sit around doing nothing. Not like him at all.

Ramirez had spoken to Cooper just before he left his house, and Cooper was all fired up. He figured that, using data from the Department of Motor Vehicles, he'd be able to narrow down the list of possible cars and owners to no more than twenty. Cooper reckoned the case would be wrapped by the end of the day. Ramirez wasn't so sure, though. The computer would help, of course, but it wasn't infallible. And besides, as he'd pointed out to Cooper, what if the car was registered out of state? No one had been able to say if they'd seen a California license plate. He'd called Frank back on that one and had been told the UPS guy hadn't seen a plate, or hadn't mentioned one. Frank was going to call the guy back and check. Damn, it was all so close, and yet what did they have, really? A ton of circumstantial evidence. The wall they were building around the killer was going up just one brick at a time.

Frank had tried to call Ron Golding back, but Golding had left for work. He cursed. He should have thought to ask him about the license plate. Damn, all he could do now was wait and hope that the guy got the message from his office, then called him soon. Maybe he'd mentioned something to the desk officer, he thought, deciding to go down and check it out before the shifts changed. He needed the paperwork anyway.

He grabbed a couple of coffees from the machine and made his way to the desk. Marty was on the phone. He smiled when he saw Frank and moved the phone away from his ear, rolling his eyes. Frank handed him the coffee and mouthed a "What's the problem?" at him. The desk officer covered the phone and whispered that it was a hysterical broad down at the marina. Some lunatic had run over her dog. *Deliberately*, she said. Frank smiled and nodded as he reached over for Marty's smokes. The desk officer continued talking gently to the woman.

Frank shook his head and lit a cigarette as he searched Marty's desk for the paperwork on Ron Golding's call. He glanced at the report the desk officer was filling out: Alison Kenyon, 15 Galleon Street. He wondered why it sounded familiar. Alison Kenyon? He glanced at Marty and saw the cop had his hands full with the woman. Alison Kenyon? Damn, wasn't she the woman who had called in the report on the plant-pot incident way back in December? That call-in had been one of the five he'd noted as long shots worth checking.

He hurried back into the task-force room and grabbed the pile of files from his desk. The name on the third file leapt out at him. *Alison Kenyon, 15 Galleon Street, Marina Del Rey*. It was the same woman. He read through the report again, smiling to himself. The damaged car was a Porsche. He looked at the date; December 15. Several days after the black kids were murdered. Coincidence? Probably. Tina had said the incidents would have taken place prior to the first killings. Still . . .

He picked up the phone and buzzed the desk. It was busy. He wondered if Marty was still talking to the woman.

Standing and stretching, he began pacing the office, feeling the place closing in on him. The mornings seemed to be the worst. That was when he missed Susan the most.

He was hungry, and the thought of fresh coffee and food made his stomach growl. He glanced over at the clock and saw it was a little after seven-thirty. Cooper would be in in about forty-five minutes, and Ramirez wouldn't be call-

ing for more than an hour. He decided to go down to the
marina, talk to the woman, and get something to eat at
the Rose Café. Kill two birds with one stone.

He scribbled a note for Cooper, telling him he'd gone
to talk to the woman and then for breakfast, and went out
through the rear of the station house. The first thing he
needed was a car. The car pool was a couple of blocks
away, and the walk made him feel better.

It was going to be a pretty day at the beach, Frank
thought as he drove down toward the peninsula. The sun
was warm already and there were dozens of kids and young
married women heading for the beach. Yeah, on mornings
like this, California was a great place to live. There weren't
many other places in America, or the world, where you
could head for the beach at the end of February. He glanced
at the address. Galleon Street. That would be about half-
way down the peninsula, after Washington Boulevard. He
remembered the streets were all named after something
nautical and alphabetized in descending order from Washington Boulevard down to the end of the causeway that
separated the peninsula from El Segundo.

He saw Galleon and pulled the car over and parked.
Sure was a ritzy area, he thought as he located the woman's
building.

Damn nice building she lived in, too. A huge wooden
structure with floor-to-ceiling windows and a spectacular
view of the ocean, especially on days like this. Must be
nice to see the ocean and hear the waves breaking as you
went to sleep, he thought. He glanced at the slip of paper
in his hand: 2A. Her apartment was on the second floor.

It was a security building. He saw the names on the board and the telephone codes against each name. Locating her name, he saw that he had to dial 344. He dialed and waited. No answer. Damn, he hadn't figured that. He dialed again and listened to the ringing on the other end of the phone line. Nothing. He was about to replace the receiver when he heard her voice, metallic and scratchy.

"Who's there?"

"It's the police, Mrs. Kenyon. I wondered if I could speak to you about what happened to your dog this morning."

"I don't understand. The officer I spoke to a little while ago said there wouldn't be anyone available for a few days," she said, and then went on before he could respond. "All right, come on in." Frank heard the front door buzz and entered the building.

She was waiting for him at the far end of the hall when he got off the elevator. He could see she'd been crying. Poor woman. The dog was probably all she had, he thought. He decided to be gentle with her.

"Do you have some ID, please?" she said, backing up across her front-door threshold. Frank smiled. If he'd been a mugger, he'd already have made his play. He showed her his ID, and she guided him into what was indeed a huge and spectacular home.

"Would you like some coffee, Sergeant? It's freshly brewed," she said.

"Coffee sounds great. White, no sugar, thank you. Call me Frank, Mrs. Kenyon," he said, wishing she wouldn't keep staring at him like that. She had those beautiful steely eyes that reminded him of his mother. They were the kind that looked right through a person.

She showed him into a stunning sitting room, tastefully decorated with touches of fragility. He was reluctant to sit on the tiny chair she'd indicated. It looked as if it would collapse. The wooden floors gleamed. Everything was spotless, meticulously kept. He wondered what her husband did, had done.

She brought him a mug of coffee, and he smiled at her reassuringly as he sipped it.

"I realize, Mrs. Kenyon, that you've already related what happened to the desk officer you spoke to this morning, and that it's painful for you, but could you describe exactly what happened once again?"

"Certainly," she said, dabbing at her eyes with a tissue.

"I had Dani for eleven years. He was all I had, really. We were out walking this morning, as we always do, and I'd let him off his leash. At that time of the day, there are very few cars to worry about. Anyway, we'd almost finished our walk and we were on our way back here. Dani was sniffing around the flowers in one of the condos at the end of the peninsula. I saw the underground gate open and heard a car engine revving. It must have startled Dani, because he stopped sniffing and stood, watching the gate opening. I'd turned to go over and releash him when the car flew out of the underground garage and hit Dani. The driver made no attempt to avoid him and didn't stop. I saw the driver smile and wave his arm in the air, as if he'd intended to hit Dani all along. Just like the other time," she said, dabbing at her eyes again.

"What time did you say it happened?" he said.

"A little after seven. Why?"

"Well, and please don't misunderstand me, it was only just light, right? And you said the car came out of an underground parking garage. Very fast. Perhaps the driver was in a hurry and didn't see Dani. Was he a small dog?" he asked, and saw the fire in her eyes, the start of the anger. Damn, she was convinced; wasn't she?

"Yes, he was a small dog. Very small. But he saw him. I was there, and I saw what happened. The driver saw him. Aimed at him and accelerated his car just before he hit Dani. It was like the last time. Nothing happened then, either, did it? I knew then that the man threw his plant at me and my Dani. You aren't going to do anything about this, are you?" she said, and he saw the bitterness in her eyes. He was surprised by the force of it. Too many disappointments and lies in her life? he wondered.

"Tell me about last time, please."

"I already told it, twice," she said, getting up from her chair and taking his coffee mug, the anger evident. "What happened is all on file, and I retold it to the officer this morning. The man threw a plant at me and my dog sometime before Christmas. Dani was sniffing around the car, and the next thing I see, this man is standing on his balcony throwing a plant pot at us. It missed and smashed the car's windshield."

"I believe you. I'll go and talk to the man and see what I can find out, okay? Where, exactly, does he live?"

"The last street on the peninsula. The large condo right on the beach. You can't miss it; it's very ostentatious."

"One last thing. Do you know what type of car hit Dani?"

"The same one as the plant hit. I told the policeman that this morning. It was a Porsche. A black one. I don't understand. I went through all of this already," she said, and she stood, crossing her arms in front of her.

"I know that, Mrs. Kenyon. It's police procedure, that's all. We always review the story with the people involved. Several times, usually, to see if the witness can remember anything that was missed in the original statement. No offense intended. I'll go speak to the man, and I'll call you. Do you remember what kind of Porsche it was?" he said, standing and walking to the door with her.

"What?"

"I asked if you remembered what kind of a Porsche it was. What model."

"It was a Porsche, is all I know, a small one. I didn't know there was a difference," she said. Frank smiled. A kindred spirit. As he left, he promised to call her.

Another dead end, Frank suspected as he walked back toward his car. It was very possible she was seeing it one way when it had happened another way. The retelling of the plant-pot story had convinced him she was in all likelihood targeting the neighbor. The version of the incident he'd read in the original report had the man aiming just at the dog. Today, she'd revised her story to make it seem as if the man was aiming at her as well. Probably figured she wouldn't get any action otherwise, Frank thought.

He drove toward the end of the peninsula, wondering

which house it was and keeping his eyes open for a parking
spot. He tried getting Ramirez on the radio, but he was
apparently out of his car. Must be in one of the dealerships,
he thought, hoping Ramirez would have better luck than
he was having.

The condo was huge and fairly new. Frank was wondering how many people lived in the building. The parking
structure was empty. He'd gone over to the metal gate and
looked into the parking area: no cars in the garage at all.
Glancing around, he decided that the driver had probably
not even seen the damn dog until he hit it. He should have
stopped, though. Most people would stop, wouldn't they?
He walked around to the front of the building and glanced
at the mailboxes. Only two names: V. Perry and A. C.
Christiensen. Big place for two people, he thought, glancing at his watch. It was 8:40.

Absently, he walked out over the sand toward the ocean.
There were kids and surfers, and he decided to have a
smoke, wait a while, and see if the guy came back. If not,
he'd try Ramirez again before going to get something to
eat. He felt close to Susan at this moment; she was filling
his thoughts. They'd spent so many happy times at the
beach over the years. He'd taught her to surf and windsurf.
He watched the people and gave in to the memories.

Ramirez had struck out at the first dealership and had
almost decided to give the second one a pass. If it wasn't
so close and on his way, he would have. He saw the
dealership and pulled over. It was eight-thirty. He parked
and was walking slowly toward the showrooms, taking it
all in. He was astonished at how many Porsches and Vol-

vos they had on the lot. Millions of dollars' worth of inventory. The showrooms were spectacular: beautifully carpeted and gleaming. Oak and glass furniture everywhere. Everyone in the place wore suits. Nice suits, wools and silks, all expensive looking.

He went up to the reception area, and a beautiful girl asked him if she could help him. He felt her eyes giving him the once-over, checking out his shoes and suit. Obviously, she was less than impressed. He felt himself getting angry and spoke more roughly than he'd intended, shocking the girl.

"Tell the sales manager the police want a word with him. Now," he said, flipping his ID at her and smiling coldly.

The girl stared at him and then shrugged and pointed at a huge glass-encased office in the center of the showroom.

"Mr. Meyer's in the office over there."

He walked over, feeling the girl's eyes boring into his back, and knocked on the office door. Meyer opened the door and introduced himself, waving him into the office, offering him a seat. He was young and immaculate. Looks more like a banker than a car salesman, Ramirez thought.

"What can I do for you, Detective Ramirez?" Meyer asked after seeing Glen's ID. His voice dripped with phony respect.

"I was wondering if you could check your records and see if one of your customers has purchased both a black Porsche 930 turbo and a white Volvo 760 turbo station wagon," he said.

Meyer smiled at him and pulled open one of his file cabinets.

"I don't think so," he said, hardly glancing at the files he'd pulled out of the drawer. "We haven't sold all that many 930 turbos, and I know most of the customers who bought them personally."

Ramirez stared at him for a long moment, despising the man's arrogant attitude and wanting to get the hell out of there. But he waited until Meyer read through the files more thoroughly.

"Like I thought, Detective, none of my Porsche customers purchased a Volvo wagon. Sorry."

Ramirez nodded, stood, and walked toward the door. "Thanks for your help."

Suddenly, as he was about to leave the office, he had an inspiration. He turned back toward Meyer and smiled. "I just thought of something. Did any of your 'personal' customers bring their Porsche 930s in for repairs or service in December and receive a Volvo wagon as a loaner?" *Why hadn't he or Cooper thought of the loaner angle earlier?*

Meyer stared at him and adjusted his gold-rimmed glasses. He cleared his throat, shuffling some papers, not looking at him.

"Checking the records won't be necessary, Detective Ramirez. It was Mr. Perry. Why do you want to know?" he said softly. He was uncomfortable, and it showed.

"How can you be so certain that it was Mr. Perry?" Ramirez asked.

Meyer folded his arms and glared at him.

"Because I handle Mr. Perry's account personally. He's a very valued customer of mine. I loaned him *my* Volvo, as it happens. It was an unusual request. A Volvo isn't exactly Mr. Perry's sort of car, if you know what I mean," he said, smiling that imperious smile again, back in control as he steepled his manicured nails. Ramirez had had it with being nice to this prick.

"I appreciate your help, Mr. Meyer. Now, if you'll get me Mr. Perry's address and phone number . . ." he said with an edge to his voice. He walked back toward the desk and reached for the telephone. "May I use the phone?" he asked. Meyer nodded and pointed at the single red phone on the opposite end of the desk, away from the phone Ramirez had started to reach for. "Thank you," Ramirez said sarcastically. "We have reason to believe that Mr. Perry can assist us in a murder investigation. Your full assistance will be appreciated." He shot Meyer a menacing look and saw the man's face grow ashen.

Meyer's hands shook as he took a set of keys from his pocket and opened his desk drawer. He drew out another file and scribbled down Perry's address and phone number.

"The car's outside. The file and records are here," Meyer stammered, handing Ramirez the file and the paper with Perry's address. "Of course I want to assist the police all I can. But I can't believe Mr. Perry would be implicated in a murder investigation. Surely you must be mistaken. I've known Mr. Perry for eleven years."

Ramirez ignored him and called the station, reading the address Meyer had jotted down. Son of a bitch was a local, like Frank and Tina had figured. He glanced at his watch. It was 8:47.

"Put me through to Frank Morrissey."

"Frank isn't in. He was trying to reach you. He's in the marina. Cooper was trying to get him on the radio just now. He's not in the car."

Jesus Christ, Ramirez cursed silently. What the hell was Frank doing in the marina?

"Put me through to Cooper."

"Sorry, his line's busy. Want to wait?"

"Interrupt his call. Put me through now. *Now*," he yelled. He felt his heart pounding.

"Hi, Glen. What's the problem?"

"Listen, Coop, and listen good. Frank is somewhere in the marina. Doing what, Christ knows. The killer lives in the marina. His name is Perry, and this is the address." He read the address over the phone. "And get a team over there right away. And get on the phone and find Frank. I'm on my way to the marina now."

"Wait a sec," Cooper said. "Frank left me a message. He was going to talk to some woman on Galleon Street. That's only a few blocks from where this Perry guy lives. Do you think he . . ."

"Holy fuck," Ramirez said, and hung up the phone.

The gym hadn't helped. The pain in his head was blinding him and his stomach was wrenched by spasms. The pleasure of squashing the dog had departed too quickly, and he knew it was the damn girl's fault. She'd spoiled everything.

He'd called the airlines from his car, and there was a flight to Seattle at 10:30. It was 8:45 as he pulled into the underground parking, and he figured, if he hurried, he'd be able to make the flight. Damn the girl. Damn her to hell. He wished he could take the gun on the plane. He hefted it in his hand as he ran up the stairs and into his apartment. The anger was starting again, swirling smokily and red through his eyes. Christ, she was going to pay for this. The house smelled bad, and he yanked open the sliding glass doors with a crash, smashing a vase and a hanging plant. The cool sea breeze felt good as he gulped in the air, then froze. He shook his head, and the image stayed there. He couldn't believe it. . . .

It was Morrissey. Standing there twenty yards from his house and smoking a goddamn cigarette. So she'd betrayed him already. The anger consumed him, and as the energy flowed through his body and the mist overtook him, he knew it was going to be his day. First the dog, now the stupid cop.

He saw the cop throw down his cigarette and say something to a passing teenager, then turn away from the crashing surf. His mind was whirring, and he wondered why the cop had chosen to come here alone. Avenge himself for his wife, he thought, and smiled. *Stupid, arrogant prick.* As the cop walked toward the house, Vic ducked back off the balcony, watching him through the window. He glanced along the beach, to the left and to the right. People, plenty of people. No more cops, though. This was going to work out well. He rammed the gun into his sweats and ran out of the room and down the stairs, deciding to take the cop as he came into the house.

This time he'd do it right and take his time. No goddamn interruptions. Then, after, when he'd been made stronger and saw the pathetic cop lying lifeless on the floor, he'd get the bitch and it would be game, set, and match.

Frank had had it with the beach, as pretty as it was. His stomach was growling, and he'd decided the guy was probably gone for the day. Too bad; it would have been another loose end tied up and filed. He wondered idly what the guys in the condo did for a living. Whatever it is, he thought, it must pay big bucks. Glancing up at the condo's balcony, he noticed that the window was open; the curtains rose and fell in the gentle breeze. He wondered about that. Maybe the guy was coming back soon. He changed direction slightly, walking toward the garage again. Still no sign of a car. Deciding on the spur of the moment to try the front again, he was startled to see the Porsche, like some great, fat, black predatory cat, sitting outside the front door, waiting for its owner. So the dog killer was back? Slowly he walked toward the car and heard the ticking of the engine as it cooled down. He saw the rent in the off-side front, just under the headlight, where the car had impacted with the dog.

Vic was standing in the shadows of the front door, out of sight, watching as the cop examined his car. He was getting more furious with every second, wondering why the stupid cop was dicking around. Finally, he saw the cop straighten up from his inspection of the front fender and walk slowly toward him. Amazingly, he hadn't drawn his gun. Vic smiled then, glad he had opened the door a crack and melted back into the shadows.

''Come to me, death,'' he whispered, feeling the cool, reassuring metal of the gun in his hand. It was obvious that the cop was more stupid than he'd figured. This was going to be so easy, he thought. He suddenly realized that Morrissey didn't know what he looked like.

Frank was close to the front door now, and frowning as

he noticed the door was slightly ajar. He hesitated a moment, then remonstrated with himself. *Get this over with, Frank, then get something to eat.* He pressed the buzzer and waited. Nothing. He pressed it again, holding his finger on it for several seconds. Nothing. Strange, unless the guy's in the bathroom or something, he thought, wondering if the dog killer was Perry or Christiensen. Screw it, he decided. He pushed open the door and went in.

Vic was beside himself, watching the cop dithering with the goddamn buzzer when the stupid door was open. What was the cop's problem? he wondered. He felt the tightening in his head and around his eyes, wanting to smash the cop's face in with the gun barrel. Finally, Morrissey entered. Vic was astonished to see he still hadn't drawn his weapon.

Frank pushed open the door and saw the bank of elevators off to his left. He felt a tug in his gut. Something was wrong. He saw the movement then, out of the corner of his eye, and he'd barely reached for his gun when the cold metal was pushed violently against the back of his head.

"So finally we meet, Morrissey," a strong, confident voice said softly from behind him.

Frank could feel the gun digging into his neck, and he stiffened. The man—he knew it was the one they were looking for—hadn't fired. That gave him some kind of an edge. He wondered fleetingly why the guy hadn't shot him, and put the thought out of his head. *Concentrate.*

"The game's over. Put the gun down," Frank said firmly, moving slightly and trying to see the killer's face. It was a bad move; the gun came down on his head, gouging it and ripping a painful rent in his neck. He bit back the pain and smiled as he used to do in a big ballgame when the other team's tackle had flattened him.

Vic froze. The cop had actually smiled. Images of the bikers and the thugs at school and all the others floated vividly into his mind, cutting across the redness and settling in the center of his vision. His breathing became more difficult as his chest tightened and the grip on the gun intensified.

Frank felt the killer stiffen and the pressure on the gun tighten, then slacken, as the man slammed him against the wall near the stairwell. Then a blur, as the killer's arm swung back, followed by bursting lights in front of his eyes. He felt his guts lurch and the bile in his throat as his legs wobbled.

"Get the goddamn smile off your face, cop. Think you're tough, huh?" Vic said as he pummeled him with the pistol.

Frank heard the crunch of his nose, then his jaw, and felt the red-hot pain of his skin separating as the killer smashed the gun repeatedly into his face. He wondered bleakly why his smile had enraged the killer. Did it mean something? *Concentrate, Frank. Think.* Fighting to keep from falling, he smiled again and spat a red, bloody wad at the killer.

Vic felt the rage and the pressure on his finger taking the slack up on the trigger, and he hesitated. The cop was laughing at him, just like all the others. He wouldn't shoot the bastard. Not yet. He had to regain control. Make him afraid. Make him beg for his worthless life. Morrissey's

slutty wife hadn't been afraid of him either, he thought
angrily, feeling the tremors starting deep within him.

"Arrogant bastard," Vic screamed, ramming the gun
into Morrissey's ribs. "Take out your gun, nice and slowly
now. Throw it over there. Do it *now*," he said, teeth bared.
He watched the cop do as he was instructed.

Then his finger tightened on the trigger. And Frank saw
madness on the killer's face. There was something more
in those eyes, though. A flicker, a shadow of fear. What
was he afraid of? Frank's confused brain screamed at him.
The killer was holding all the cards, and yet he was afraid.
Why? Frank took a desperation shot.

"What's the matter, friend? What are you afraid of?
Death? Christ, dying's easy. Go ahead, pull the trigger. I
don't give a shit. Not now, not anymore. What's the problem? Lost your nerve? Go ahead, pull the fucking trigger,"
he said simply with the most indifferent shrug he could
manage. He saw the killer's eyes flicker and a small tic
start beating furiously over his left eye and the fine sheen
of sweat covering his face. He wondered again what the
hell the killer was afraid of.

"You think you're real damn smart, don't you, Morrissey? You're just like the rest of them. Always under-
estimating me. Well, no one will ever underestimate me
again, will they? Not now," Vic said, and his face was
no longer twisted and demented looking. Frank felt the
first prickle of real fear as he stared at him. He was about
to respond when the man smiled and relaxed his grip on
the gun a fraction.

"You've got nerve, Morrissey. I'll give you that. You

actually thought you could haul my ass in, didn't you? If
it wasn't for the damn girl, you wouldn't have had a clue,
would you? You're pathetic, just like your partner and that
pretty little wife of yours and all the others. Look at you,
you still don't understand who I am, what I am. Do you?
You're all the same. Pathetic little people in a pathetic
little world. Well, it's my time now, and you're mine,"
he said. Frank saw that the man's eyes had again become
unfocused. He noticed the whitening of the man's finger
on the trigger. Then he heard it, faintly at first but growing
stronger. He smiled cheerfully and looked at the killer,
locking into his eyes.

"Hear that? They're coming for you, friend," Frank
said, watching the naked terror come into the man's eyes
again, stronger this time. The man's lips trembled and he
tore his eyes away, faintly shifting his body.

Frank moved, slamming his fist into the killer's face
and lifting him off his feet. Using his head as a battering
ram, he butted the killer again and again, feeling the man's
body slackening. *Get the fucking gun!* Frank's brain
screamed. *Get the goddamn gun away from him!* Using
both of his hands and gripping the man's right arm, Frank
swung him around and into the stairwell. He smashed his
elbow again and again into the man's face. The sound of
the gun discharging was deafening, and Frank heard the
bullets impacting dully into the wall as the killer refused
to release his grip on the gun. The man was bloody and
battered, and still his grip on the gun was viselike, desperate. Frank felt his own strength weakening.

Letting out a roar, Frank hit him again and slammed his
wrist into the wall with all his strength. He heard the clunk

of the gun hitting the floor, and with its loss a limpness overcame the killer. And then it was over. Frank reached down, picking up the gun.

"Move one muscle, asshole, and you're dead," Frank said. "Understand that? One move and your goddamn head gets splattered all over the wall." He was surprised to hear that his voice didn't shake when he spoke. In the distance he could hear the sirens getting closer, and he wondered how they'd reacted so fast. The killer was staring at him, his mouth slack and his breath coming in great, ragged gasps. His face was torn and ruined. White bone protruded from the swollen left check.

"So when did the bitch tell you?" the man said, twisting his face and lips, looking totally insane. Frank watched him closely and wondered what the hell he was talking about. That was the second time he'd referred to a girl. *Let him talk*, he thought. *Play along with him.*

"Last night, the girl told me all about you," Frank said. "About all sixteen of them. What I want to know is, why? Why did you kill them?"

Vic spat blood and teeth onto the floor. Cops, he thought. So naive, so ignorant. He smiled then, and his eyes shone as he ran his tongue over his ripped, torn lips.

"Why don't you just come out and ask me why I killed your beautiful wife, Morrissey," he said, grinning. "Go on, ask me. I'll tell you, but you won't understand. Shit, if you had any brains, you wouldn't be a cop, would you? As for the girl, she was stupid and didn't know anything. It was eighteen, cop, not sixteen. It was eighteen. Paybacks, cop. Paybacks. My time . . . no more dealing with shits like you and all the rest of them. He wasn't here to see it, and that's too bad, but you saw it. You saw how I did, didn't you? If the bitch hadn't betrayed me, you'd never have found me, would you?'' he said, and started to laugh. Frank just stared at him and fought back the urge to shudder. What was the mad bastard talking about?

''I should have killed her, cop. I could have, and I let her go. It was the only mistake I made. I should have known she'd betray me just like all the others.''

Frank saw the killer's shoulders slump; the anger that had resurfaced when he was talking about the girl had gone. His eyes had turned glassy and lifeless. He was staring off someplace Frank didn't know. Didn't want to know. Frank stared back at him. He felt empty, drained, and incredibly fatigued. He glanced at the gun in his hand. It seemed far away, alien. He pointed the gun at the killer, aiming it at the man's forehead.

''How does death feel, friend?''

And he saw it in the killer's face; the bastard was afraid to die. Huge wet tears were brimming in his dead, crazy eyes, ready to be unleashed and cascade down his face. Frank's finger tightened on the trigger, and he looked into the man's eyes.

''Don't kill me, Morrissey. Please, don't kill me. Please, don't . . .''

Frank stared at him. Killing this sad excuse for a human being wouldn't bring Susan and Tony back, would it? He shuddered then, seeing the image of his wife floating eerily in front of his eyes. What had she said? You'll do what's right, Frank. You're a good cop. *Christ, Susan, what does being a good cop mean? What's right? Your death? Tony's death? All the others?* Damn, he wished he understood the *why*.

He stepped closer to the killer and stared deeply into his eyes. Slowly and carefully, he pulled back the hammer of the gun. He saw the stark terror on the killer's face as he put the gun into his mouth. He smelled the foul smell as the man defecated. Somewhere in his mind, he heard the slamming of car doors behind him, the chopper hovering overhead. He felt someone edging closer, not wanting to panic him, afraid of the gun's discharging. Slowly he took up the slack of the trigger, saw his finger start to whiten.

"Don't pull the trigger, Frank. Not now. It's over," Ramirez said softly, pleadingly.

Frank pushed the gun harder into the killer's mouth, feeling his own sweat as it poured from his face, into his eyes, stinging and making him blink. He pushed the gun harder, feeling the barrel biting into the flesh at the back of the killer's throat, and he saw the tears, fat and huge, rolling down the terrified man's cheeks. A second passed, and then . . .

"Bang bang," Frank said, and withdrew the gun. He turned to Ramirez and said, "Cuff him and read him his rights."

EPILOGUE

They had finished their meal, and his coffee was getting cold. They hadn't talked much. There was so much inside of him. The fullness of all the words in him sat heavy in his gut. He was glad they had decided to have dinner. He had thought he might be able to tell her how it was with him. But the words wouldn't come. He felt them, thought them, and yet couldn't articulate them. She was asking him something. It seemed as though she was far away and he couldn't hear the words.

"Sorry. What did you say?" he asked softly, avoiding her eyes.

Tina looked at him closely. He wasn't with her at all. She felt the melancholy sweep over her, the sadness creeping through her body and weighting her limbs. It had been too damn soon. She wanted to cry. For him, but mostly for the pure, goddamn unfairness of it all. And for herself too. She saw his hand on the table, and she wanted to reach out to him and hold on to him, tell him that it would be all right. But it wouldn't be all right, would it? Not for him. His wound was open, huge, still fresh and bleeding. Maybe time would help. Maybe.

"I was asking what you were going to do, whether you'll be going back to the department," she said softly, patiently, trying to reach into him, grab a part of him, make him respond and communicate with her.

He hadn't thought about that, not really. He had three months to decide, didn't he? Right now, he didn't have a clue. He certainly didn't *need* to stay on. Susan had made sure of that. There was enough money to last him forever. What was it John Kennedy had said about asking not what your country can do for you, but what you can do for it? Fucking great sentiment, John. But then what? When you have given and given, and everything that meant something to you has been taken away and without a reason . . . He sighed. She was waiting for him to answer her. She meant well. And she was a good person. He didn't mean to exclude her. It was just happening that way, that's all. To hell with the department.

"I don't really know, Tina. If I had to decide today, I wouldn't go back. In a month or two, who knows? I think . . . I think I would like to leave this place now, if you don't mind," he said. He picked up the check and moved slowly toward the door. She got up and walked back with him. Miles away from him. Wanting to close the gap and not knowing how.

What could she say? She had tried, and she did care.

"Sure. Thanks for meeting with me, Frank. Listen, you have my number. If you need to talk sometime, give me a call. Okay?" she said, and managed a brave smile. She hoped he would call. Maybe he would. Later, when he felt he could get on with the living part again.